W9-BGZ-638

Playing the Game

Playing the Game

IAN BURUMA

Farrar, Straus and Giroux

New York

In memory of Dhiren Bhagat and
Bernard Edward Schlesinger

Library of Congress Cataloging-in-Publication Data
Buruma, Ian.
Playing the game / Ian Buruma.—1st American ed.
"First published in the United Kingdom by Jonathan Cape Limited,
London"—T.p. verso.
I. Title.
PR9130.9.B87P57 1991   823—dc20   91-13646   CIP

Excerpt from "The Joker in the Pack" in Dyer's Hand and other
essays by W. H. Auden, reprinted by permission of Faber and Faber
Limited, and of Random House, Inc. Copyright © 1960 by W. H.
Auden. Excerpt from Cricket Country by Edmund Blunden reprinted by permission of the Peters, Fraser & Dunlop Group Limited. Excerpt from Oscar Wilde by Richard Ellmann, copyright ©
1988 by Richard Ellmann. Reprinted by permission of Alfred A.
Knopf, Inc. Excerpt from Thy Hand, Great Anarch! by Nirad Chau-
duri, reprinted by permission of Chatto & Windus Limited

Since no fiction can exist without facts, I would like to express my
debt to some of the sources of my fancy. First of all, Alan Ross's
excellent biography of Ranjitsinhji, entitled Ranji, Pavilion Books.
Also to Clive Ellis's C. B.: The Life of Charles Burgess Fry, J. M.
Dent and Sons, and to C. B. Fry's own Life Worth Living, Pavilion
Books. And, finally, to Ashis Nandy's The Tao of Cricket, Penguin
India, one of the finest and quirkiest books on cricket ever written.

Cricket: A Short Introduction

SINCE SOME of the cricket terminology will be, to American readers, a little arcane, I shall explain the gist of the game as briefly as I can. As in baseball, there is a pitcher, or 'bowler', who dispatches the ball at a batter, or 'batsman', who can score points, 'runs', by hitting the ball without its being caught in the field. But there, really, the similarity ends.

In cricket, two teams of eleven men (or sometimes women) each have an innings, or two, depending on the length of the game – a so-called Test Match, or international game, goes on for five days. The idea is to get ten batsmen of the other side out, conceding as few runs as possible. With exceptions, too complex to get into here, all eleven players come in to bat. Only when one side is 'all out' does the innings of the other side begin.

The side which scores the most runs wins, but only if it succeeds in getting ten men of the opposing side out, for otherwise the match ends in a 'draw' – not the same as a 'tie', which is when both teams score an equal total, a very rare occurrence.

The game is played on a field, which is usually a squarish rectangle, depending on the location of the ground. The batting and bowling take place on a narrow strip in the middle of the ground, called the 'pitch', or sometimes 'wicket'. On either end of the pitch or wicket are three sticks, called 'stumps', with shorter sticks on top, called 'bails'. These stumps and bails, somewhat resembling a gate, are the 'wickets' which the batsmen have to defend. They are 66 feet apart.

While the bowler bowls at one batsman, bouncing the hard red ball – of about the size and weight of a baseball – on the pitch once, another batsman waits at the bowler's end of the pitch. When the batsman being bowled at hits the ball out of reach of the fielders, who are strategically placed around the field, the two batsmen run in opposite directions, changing ends. (They do not have to run.) If they run only once, it is the turn of the other batsman to stand in front of the wicket to receive the bowling. Every run between the two wickets constitutes a run. After every six balls, an 'over' is declared, which means that another bowler will bowl from the opposite side of the pitch at the other batsman.

There are various ways of getting a batsman out. He can be caught in the field, or he can be bowled, which means that his wicket is hit by the ball. He can also be judged LBW, or 'leg before wicket', which is when the ball hits his leg in direct line of the wicket. He can be 'run out' if a fielder throws the ball back to the wicket before he reaches it safely.

To score runs, batsmen can hit the ball in a variety of ways. They can drive the ball to the left, or 'leg' side, or to the right, or 'off' side. They can 'hook' it behind the wicket to leg, or 'cut' it behind to the off side. (They can hit the ball in any direction: there is no foul territory, as in baseball.)

Ranji's most famous stroke was the 'leg glance': he would lean forward on his front foot, as though to simply push the ball back to the bowler defensively, and at the very last minute, with the silkiest of touches, flick his bat to the leg side to help the ball on its way to the boundary behind him.

The boundary, by the way, is the border of the field. If the ball crosses the boundary without touching the ground, as in a home run, the batsman scores six runs, or as people sometimes said in Ranji's time, a sixer, and when it touches the ground, four runs.

The types of bowling can be roughly divided into slow and fast. Fast bowlers rely on pace, though some swerve or swing the ball in the air, like a curve ball in baseball, and slow bowlers rely on spinning the ball, to produce 'leg breaks' or 'off breaks'. A leg break turns towards a right-handed batsman from the leg side, after hitting the ground, and an off break does the opposite.

Since cricket was originally an English game, it is imbued with the clubby snobbery Anglophiles find charming. The most famous club is the Marylebone Cricket Club, or MCC, whose members are proud to wear the orange-and-yellow-striped tie which is as distinctive as it is hideous. The club's headquarters is Lord's Cricket Ground in London, considered, by Ranji and everybody since, the Mecca of the game.

There are other more obscure clubs, whose ties vie with the MCC one in garishness, and whose rules of admission are as arcane as those of the game itself. I Zingari is one of these. Its colours are black, red, and gold. The club was founded in 1845 by the Hon. F. Ponsonby, later Lord Bessborough, during supper at the Blenheim Hotel. Their first game was against Harrow school. Ranji was not a member, since he didn't go to a grand enough school, but would certainly have played against them, perhaps for the Gentlemen of England.

It was only after World War II that the distinction between Gentlemen (amateurs) and Players (professionals) was abolished. Before that they had separate dressing rooms, even when they played for the same team, as well as separate entrances to the ground, and they would not sit together for lunch or tea. Gentlemen were identified on scorecards as Mr So-and-so, while Players were simply So-and-so. Ranji, naturally, was always a Gentleman, and never just a So-and-so.

Playing the Game

Prologue

'He loved England! though not quite in the English way.'

Esme Wingfield-Stratford, about Benjamin Disraeli

I AM NOT quite sure when the legend of Ranji first impressed itself on my mind. Perhaps it was round about the time when, aged ten, I was taken to a restaurant by my grandfather and I spotted a man wearing an I Zingari tie. Such arcane knowledge of English life impressed my grandfather. At least I think it did. Not that he was a cricketer, let alone a member of I Zingari, but such connoisseurship amused him, especially when it came from a boy growing up on the Continent, a boy who loved England, though not quite in the English way.

But I was speaking of Ranji. I remember what it was that first struck my fancy; nothing more than a fleeting image, really; of Ranji coming in to bat, wearing a silk shirt buttoned up to the wrists – 'to hide his dark skin', so they said.

It is no exaggeration to say that Ranji's silk shirt was one of the icons of my youthful imagination, along with my grandfather's brass army buttons, his Old Uppinghamian tie, and his first aid kit from the trenches in Flanders. But whereas my grandfather's relics were the badges of Englishness, earned (so he might have put it) by the son of German Jews, Ranji's shirt was something more exotic, more flamboyant, akin to the wristy flicks of his bat, the silky strokes off his legs. As a contemporary British enthusiast observed, admiringly one presumes: 'He never played a Christian stroke in his life.'

Not that I was attracted especially to the mysterious East. It was as an English legend that Colonel Shri Sir K. S. Ranjitsinhji, KSCI, the Jam Saheb of Nawanagar, caught my imagination. (The mysterious East was itself an English legend, but I was not to know that then.) And an English legend he was, as English as Kipling; that is to say, his was the Englishness of dreams, the Englishness of my dreams, meaning, not really English at all. But

3

Ranji, the Indian from Gujerat, was an English folk hero, not simply the greatest cricketer of his time. He was a fairy-tale prince in an age of steam engines, steel bridges, and the first motor cars. He was so famous that children sang songs about him, and grown men wept when they saw him play.

The Englishness of dreams. My choice of heroes followed a predictable course: Benjamin Disraeli – not so much the wooer of Queen Victoria, as the young orator in velvet and ringlets, titillating the English with his mysterious Oriental outrageousness – and after Dizzy, Oscar Wilde, the Irishman in silk knee-breeches subverting English codes with nothing but his genius.

I have often imagined the three together, at Lord's perhaps, Ranji having just completed a century, entering the pavilion to a standing ovation from the English crowd: 'Good old Ramsgate Jimmy! Hurray for Run-get-sinhji! Bless your heart, Black Prince!'

Dizzy: Well played, Your Highness.
Ranji: Thank you for your kind praise, sir, but I am afraid my performance today lacked discipline. I should never have got out.
Oscar: On the contrary, my dear Prince, the way you lost your wicket was a thing of quite extraordinary beauty, the exquisite nobility of failure, the one thing, I believe, that English philistines can appreciate.
Dizzy: How true, Mr Wilde, how true.
Ranji: We know how to play the game, gentlemen. Indeed, if I may say so, the genius of our noble race, under British tutelage, adds lustre to our Empire, and to the greatness of our gracious Queen-Empress.
Dizzy: Ah, the nobility of race . . .
Oscar: . . . Our dear, dear Queen . . .

It is of course but a fancy. They couldn't have met at Lord's. One year after Ranji first played cricket for Sussex, Wilde was on trial. Disraeli had been dead for thirteen years. Oscar and Dizzy did meet once: 'I hope you are very well,' said Oscar. 'Is one ever well, Mr Wilde?' replied Dizzy. I believe that is all that is recorded of the conversation.

But I like to imagine my three heroes sharing, without actually admitting it, a huge joke, a joke on the English, and, perhaps, ultimately on themselves. I like to picture them as pranksters, jesters, practical jokers. But I doubt if they – even Wilde – saw themselves that way. I doubt if they ever could have looked one another in the eye and collapsed laughing at the absurdity of it all. Perhaps if they could they would no longer have been so compelling.

'Dandyism', wrote Baudelaire, 'is a kind of cult of the ego . . . It is the pleasure of causing surprise in others, and the proud satisfaction of never showing any oneself. A dandy may be blasé, he may even suffer pain, but in the latter case he will keep smiling, like the Spartan under the bite of the fox. Clearly, then, dandyism in certain respects comes close to spirituality and to stoicism . . . Dandyism is the last flicker of heroism in decadent ages . . . Dandyism is a setting sun; like the declining star, it is magnificent, without heat and full of melancholy. But alas! the rising tide of democracy, which spreads everywhere and reduces everything to the same level, is daily carrying away these last champions of human pride.'

I thought of Ranji, dying in his splendid palace, his loneliness relieved only by the presence of his parrot. The audience for his pranks, the British, had let him down, as invariably happens when the dandy's sun finally sets. I hadn't actually thought of Ranji for a long time, not since I was haunted as a child by the image of the fluttering silk shirt, buttoned to the wrist, hiding the dark skin. I had, in fact, completely forgotten about him until I read a description of the room in which he died.

The room, in the Jam Palace of Jamnagar on the coast of Gujerat, was kept as a shrine, left exactly as it was at the time of his death in 1933. There were his glass eyes, neatly laid out like my grandmother's marrows at the village fête; there were his slippers, his letter from George V's secretary, his old cricket bats, stained dark with patches of English soil, the army uniform he wore in France during the Great War, and a photograph of his

English friend, C. B. Fry, resembling a Greek god with a bat. And there was the empty cage of Popsey, the parrot.

I wanted to see that room. I felt that in that bric-à-brac I would find something that would make sense of the army buttons, the I Zingari tie, or the stories of Dizzy and Oscar; something that might tie all the dream images together into a meaningful whole, that would lend coherence to this peculiar love of England.

I

'To be once déraciné is to be for ever on the road.'

Nirad C. Chaudhuri

IT WAS COLD when I arrived in Delhi. Men emerged from the early morning fog wrapped in blankets to keep out the desert chill. As I rumbled through the sandy suburbs in the old Ambassador taxi (Indians, quite perversely, defend this piece of antiquated, gas-guzzling machinery, copied from a 1950s British model, as though it were part of the ancient Indian heritage – the spirituality of backwardness; British romantics defend it too, for they hate to see any change in India that wipes out traces of the Raj), as I rumbled through the suburbs, I thought of Inder. It was for his funeral that I had come to Delhi. He had died suddenly, horribly. But the details of his death are less important than what he had meant to me, as a friend, as a guide, as an occasional adversary, and, most pertinently for the story I am about to tell, as the one who showed me the way to Ranji's shrine.

My quest for the shrine was the excuse for an assignment to write about India, but soon the details of Ranji's life began to obsess me. I wanted to know more and more, as though the accumulation of facts would somehow bring the cricketer alive again. What was supposed to be a short trip turned into an endless search for more bits of information, mere shreds usually, which, together, might one day form a coherent tapestry. And always there was Inder, hovering around somewhere, my Indian lodestar.

I first met him at a dinner party in Delhi hosted by an Australian called Wayne. Wayne was, as they say, a character. He looked like an Oxford don in the days the first Ambassador rolled off the assembly line: tweed suit, horn-rimmed glasses, brogues. Wayne aspired to success in London, another model that smelled of the 1950s. His ideal was the London of Cyril Connolly, a Mecca of civilisation, a repository of fine first editions (which Wayne collected) and wine connoisseurship – Wayne prided himself on his passion for wine, weighing and slushing and gurgling the precious fluid in his mouth, with a look of rapture on his round, fleshy face. Wayne spoke in soft drawing-room English, and almost succeeded in hiding his Antipodean origins. But, once in a while, as though to balance this precarious act, upon which his easily bruised identity rested, he would come up with a gross Australian obscenity, spoken in a broad Sydney accent. There he would sit, in a smart restaurant, cradling his wine glass daintily between thumb and index finger, watching the waitress slide by. Then, suddenly, it would pop out, irresistibly: "Whoah, look at that Sheila, sport . . . wouldn't mind exercising the old armadillo with her . . . '

It was Inder, however, who had fascinated me from the beginning. This much I knew about him: he was born in Delhi, educated there at an English school, and went on to Cambridge, whence he returned with a perfect English accent. He was known at Cambridge as a dandy – once startling his guests at a tea party by appearing in a striped shirt and bow tie under an achkan – and a poet, with a special fondness for Shelley, whose poems he recited whenever the mood struck him, which was often. Inder was a small, thin man, who tended to get excited when holding forth on a favourite topic, and once the words flowed there was no stopping him.

At that dinner party in Delhi, he told us the story of his youth. Inder's father was an Indian nationalist who believed that adopting Western civilisation was the only way forward for an independent India. By Western civilisation he meant one thing in particular, what he, and generations of English schoolmasters, missionaries and sergeant-majors called discipline. British discipline would make India great again. He volunteered for the Territorial Army, but was rejected since he was not a member of one of the martial races. He then adopted the name De Souza, was accepted and had a good war. When he became seriously ill in 1946, he left instructions with his wife that Inder was to be educated at an English school, where they would make a man of him, teach him discipline, fairly and firmly. Inder's mother spoke

8

no English herself, but complied with her husband's wishes after he died in 1947, the year of Indian independence. And so Inder went to an English school in Delhi, where the Anglo-Indian teachers made a man of him by putting him in the boxing ring with much stronger boys. Week after week, his mother would sit at the ringside, dressed in her sari, watching in silence as her boy was mauled, over and over again. He would have screamed with pain and humiliation if he had not been held back by the memory of his father, who would have disapproved deeply of such unmanly behaviour. And so Inder bore his fate as silently as his mother, for they both knew that this is what his father had wanted. Inder finished his story with a peal of laughter, followed by a series of snorts.

I soon met Inder again at a party celebrating the 'Sesquicentennial Anniversary' of *The Times of India*, for whom he wrote a stylish and provocative weekly column. I could hear him hold forth in a crowd of saris and cashmere shawls. Inder was dressed in a striped shirt, a bow tie and a white linen jacket. 'England is of course absolutely dead,' he said to a nut-brown man, who wagged his head in agreement. 'Quite true,' said the man, creasing his brow to stress the seriousness of the point he was about to make: 'England died of her own power. Of materialism, of greed, of arrogance. England is now quite irrelevant, indeed quite irrelevant.'

The man made off to the long row of silver trays, arranged on the front lawn of a Palladian villa. They contained Italian, Chinese and Indian food. He piled spoonfuls of all three on to his plate, creating a greasy mountain of pasta, sweet and sour sauce and curries. A one-eyed guest in an embroidered shawl dunked his roti into a wet curry and bit off a large chunk. He grinned at me, yellowish oil seeping through his teeth, and said: 'This is what is known as conspicuous consumption.' When I nodded politely, he observed that 'Britain is the most underdeveloped country in the First World and India the most Third World of the Third World.'

I pondered this. The man turned away. I asked Inder when England had died.

'My dear, when she lost the courage of her own convictions. That's when England died. England created a ruling class in India of Fabian socialists, still trying to catch up with the 1930s. What we lack here is an intelligent Right, Indian Tories who can properly defend the only thing that holds this society together . . . ' He snorted, as he always did, when working up to a statement he knew would provoke protest.

'And what is that?'

'My dear fellow, the caste system of course. This is something the British understood perfectly well during the eighteenth and much of the nineteenth century. But when disillusion with their own society infected the British, things began to collapse in India. They tried to civilise us without believing in their own civilisation. So we ended up with the worst of both worlds – ashamed of our own traditions and no principles to take their place.'

We were joined by the man eating the greasy mountain. A crusty film of curry and tomato sauce had congealed around the corners of his mouth. 'Naturally,' said Inder, his eyes glinting behind his spectacles, 'we benefited enormously from the British Empire.' The man flushed with anger. 'That is totally absurd,' he said, 'totally absurd. We had democracy in India thousands of years ago. Look here, when the Britishers were still going round in bearskins, we had a first-class culture here.' Inder was in his element: 'Oh, come on,' he bellowed in his best Cambridge accent, 'without the British, we wouldn't have had modern science.' The man could hardly contain himself: 'Totally absurd. We invented science . . . The number zero, what about that! You must admit we were the first to have the number zero.' Inder beamed with pleasure.

I watched a group of mime artists in white face dancing between the Doric columns of the colonial mansion. They were mimicking the various stages of making a newspaper – the reporting, the editing, the printing.

'I could only marry a north Indian girl,' Inder suddenly said after his victim had stomped off in a rage. This time he had managed to bait me. Why should he, an Anglicised Cambridge graduate, insist on a north Indian wife? Why, I said, insist on anything so specific, why not marry somebody you love?

'Oh dear, Love, what does it mean?' he snorted. 'Love is for poetry. I admit it, I'm always falling in love, but marriage is quite a different thing. We must carry on our civilisation as a link in an ancient chain. You see, I insist on preserving our differences. I say this as a Punjabi, of course.'

'But Inder,' I said, the liberal in me stirring, 'you sound like a racist.'

He saw this coming: 'There is nothing wrong with racism. Yes, I admit it, I am a racist. Racial and cultural distinctions must be preserved. Without them, we would end up like the Caribbean, a huge, meaningless, deracinated melting pot, driven by nothing but greed. Enoch Powell is quite right.' He paused, and briefly scanned the crowd, in the hope, perhaps, of having provoked some sensitive Indian sensibilities. 'There is no reason why the English should accept planeloads of darkies descending on them. Powell wants the Indians to go back home precisely because he respects us. My dear, as Aziz observed at the end of *A Passage to India*, we can be friends now, but only if we stay here, and you stay there.'

Inder's reputation in Delhi was decidedly mixed. Many people found him snobbish and arrogant. It is true that, like all dandies, Inder was fastidious. He felt disdain for those whose appearance and manners fell short of his high expectations. An awkward pair of shoes or a carelessly chosen tie could cause intense irritation. He was sensitive to the surface of things, because from an early age he had imbued them with meaning. A tweed jacket was not simply a garment; it stood for something and it suggested a whole lot more: a vision of England, a badge not so much of Englishness, as of Anglophilia, perhaps of civilisation itself.

'Have you noticed', he once said, 'how foreign writers in England always wear loud tweed jackets?' I confessed that I had not. He giggled and reached for his bookcase, from which he produced two books. He showed me the dust-jacket photographs of Arthur Koestler and V. S. Naipaul. 'Look at them,' he said, 'just look at them. They're like a bunch of bookies.'

Inder's dandyism was often taken by Indians as an effort to imitate the British. I think it was more complex than that. There was an element of bravado, of conscious theatricality about his posing. His attitude towards himself, as much as towards the rest of the world, was one of ironic distance. Moreover, to me, he seemed most Indian when appearing most English. The way he recited Shelley or Milton at dinner parties, smiling happily, especially if he noticed a wince of irritation on the face of a fellow guest, was the way an Indian pundit showed off his knowledge of the Vedas. He was, so to speak, displaying the badge of his caste; that of the Cambridge Indian. I thought I even detected a slight Indian wag of the head, a little flourish of triumph, but I may have been wrong.

Inder made a modest living as a writer, but had many grand friends, not so much among the Delhi *nouveaux riches*, whom he despised, but among artists and the more raffish aristocrats. One of these was an elderly Rajput lawyer with vague family connections with the Maharaja of Alwar. Inder liked elderly men, eccentrics like himself, who enjoyed being contrary; the crustier the better. Cantankerousness amused him.

The lawyer, known to his friends as V. G., lived in a mouldy white villa, built during the Raj for middle-ranking civil servants. Creepers cracked the walls and the garden had gone wild. But V. G. didn't seem to notice. Weeds didn't bother him. There was nothing casual about his appearance, however. He was a tall man in white trousers and an orange scarf, tied neatly round his neck. He ushered us into his house with the expansive gestures of a grand seigneur. The other guests included an elegant middle-aged Indian lady in a sari and a young Englishman named Dodwell, whom everyone called 'Dodsy'. Dodsy, I was told, had been to Eton with the Maharaja of Jodhpur. He spoke with the soft lisp and slight stutter that make so many upper-class Englishmen unintelligible. He also had the disconcerting habit of forcing his thin lips into a smile which disappeared as soon as it had formed, as though it were a shameful expression that had to be suppressed. I didn't care for Dodsy.

12

V. G. asked us what we wished to drink and pressed a buzzer next to his chair. An old servant shuffled in silently, and without looking up V. G. placed his orders.

'What is it you would like to know?' he asked. This kind of question always throws me. I had been told that V. G. had gone to Mayo College, the most famous princely school in India. I stammered something about English public schools in India and how the aim, under the Raj, had been to turn Indians into English gentlemen.

Perhaps he misunderstood my question. But it seemed I had offended him. 'What makes you think, my dear fellow, that we had to be taught how to be gentlemen, as it were? I deny that there does not exist in India a concept of behaviour that is in any way inferior to the Britishers' code. What did they teach us at Mayo . . . ?' V. G. paused dramatically. ' . . . To eat with knives and forks. Rather a middle-class accomplishment, wouldn't you say?'

Dodsy flashed a thin-lipped smile and lisped: 'Perfect, perfect.'

V. G. mentioned the gentlemanly virtues of the Rajput race. He spoke carefully, clearly enunciating every fruity vowel, a bit like an ageing matinée idol with a drink too many under his belt.

'To a Rajput,' he began, 'it does not matter if you win or lose a war, as it were, but you must die honourably. We are like the samurai, and you cannot say they have no gentlemanly tradition, so to speak. As children we were taught to stand the sight of blood. We had to watch as goats were slaughtered and were not permitted to avert our eyes for one second . . . '

'Splendid, splendid,' whispered Dodsy.

'What did Mayo teach us? The creativity of the English language. I can appreciate the creativity and wonder of European civilisation. That opening of the door, as it were, was a great thing. What values did we learn, what higher values? None, my friend, none whatsoever. It was a boarding school, so I learnt how to deceive, how to play jokes on people, how to pretend to work to satisfy our masters, how to use my charm to gain popularity, in short, how to be cunning to survive. I don't know whether that is a quality for a gentleman to be proud of, do you?'

Dodsy's mouth twitched in and out of a smile. He said nothing.

'I am afraid', V. G. continued, 'they tried everything to make me an English gentleman. But they never succeeded. I am still a backwoodsman from Rajputana . . . '

The lady in the sari came to life. 'Oh nonsense,' she said. 'You're just being absurd . . . '

'You think so? You should see my village.'

'Yes, but you weren't a backwoodsman.'

'Oh yes, oh yes. But we did have a sense of honour. At boarding school we merely learnt how to be cunning.'

'Maybe that's in the genes of Rajputs.'

'No, no, not cunning, we are not cunning. We are honourable. You see, there is a great difference between living a life of honour and a life of virtue, which was taught us in school. A life of virtue is middle-class, Victorian, prudish, whilst a life of honour . . . well, I heartily recommend you read this book . . . '

V. G. handed me a book entitled *The Annals and Antiquities of Rajastan* by Colonel James Tod. I looked around the room, at the chintz curtains, the open fireplace, the English furniture, the *Diaries of Evelyn Waugh* in the bookcase.

Inder remained silent during the interview. He watched my reaction to his old friend with the air of a man enjoying a good night at the theatre. As we left the villa to step into the cold Delhi night, he tossed a red woollen scarf over his left shoulder and turned to me: 'Don't believe a word he says.' I could not make out whether he meant this. But it seemed pointless to ask, for he would never have told.

'You must meet Jai.' This was one of Inder's favourite propositions. There was always someone new to meet, and Inder would always watch the result with his amused expression, his eyes blinking innocently behind the gold-rimmed glasses, perched a little askew on his thick nose. This latest introduction was not just to another eccentric with outrageous opinions or strange personal habits. To be sure, Jai was outrageous and had a reputation for extreme drunkenness and womanising – always white and usually British women, susceptible to the charms of mysterious Orientals. But that is not what interested me. The reason for Inder's introduction was that Jai happened to be related, I was never quite sure how, to the princes or rather, Jam Sahebs, of Nawanagar. That is to say, he was related to Ranji.

He was more than an hour late for our meeting in the coffee shop of a huge, modern, French-run hotel, a favourite meeting place for young Sikh businessmen in blazers, New Delhi yuppies and Air France stewardesses. English, spattered with the odd phrase in Hindi or Punjabi, was the dominant language in this palace of sheet-glass walls and fake Olde English and Mughal interiors. Inder, not known for punctuality himself, was annoyed and fidgety. It was, after all, his show. We spent the time gossiping about journalists in London, all of whom he knew, a few of whom I had met.

'Dicky always says that however much he detests the vulgarity and breakdown of civilised life in Britain, he will always live there.' Inder was on his favourite subject. 'He is absolutely right of course. I have nothing to say about any country but India and my poetry can only be rooted in the landscape of the Punjab.'

'But you grew up in Delhi and came of age in Cambridge.'

'Irrelevant, quite irrelevant. I believe one is born with a mental landscape, the result of generations of art, scholarship, and culture. One's landscape is part of one's language, one's classical literature, one's myths. Culture is like a great tree, from which its branches, us, cannot be severed without dying.'

A young man in jeans and a polo shirt lurched towards our table. He greeted Inder by folding his hands and wagging his head. 'I am being so very sorry about being late,' he said in the accent of a stage Indian. He then turned to me and said 'How are you, mate?' in broad Cockney. I laughed politely, assuming this was meant as a joke.

He ordered champagne, an odd and expensive drink in India, and attempted to describe a cure he had just taken in a California clinic for alcoholics. 'It was a fucking gas,' he said. 'It was being bloody marvellous,' he repeated for Inder's benefit. I was trying to make out whether this tiresome way of speaking was a conscious effort to amuse or whether it was part of Jai's persona, like a nervous tic of which he was no longer aware. His manner fascinated more than what he actually said: London gossip alternated with stories of palace revelries and hunting parties for European aristocrats.

'Yeah,' drawled Jai, 'Ranji. 'Course you know the famous story about him.' I asked which one. 'Well, see, he was playing the Australians. Two guys, an Englishman and an Aussie, were watching from the pavilion, when Ranji hit a six. A huge, fucking six. The Englishman turned to the Aussie and said,' (here Jai affected the accent of a typical toff) '"a prince, you know." Then, the next ball, Ranji was bowled. "Bloody nigger," said the Englishman.'

I laughed. Inder smiled. But Jai howled so uncontrollably that I thought he might choke. He hooted like an owl. He dabbed the tears from his bloodshot eyes with his napkin. And when the spasm of mirth gradually subsided, Jai said: 'You must meet . . . ' But for the Cockney he sounded like Inder. 'You must meet Binkie.'

'Binkie?'

'Yeah, Ranji's nephew. A real character, Binkie. And I can tell you one thing . . . '

'Yes?'

Jai leant forward, his face still remarkably handsome under the bloated traces of debauchery: 'Ranji really hated the Britishers.' I didn't notice it at first, but he had said this without a trace of a Cockney accent.

The train to Jodhpur smelled, not unpleasantly, of curry and toilets. The monotony of the arid landscape, pale yellow with blotches of ochre, was relieved here and there by clumps of bush. We were in the part of India they call Land of the Dead. Inder and I had been arguing about religion, an argument which was to end in a row.

We were sitting in the old library of a former palace in Jodhpur, where I found a copy of Ranji's *The Jubilee Book of*

Cricket in the carved teakwood bookcase. It was 'Dedicated by her gracious permission to Her Majesty the Queen-Empress'. The library was actually little more than a ramshackle room where the old world charm of the Raj was preserved in all its faded glory. Dusty peacock feathers still adorned the gaudy Chinese vases, and splotched old menus of long-forgotten banquets were displayed on the side-table like museum pieces for nostalgic tourists. A party held in honour of the Maharaja of Bissau in 1928 began with a Cocktail Panachée and continued on through a Crème Madrilène, a Gigot d'Angelet, and Plats Indiens, to finish with a Surprise de Boudoir Turck. After the banquet there was dancing to the music of Ivor Novello tunes played by a band from Goa.

Englishmen love this kind of thing. It reminds them of BBC dramas, of their collective dreams of Englishness, so glorious, so poignant, so bitter-sweet in the resentful seediness of contemporary little England. I am not an Englishman. There is nothing for me to feel nostalgic about. Yet the poignancy of such places isn't lost on me. The grandeur of these pathetic artefacts of the past lies precisely in their air of fakery, of fantasy, of striving for an effect, vaguely perceived, and clumsily executed. To invent is to be human.

It was then that I had my first spat with Inder. I made a disparaging remark about gurus. I said that most were imposters who got rich by exploiting the credulity of confused people. Inder began to shout: My remarks were both patronising and wrong, he said, for there was ample proof that some gurus did indeed have the power to perform miracles and if I refused to believe this, well, that was due to my own spiritual shallowness and crude materialism. Surely I had to admit that there was more to life than meets the eye, indeed that there is a hidden dimension unseen by all but a select few with special powers of perception.

That there might be forces we cannot see I didn't deny, but still I was highly suspicious of people claiming special access to these mysteries, especially when they peddled some kind of salvation. I have always found it odd that some parts of the world seem to be inundated with gurus, ghosts and other miraculous phenomena, while others seem to have none. Was it a question of climate, of landscape, of language? Inder maintained that there was a perfectly reasonable answer to this: whereas rational faculties have been overdeveloped in the West, the spiritual mind is a function of the East, the product of thousands of years of effort to bypass discursive thought and plumb greater depths. No major religion, he said, had ever come out of the West.

True, true, I said, but isn't philosophy a higher form than religion? That, Inder said, is precisely where Indian civilisation is superior: philosophy and religion are indistinguishable. Surely, I said, your average guru is hardly a philosopher. No, said Inder, but even if you came across one who is, you wouldn't be able to tell. You're too blinded by your cultural prejudice. And that was that. He said no more. And turned to his copy of *Sketches by 'Boz'*.

I went out for a trip in the hotel owner's jeep. As we sped through villages into the desert, the hotelier, a friendly raja, who drove at enormous speed, pointed out how much better the maharajas had taken care of their people than the Indian government. We drove past primitive wells, 'built by the Maharaja and used all the time by the people'. As for the modern water tank, a functional looking edifice made of concrete, the Raja dismissed it with a gesture of contempt: 'Built by the government, not used by the people.' The same story with the roads: a dirt track built by the Maharaja, loved by the people; tarmac roads, built by the government, 'not suited to our people'. There was a third road, or, more accurately, a camel track between the dirt road and the tarmac, which seemed to contain by far the most traffic, mostly camels and ox-carts. The maharajas, I should realise, understood the people, because they lived amongst them, were born from the same soil, whereas the government was an alien and impersonal intrusion in the lives of folks no Delhi-wallah could hope to understand. The Delhi-wallahs only brought greed and injustice.

The villagers, dimly seen through the clouds of desert dust kicked up by the Raja's jeep, greeted him as 'Bapu', 'father'.

Their faces beamed up at us, in the hope of at least a glance their way. The Raja looked straight ahead, only once in a while acknowledging their presence with a quick wave, rather like swatting a fly.

'You are seeing that every caste and community has its own dress,' he explained. 'They're all happy in their own way.' We stopped here and there for the Raja to take care of his people; sweets were pressed into small hands, and eyedrops from a little bottle kept in the Raja's inside pocket were squirted into the milky eyes of grateful trachoma victims. 'India is so damned complicated,' said the Raja, 'and, if you'll forgive me for saying so, Westerners so damned ignorant. You're always bloody banging on about the so-called untouchables. Let me show you some untouchables. They are perfectly content.'

We drew into a hamlet and stopped in front of a small house. I could hear the clanking sound of somebody banging a tin. We entered the house. A thin, dark man in a grubby shirt greeted us without smiling. His children, dirty and snotty-nosed, kept their distance. The house itself was spotless. Because of the caste taboo, we couldn't enter the kitchen, nor could the man, who spoke in a servile whine, offer us anything to drink. All we were permitted to do was look round, as the man rubbed his hands over and over on his shirt. There was a picture on the wall of a maharaja sitting on a white horse. 'One of my ancestors,' said the Raja with great satisfaction. 'They worship the maharaja here, you see, it is their religion.'

The desert air was freezing as we bowled along in the jeep. My eyes watered in the wind. The Raja looked impassive, his waxed moustache firm, his eyes protected by a smart pair of dark aviator glasses. I thought of Inder and his defence of caste. It was all about pride, he had said, about belonging. It rooted people in the cosmic order, without which life would be meaningless. Robbing a man of his caste would leave him naked, lonely, adrift in a world that no longer made sense. All happy in their own way. Everybody in his own dress, his own colours. Rooted in the cosmic order. It all seemed so perfectly logical, so enviably well worked out. We skirted the outside of Jodhpur, a wasteland of tumbleweed, sand and squalid huts. Women in colourful rags were digging beside the road.

'Terrible,' said the Raja, 'very terrible. You see, they left their villages. Looking for the bright lights of the city. Their way of life destroyed. No morals. Damned, damned shame.' The Raja's lips formed a straight thin line of stern disapproval.

Back in the desert: nothing but sand and rock and the occasional camel train. The Raja smiled, the waxed wings of his moustache pointing to his ears: 'Life is just as it was out here, before it was disturbed by the Britishers.'

'How was it disturbed by the British?'

'Oh, you see, they built railways, electricity, all that bloody nonsense.'

'That, surely, was not such a bad thing.'

The Raja's face remained impassive, only his voice betrayed some emotion. 'It was nothing, nothing at all. Look what we achieved in forty years of independence. Compared to that, a hundred years of the Raj was insignificant, totally insignificant. The Britishers may have built electricity, but we have nuclear power-stations. The Britishers gave us a few cars, Rolls-Royces and whatnot, but we have our own Indian cars now. Of that we are proud. One thing, though, we have lost, and that is discipline. The Britishers taught us discipline. But we have lost it. Indians have forgotten discipline.'

It was a painfully slow trip to Rajkot, the landscape hardly changing from desert to scrubland to desert again. I no longer had Inder to argue with, for he had returned to Delhi. I tried to imagine how Ranji must have felt, on his way back from England, thinking perhaps of his house on the Thames or the Brighton Esplanade, as he rolled back home over dried up river beds and the khaki soil of Gujerat. He intensely disliked the heat of Indian summers. The humidity had a bad effect on his asthma. So he was always glad to return to England and, later in his life, to Ireland. Yet it was here, in Rajkot, in a Victorian Gothic building in the sand, that he learnt how to play cricket and be an English gentleman.

You used to be able to see Rajkumar College from a distance, its twin towers the only tall buildings in town. It is now dwarfed by shopping emporiums, built on the other side of the dusty Maidan, where Mohan Lal's Magic Circus tent was pitched. Young boys played cricket there. Villagers carved crude cricket bats, which the women sold on the edges of the Maidan. They made and sold the bats during the day and curled up in their shawls at night.

I arrived on Independence Day to find an Old Boys' cricket match in progress. The O. B.s were dressed in blazers, old school ties and tennis shorts, and were having an excellent time. They called out heartily in a mixture of English, Gujerati and Hindi. 'Good shot!' they cried from the pavilion, where I was examining an old photograph of Ranji. 'Bad luck, sir!' they shouted as one O. B. got himself out playing across a leg break. 'Nice one, Shiva!' they yelled, when Shiva, playing for the School, returned the ball right over the stumps.

An English voice boomed suddenly across the ground: 'Great fun, great fun!' It belonged to the headmaster, Mr Haylock (Tonbridge and Balliol). He was a genial man in his early sixties. His shock of white hair stood out against a florid face and a canary-yellow scarf knotted round his neck. 'Jolly good show,' he said, and introduced me to some of the Old Boys. There was a large man in shorts, who asked me to call him 'Pat', since he was from Patiala. A group of younger men complimented their old headmaster effusively. School, they said, had been the best time of their lives, and all because of Sir. One thing they would never forget: the kindness of Sir.

'Oh, nonsense, nonsense,' said Mr Haylock, a broad smile creasing his crimson face. He wrapped his arm round Pat's enormous waist, his hand not reaching further than the spine, which he patted with affection: 'You're all lovely boys, lovely boys.'

I was offered lunch in Mr Haylock's bungalow, which was furnished simply, rather like an English country vicarage: white walls, sofas with chintz upholstery, some Indian nick-nacks, silver-framed photos of Mr Haylock's mother and sister and of various O. B.s, some of them dressed in army uniforms. We had cold fried eggs, green peas, kedgeree, a mild curry served with rice, and a custard; all a little like Mr Haylock's accent: hearty public school with an Indian lilt.

It was tempting to see the Englishness of Rajkumar, the 'good shots' and 'good lucks', the portrait of Queen Victoria in the Assembly Hall, the striped blazers and the sentimental talk about Sir, to see all this as a caricature, an absurd, Wodehousian drama in the desert. Some Englishmen might find it charming, like discovering a forgotten family heirloom in an obscure antique shop. Rajkumar College is of an England which no longer exists, or perhaps it only ever existed in India, as a piece of Raj theatre. The best years of our lives, the kindness of Sir – these were not the expressions of Indians trying to be British, any more than prayers in Arabic by Indian Muslims are an attempt to mimic Arabs. No, Pat and his blazered friends were Indian through and through, as Indian as the portrait of India's Queen-Empress in the Hall.

The O. B.s were gathered there to hear Mr Haylock deliver his Independence Day speech. Bright sunshine, filtered through the stained-glass windows, formed pretty patterns on the wooden floor, as Sir, dressed in a black gown, strode to the dais in a manner that signified the dignity of the occasion: not too fast, not too slow, head held high, eyes straight ahead, earnest yet benign. There was a hush in the Hall as he began his speech haltingly in Hindi. The only time he spoke in English was when he quoted from a patriotic speech made by Nehru on the first day of Independence in 1949. The phrases, so typical of Nehru – character, individual integrity, responsibility, discipline – were those of a Victorian English gentleman. And they got the greatest applause.

'Ah, Ranji,' said Mr Haylock, adjusting his yellow scarf, as we were served tea and cake in the bungalow, 'yes, yes, great fun, great fun. Let me tell you a story.' And he told me this astonishing tale: Quite recently Ranji's great-niece was visiting London. She hired a cab to get to her hotel from Victoria Station. It was summer. The driver opened the glass partition and politely asked her whether she would mind if he listened to the Test Match on the wireless. Indeed, she said, she would not. In fact, she took rather an interest in cricket herself. The window was shut, but soon the driver opened it again. Why was she interested in cricket, he asked, she being an Indian lady. Ah, she said, a relative had once been quite a useful cricketer. Once more the window was closed, only to be opened shortly after. And who, the driver asked, might her relative have been? Oh, she said, a gentleman called Ranjitsinhji, the Jam Saheb of Nawanagar. Good Lord, said the driver, and pulled up the cab, good Lord, a relative of Ranji! His niece, she said. Well I never, he said, and for the rest of the week he drove her wherever she wished to go and refused to take a penny.

It was an almost inconceivable story. But Mr Haylock assured me it was true. No doubt he believed it was. It made him seem oddly out of touch with contemporary Britain, where taxi drivers simply do not talk, let alone behave this way. Had something happened to the story in the retelling, perhaps? Could this be an English story, a Victorian morality tale, which had been gradually transformed into an Indian myth? Or was it perhaps the other way round: an Indian myth turned into an English story?

Mr Haylock was proud of his boys. He told me they all knew about Ranji, the most famous Old Boy. In his office I noticed a cricket bat, an oil painting of Chester Macnaghten, headmaster of the school in Ranji's time, and a picture of Ranji himself. There was a soft knock on the door. 'Come in,' cried Mr Haylock. A small, dark boy of about eleven entered and wished us both good morning. 'Please sir,' he asked, timidly eyeing his brightly polished shoes, 'may I be going up to the computer lab, sir?'

'Not be going, Rajiv, a simple go will suffice. Yes, you may go up, but not before you have recited "Gardiner's Tribute" for our guest here.' Mr Haylock winked at me. This time it was I who examined my shoes. 'They all know it by heart, you know,' said Mr Haylock.

Rajiv blushed to a darker brown. 'Yes sir,' he almost whispered and began to recite the famous lines; famous, that is, in

India, no longer in Britain, for this, too, had become an Indian story: 'The last ball has been bowled. Round Lord's, the grandstands are deserted and forlorned . . . '

'Forlorn, Rajiv, f-o-r-l-o-r-n.'

' . . . deserted and forlorn. We have said farewell to cricket. We have said farewell to cricket's king. The game will come again with the spring, but the king will come no more. There have been kings before him to whom we have joyfully bowed the knee. Yes, there were giants before the Jam Saheb, and yet, I think, it is un . . . un . . . undoo . . . '

'Undeniable.'

' . . . it is undeniable that, as a batsman, the Indian will live as the supreme exponent of the Englishman's game.'

'Quite right, quite right. Now run along to the lab, my dear boy.'

Mohan Lal's Magic Circus tent on the Maidan was lit up like a beacon at night. The batmakers and sellers were fast asleep in their rags. I trudged towards the circus through the sand and heard wild dogs sniffing around in the dark. It was light and cosy inside the tent, with hundreds of shiny eyes riveted to the stage. Mohan Lal himself appeared, dressed like a fairy-tale maharaja. He was a fat man and beads of sweat made his make-up run in small streams down his beaming face. Coloured glass glittered from his turban and his body was wrapped in swirls of gold and blue satin. He told jokes in Gujerati and produced white pigeons from a silver box. The crowd cried 'Ooh!' when he pulled a seemingly endless handkerchief from his sleeve. And then, with a wink and a leer, Mohan Lal announced his *pièce de résistance*, the act we had all been waiting for: he would saw a young woman in half.

The tent went dark, sounds of thunderclaps and Bombay film music filled the air. A new set was noisily cranked on to the stage, partly obscured from our view by a satin curtain with silver stars stuck on. The Bombay film music changed to a disco tune, the curtain went up, the lights came on, and there was Mohan Lal looking quite malevolent in a long, white doctor's coat, with a stethoscope round his neck and a glinting mirror mounted on his head. He leered into the green spotlight and the children screeched with pleasure.

His operating theatre was a torture chamber filled with saws, knives, scissors and grotesque, bleeping machines. A plump young woman, dressed in tights, lay down on the operating table, where Mohan's assistant strapped her into a shining white box. Mohan then picked the meanest looking chainsaw and little red lights blinked on the bleeping machine. The nightmarish lab was twitching with evil. Mohan Lal's magic was science run amok.

'When in Rajkot,' Inder had told me after our row had subsided, 'be sure to see Jacky.' I had scribbled the address in my notebook. Jacky was actually called Jagdish Bathia. He had been a keen cricketer once and, so Inder said, would be a useful contact, for he knew Ranji's nephew, the man everyone called Binkie. I knew little more about Binkie than the fact that he lived on a boat somewhere near Jamnagar and that he was an eccentric. Since I wanted to visit Ranji's old palace, he was important, for the current Jam Saheb was never at home. Binkie, as the nearest relative, was the only one who could give me permission to see where Ranji once lived. People didn't actually go for the garlic cloves at the mention of Binkie, but there was something disconcerting about the way everyone referred to him as 'a very strange man'.

Jacky was no exception: 'Binkie-sahib, yes indeed, a very, very strange man.' Then, silence. Jacky was not a talkative person. He pondered my questions for a long time and answered in single sentences. I asked him about Ranji. He thought for a while. Then at long last: 'A very, very great cricketer.' Could he think of anything else that might help me understand the great cricketer? Silence. 'A very great English gentleman.' An English gentleman? 'Yes, yes, an English gentleman. He was an English gentleman.' Silence.

I didn't know what more to say, so we sat side by side, in the cricket pavilion, staring at the field where Ranji scored his first runs, meditating about the meaning of it all. Then, to my immense relief, out of the blue, an anecdote: 'In 1901 Ranji scored 285 Not Out against Somerset, a very, very fine innings. The crowd rose to applaud him all the way back to the dressing-room, but as people patted him on the back, congratulating him on his great feat, Ranji pointed to two red smudges on his pads. "The bowler hit me twice," he said, shaking his head. "The bowler hit me twice. No good at all." That's what he said, "No good at all."' Jacky smiled for the first time and looked wistfully across the field, where a white cow was pissing, leaving a dark stain in the dust.

I asked Jacky about cricket in India today. Again his answer took a long time coming, but I had learnt to be patient. Cricket was no longer cricket, he said. 'No discipline on the field, no discipline off it. Cricket is a gentleman's game and Ranji was a great gentleman, a very, very great gentleman.'

'What about the present Jam Saheb?'

'Oh, yes, yes indeed, but he's usually abroad. You will not be able to see him. Binkie should be able to help you. A strange man, but a good man. He will help you. But you must remember one thing. You must call him Your Highness. He insists on it.'

'Is he a prince?'

'No, not really . . . well, a strange man, very strange. Just remember – Your Highness.'

I was beginning to feel a little apprehensive about my visit to Ranji's old town. But I was intrigued all the same, especially when an elderly doctor on the rattling bus to Jamnagar creased his brow and said: 'I'm telling you, my friend, you're coming to our town at a very sad time. You will be seeing it at the nadir of its history. You will be seeing the disintegration of a very great family.'

My only contact in Jamnagar was an old cousin of Jacky's, called Mr Patel. Jacky did not tell me much about him except that he used to stay with Ranji in England when he was a child. I called Mr Patel from my hotel. A man answered: Oh, you want my dad, sure man, come right over.' I could hear rock music blaring in the background.

The Patels' living-room floor was covered with large cushions. There was an overpowering smell of sweet incense, as in a Hindu shrine. Any conversation was drowned out by The Rolling Stones on the tapedeck. Reproductions of Tibetan scrolls decorated the walls. A young boy in tight jeans was sprawled on the floor, asleep. The scene brought back, as in an old photograph, my days in Notting Hill Gate in 1970, when the drifting population of my basement flat included the odd Indian hippie. We lived in a perpetual haze of hash and incense and Ravi Shankar music. India represented the land of our dreams.

'Hey, man, make yourself at home,' said a middle-aged man with long grey hair. He had to shout to make himself heard above the din. 'I'm Ajit and this', he patted the sleeping boy on his rump, 'is my son Vijay. Want a joint?' As we passed the joint to and fro, Ajit gave me a brief history of his life. He had spent four years in London in the late Sixties, much of the time round the corner from my basement flat in Notting Hill. 'But London's dead now,' he said with a frown, 'quite, quite dead.' After his return to India he had made some money selling electrical goods. Then, in semi-retirement, he had decided to become an artist. His wife was also an artist, and his son, Vijay, was an artist too. Some of their works were displayed on the wall, amongst the Mandalas. These pictures, best described as colourful doodling, were as reminiscent of Notting Hill as the cushions, the incense and the continuous rock music. The family was also 'into video' and Ajit launched into a rambling discourse about 'real time' and 'reel time'. I sank back into the cushions and pretended to listen with interest. I rather wished Inder had been with me to share the experience.

'So you want to see my father?' It seemed as if I had been in the house for hours. Yes, I did want to see his father. 'Upstairs, man.' I followed his directions and as I climbed the stairs, I saw Ajit slumped on his cushion, staring at the doodles on the wall, nodding to the rock beat, caressing his son's behind.

I did not notice Mr Patel at first. His room, rather like a servant's quarters, was tiny. Once I had got used to the dark I saw him lying on a string bed, examining me with wide eyes. Bob

Dylan was wailing away downstairs. I wished Mr Patel good evening. 'And a very good evening to you,' he said, his voice surprisingly clear. 'Would you be taking some tea?' I said that would be very nice and he tinkled a little bell beside his bed.

The room was bare of furniture apart from the bed and a small chest. There was a large framed photograph of Ranji on the wall: dressed in tweed plus-fours and a hacking-jacket, hunched over a dead leopard. Tweeds in India? 'Oh yes, oh yes, always in British clothes,' said Mr Patel.

Mr Patel was the opposite of his cousin. He adored to talk – he gushed and flowed, without stopping, as though a dam, long under great pressure, had finally burst. He talked about his childhood visits to England; how he and his sisters were met at Victoria Station and driven to the house at Staines in Ranji's Rolls-Royce; how Ranji taught them English table manners – how to eat properly with knife and fork, how to drink tea, how to speak nicely, all so 'we could show ourselves to our best advantage in the choicest circles'. Every night Ranji would come up to the nursery to read them Kipling's jungle stories and Alice in Wonderland. And every morning, if the weather was fine, Mr Patel was taken in the Rolls-Royce to the local cricket ground, where the old pro would coach him in the nets. Then there were the picnics at Inkpen, the boating at Henley, tennis in the garden. And then, as suddenly as Mr Patel's memories had begun, the torrent stopped. There was not a drop more, not a single insight to be gained into Ranji's character, except that he had been an exceptionally fine gentleman.

So I gave up asking and enquired how Ranji's palace could be seen. Unfortunately, he said, the Jam Saheb was away on business, so I'd have to see Binkie about that. There was Binkie, in that picture . . . Mr Patel pointed to a small photograph on the chest. I saw a group of men posing with earnest expressions on somebody's lawn. That's the Jam Saheb, said Mr Patel, pointing out a stout man with a pigtail, and that's Binkie. If the Jam Saheb was stout, Binkie was enormous, a mountain dressed up in a white tent. His small moustache could just be discerned, protruding from his cheeks, which were like creamy hillocks squashing his nose which resembled a little cherry on top of a cake. 'A good man,' said Mr Patel, 'but a little temperamental. I hope and pray he will see you. I do hope and pray.' He folded his hands and drew them to his chest. 'But do permit me . . . ' Mr Patel clapped his hands impatiently. An elderly retainer appeared in the doorway waiting for his orders. Mr Patel scribbled a note and told him to deliver it to Binkie-sahib. 'Perhaps this will help. I do hope and pray . . . '

I thanked him and took my leave of Mr Patel and the rest of the family, who were all awake now, sprawled on the cushions, passing a joint. 'Sure you don't want to stay, man?' asked Ajit. I said I was sure. The Rolling Stones were playing an old Chuck Berry number as I quietly closed the door.

There are at least three large palaces in Jamnagar, two of them built in Ranji's time. No one ever lived in the grandest one, a wedding cake with Mogul-style domes, Doric columns and Italianate loggias, surrounded by long-neglected English gardens, now reduced to wilderness. It was completed just in time to house the guests attending Ranji's funeral, but had been empty ever since. I tried to get a closer look at the broken windows set in rather finely carved frames, at the rotting wooden doors and the dilapidated walls, caked with bird droppings, but a guard in a splendid but very threadbare uniform told me to clear off and pushed me outside the barbed-wire fence.

The Lal Palace, less grand than the empty wedding cake, but still grand enough, was finished in 1921 to put up the Prince of Wales during his Indian visit. Alas, the Prince failed to turn up in Jamnagar and the palace remained unoccupied until after Independence, when the government made it into a state guest-house. Inside the palace was a strong smell of camphor and table wax. The solid teak furniture might well have been there since 1921. And so might the stuffed leopard heads on the wall of the billiards room, the antlers in the hall, the Persian rugs on the wooden floors, the Victorian oil paintings of dead game and the peacock feathers stuck in Chinese vases. Some of the bedrooms were occupied by government officials, taking naps under the mosquito nets. One such gentleman, wearing his white Congress-wallah hat, had neglected to close the bathroom door and he was noisily relieving himself while staring at me with wide, unblinking eyes, like an owl caught in the beam of a torch.

Wandering through the crescents, squares and circuses of Jamnagar, I knew this place reminded me of somewhere else, but couldn't quite put my finger on where. The architectural style was what is known in India as Indo-Saracenic, a mixture of Hindu, European and Mogul, a kind of Oriental fantasy concocted by European engineers. Somehow, the style of Jamnagar, the abundance of palaces, the opulent villas, artificial lakes, and luxurious town houses, seemed too grand for this provincial city, as though it were trying to prove something, to play a role for which it was not entirely suited.

This is true of much Raj architecture, of course, built to impress the natives with British grandeur, with Britannia's right to rule. Most buildings of the Raj are monuments to power and invented tradition, which now, forty years on, can be sometimes pleasing, impressive even, but always a little shrill. Jamnagar is a little shrill.

Then, suddenly, I realised the obvious: it was like Brighton, with its palatial hotels, its quaint Orientalism, its theatrical elegance. For years Ranji had lived there, amidst Prinny's follies and bawdy postcards, nursing his asthma in waterfront hotels. Brighton's fantastic mixture of Georgian elegance and Indo-Saracenic-Chinoiserie must have been his inspiration. Jamnagar was in essence a dandy's town: meticulously planned, flamboyant, a heroic monument in a decadent age. Jamnagar was a town that had, so to say, invented itself.

The only monument that looked out of place was a large golden statue of Ranji, completed after his death. It overlooked the Lakotha lake, where Ranji planned to erect a line of statues of his illustrious ancestors. Ranji himself had posed for an American sculptor in Paris, called Herbert Haseldine. To lend authenticity to the work, he had a thoroughbred Kathi horse with the distinctive curled ears shipped over from India. The sculptor was so taken with the Indian stallion that he insisted on entertaining him for tea, much to the merriment of his friends. However, on his way back to India the horse broke his knees against the walls of his box, and had to be put down. The equestrian sculpture, alas, was never completed.

The road from Jamnagar to Sarodar, Ranji's native village, was so rocky that I feared for the Ambassador taxi's shock-absorbers. We were surrounded by a wilderness of parched brown earth. The only thing that grew was a kind of thornbush whose tufts protruded from the sand. The villages of khaki mud, dotted with patties of cow dung, looked as though they were not so much built into the landscape as an organic part of it. There were hardly any cars on the road, just processions of camels, bullocks and goats. I didn't relish the thought of being stuck out there in a broken down Ambassador with a driver who spoke no English. I had visions of being surrounded by bandits roaming the desert at night. I didn't like the way the driver flicked his wrist in despair every time the car was lifted clear off the road by nasty humps.

'Jam Saheb!' he said suddenly, pointing at a distant bush. He was aware of my interest in Ranji. I looked out and saw a small stone watchtower, presumably put up for one of Ranji's shooting expeditions. That is where he must have spent nights with his guests, eyes fixed on a tethered goat, whose whimpering and scent brought the wild beasts into the sportsmen's sights.

Further down the road I spotted the remains of four large Greek columns, which bore a slight resemblance to the ruins in Ephesus or Delphi. They were crumbling in the four corners of a rocky field. Jam Saheb? I asked, as though I didn't know. 'Jam Saheb, Jam Saheb,' he nodded.

The columns must have been all that remained of a party held for the Viceroy in the early 1920s. The rocky field had been a camp. The columns, twenty feet high, had been decorated with paintings of legendary heroes. There were green lawns where a few months before there had been nothing but sand and rock. For the banquet there were dancing girls and Goanese bands and fireworks and artificial flowers and fine wines ordered from

Paris. And the whole thing was illuminated by electric lights that lit up the entire area. The locals had been scared off by this display of magic. But luckily everything was dismantled as soon as the party was over.

'Sarodar,' said the driver, after we had bumped and lurched along the road for another two hours. Ranji's village, like all the others, seemed to have grown out of the dry earth. The buildings were crude mud dwellings, except two, which dominated the scene. Built on opposite hillocks, they faced each other like opponents in a petrified feud. One was a small ruined fort with four squat towers, which guarded the plain on all sides. The other was a large bungalow, built, I would have thought, in the 1930s. 'Jam Saheb,' said the driver pointing at the fort. And the other one? He wagged his head in the affirmative: 'Jam Saheb.'

I climbed up to the fort, followed by a swarm of curious urchins. The old wooden gate was locked. The boys motioned me to wait, while one ran to a nearby house, whence he returned with an older man, who grinned and showed me the key. 'Jam Saheb,' said the man. Ranjitsinhji? He wagged his head: 'Ranjitsinhji.' The door was unlocked and we entered a courtyard filled with straw and cow dung. The boys crowded round me, as though expecting a show of some sort. The man pointed to the various doors around the yard, and beckoned me to follow. The rooms were surprisingly neat. One of them, small, with whitish walls and a window with a view of the village, seemed to merit special attention. 'Jam Saheb, Ranjitsinhji, baby, very old,' explained the man. Was he born in this room? 'Ranjitsinhji,' said the man. Back in the yard I noticed a crude stone carving on the wall of a Rajput warrior brandishing a sword.

We walked to the opposite hill. There was an old shrine in the front garden with a rusty Hindu trident inside. An elderly caretaker dressed in a dhoti waited on the veranda. Definitely 1930s, I thought, as I looked at the clean Bauhaus lines of the villa. The caretaker seemed disturbed. 'Your good name?' he asked. I told him. 'You are having permission?' I lied and said I had. He asked me to sign a book and reluctantly opened the door. There was

32

nothing much inside except bird droppings and some marble fireplaces. The bathrooms were still intact though, equipped with handsome porcelain tubs. 'Made in England,' said the man who showed me the fort and his broad grin revealed a set of crimson teeth, stained with betel-nut. 'Jam Saheb, very old,' he added.

The villa looked too modern to have been built by Ranji, who died, after all, in 1933. I knew he had built a shooting lodge in Sarodar, opposite the fort. So this clearly was the site. The decaying bungalow must have been built by Ranji's successor, his adopted son. I think I understood what the man meant by very old. The fort, this villa, the Greek columns on the campsite, were as old, or as new, as everything else built in India; as old as the Mogul tombs in Delhi, as new as the Victoria Memorial in Calcutta. All are part of a timeless history now. All in time will be swallowed by the landscape.

There was a message waiting for me at the hotel. It was a hand-delivered note from Binkie. 'Now you are here,' it said in a rather messy scrawl, 'I might as well show you around the old place. Come for tea tomorrow four o'clock. My bearer will pick you up.'

A dark-skinned man of about fifty arrived in a battered Ambassador at three-thirty. He remained silent all the way to Binkie's house, which turned out to be an old yacht in Rozi harbour. One could still see traces of former elegance, indeed opulence in the yacht, which had not yet been obliterated by time. The deck hadn't been scrubbed for ages, but was made of superb wood, and the brass fittings, long turned green in the humid heat, were beautifully made in Chatham, 1911. Binkie couldn't sail his yacht even if he wanted to, for the harbour, once the pride (and main source of income, from smuggling) of Ranji's state, had silted up entirely. The yacht was beached for ever.

The silent bearer led me on board, where we were met by a slim boy in a long white shirt, who told me to wait. I sat down in a rusty cabin with nautical prints tacked on to the wall. After about ten minutes a door opened and the boy backed out, noiselessly

33

bowing to someone in the next cabin. He wrung his hands and told me to proceed.

'Dear boy,' whispered a deep wheezy voice, 'do come in.' An enormous man in what looked like a silk caftan, but was in fact only a shirt, sat on a pile of cushions like a pasha, drinking tea, surrounded by the oddest assortment of bric-à-brac: stuffed birds in glass domes, silver plates containing strings of pearls and other assorted jewellery, sporting trophies, ornamental horseshoes, hunting guns, fine Indian silk casually tossed on a pile, empty bottles of French wine, old copies of *Country Life* and what appeared to be Indian astrological charts.

He was so fat it was impossible to tell his age. He wore his hair down to his shoulders and his moon face hid what wrinkles he might have had. His arms were like giant slabs of suet culminating in braces of sausages, and his massive thighs seemed to merge with two large leather containers in the shape of cowboy boots.

'Yes, jolly good, jolly good, some tea? Or perhaps some of our local poison? Afraid I can't offer you much, old man. Frightfully poor these days. In a bloody pickle, actually. They're out to get us, you know.'

The hearty language was strangely at odds with the low, wheezy voice. It had the perverse effect of a child uttering obscenities. I wasn't quite sure whom he meant by 'they'. I assumed he was referring to the government authorities who weren't always well disposed towards the remnants of the princely families. 'Damned politicians,' he muttered. I was right.

'So what will it be, eh?' I asked for some tea. 'Jolly good, jolly good.' And a pudgy finger, squeezed in the middle by a large ring, reached for one of the buzzers beside his seat. When nothing happened, the finger registered its impatience by hitting the buzzer hard several times. At last the boy came scrambling in. Binkie ordered tea and pointed to his right leg: 'And while you're here, Ajay, could you . . . ' Ajay looked up. 'Could you . . . ?' Binkie asked again, a little more sharply this time. Ajay went up to his master, took hold of the right leg and with considerable effort managed to lift it a few inches, whereupon a high trumpeting sound issued forth from the region of Binkie's thighs. 'Aah . . . ' said Binkie, 'the bloody bowels,' and the leg was released. 'Ajay, bring me my black pills.' The boy wagged his head and silently disappeared.

'Can't even rely on one's own people anymore,' said, or rather, whispered Binkie. 'After all one's done for them. Bloody awful, I'm telling you, bloody awful. It's all coming to an end, you know. It's all over.' Binkie fell into a gloomy silence, studying the carpet on the floor, as though there were an answer to his problems in the intricate but faded Persian pattern.

I was not sure what to say, so I was pleased to see the huge bulk suddenly lurch to life again. 'Well, well, well, yes, yes, so you're interested in Ranji?' I said that I was. 'Pity the Jam Saheb isn't here. He'd be able to sort you out.' It was indeed a pity, I confirmed. 'Well, we'll see what we can do. Not a great deal, I'm afraid. Still, you might as well see the bloody place. Ajay!' The finger repeated its journey to the buzzer and hit it hard. Ajay reappeared, rather swiftly this time. 'Ajay, see our guest to the Jam Palace. If you'll excuse me, old boy, got to get some shut-eye.' I thanked His Highness for his kindness and got up from my chair. 'I say, dear fellow, would you mind . . . ' 'Not at all,' I said, as Ajay and I each took one of Binkie's arms and began to pull. 'Heigh-ho, heigh-ho,' wheezed Binkie, as slowly, inch by inch, his massive frame rose from the cushion. Ajay and I were left panting, as Binkie padded out of the cabin, like a great white rhino.

Binkie had a fine old Chevrolet, made in the 1950s, with large chrome-plated fins, now covered in rust. Ajay and I sank back into the cracked leather seats as we set off for the Jam Palace. As we left the ship behind us, he turned out to be quite a talkative boy. When he smiled he showed a set of exquisitely white teeth set in clean pink gums. 'I am Sahib's number one bum boy,' he volunteered. 'I give plenty satisfaction.' I nodded without saying anything, for I did not wish to probe further into Binkie's private arrangements. 'But he has bloody bowel problem. Many, many times the Sahib calls me.' I was relieved when we arrived at the palace. Ajay told me to wait and got out to talk to the guard. We were allowed to proceed.

With a little pinch in my arm and a merry giggle Ajay said goodbye. I was left alone in an antechamber. Soon the door opened and a very old servant appeared. The man seemed barely alive. He was thin and leathery and his lugubrious features seemed to be set forever in an impassive expression. He asked me to follow him. We walked through a wide hall, filled on both sides with oil paintings. I noted an Alma-Tadema, two Land-seers, a portrait of Gladys Cooper by László de Lombos, and a mediocre reproduction of David's *Napoleon*, riding his white horse. We entered a dining-room, which smelled of mould and dust. It seemed the windows hadn't been opened for years. There was a large oil painting, entitled *Mother India*, depicting Indra with her many arms, and another showing Buddha, meditating under the Bodhi tree. They were quite remarkably hideous. The artist, I saw, was one A. Alston, R. A.

'Come, come,' whispered the servant, when I lingered over the paintings for too long. We entered a dark, fairly large room, with that same mouldy smell.

'Jam Saheb's room,' he announced, and retired into a corner, where he stood absolutely still. It was precisely as it had been described: there was the empty parrot's cage, and there a large painting of young boys, bathing, by Henry Scott Tuke, R. A.; and there the bed, and the glass cabinet containing the crick-eter's relics – six glass eyes, like little chocolate pellets floating in cream, peering from their satin-lined cases; jewels, pins, cuff-links, medals and sporting trophies, all perfectly main-tained. Cricket bats, like the swords of a legendary warrior, were displayed in another glass cabinet. Ranji's bed was neatly made up, as though waiting for the Jam Saheb's return.

As I examined the photograph of C. B. Fry on the bedside table, I heard a hiss in my ear. It was the ancient retainer. 'Sahib,' he whispered, and I turned round to face a pair of faded velvet slippers held out for my inspection. They had the initials K. S. R. stitched on them in gold. 'Worn by His Highness,' he explained, with a tone of deep reverence.

In a handsome bookcase of carved mahogany, I noted leather-bound editions of Shakespeare, Carlyle, Herbert Spencer, Dumas père, Bryson's *Norfolk Shoots* and Ranji's own *The Jubilee Book of Cricket*. There was also a selection of Sherlock Holmes stories, a set of E. W. Hornung's 'Raffles' books, and a large number of cricketers' memoirs, most of them inscribed by their authors. But the *pièce de résistance*, a bibliophile's dream, was an edition of Tacitus, bound in Morocco, that had once belonged to Napoleon. It was stamped with a large golden N and the imperial eagle.

Next to the bookcase was a sturdy eighteenth-century English desk. Ranji was not, so far as I knew, much of a writer, so I didn't expect to find anything of great interest there. I opened the desktop anyway. I could feel the eyes of the old servant watching my every move, even though he didn't utter a sound. There was a pile of photographs, most of them in rather poor condition. One showed two English girls – twins it seemed – having tea in a garden, another showed C. B. Fry, dressed in a white tropical suit and a straw boater, standing in front of a Continental hotel. There were several pictures of Ranji himself, of course: behind the wheel of a new car; hunched over the corpse of a tiger; playing cricket; perched on top of an elephant; bowing to the King-Emperor at his Durbar in Delhi; inspecting Indian troops in France. There was a silver locket with a picture inside of an Indian lady. His mother? The servant silently wagged his head. The desk also contained Ranji's passport, identifying him as a Hindu, a Rajput and a ruling prince. Visible distinguishing features: smallpox marks on the face. In the photograph Ranji's glass eye was easy to detect.

The retainer, still standing as quiet as a statue, clearly did not approve of this rummaging through his master's shrine. Perhaps his anxiety prompted him to speak. 'What are you hoping to see?' he asked. 'Did His Highness leave any letters?' I asked in return. 'Ah,' he said, 'I think I know of what you are speaking,' and, swift as a ghost, he flitted off to another room.

As I waited for his return, I took another peek at the glass eyes, as though somehow they could be induced to look back.

Preserving a room entirely in its original state, as a shrine, is rather like embalming a corpse, as if one can hold on to life by retaining its outward forms; as though by leaving things exactly as they were, one could catch some of the living spirit, just as a photographic plate catches light, or better still, an infra-red film catches the shadows of history. I was reminded of certain S-bahn stations in Berlin, boarded up for decades, but still vaguely discernible as you roared through these cobwebbed, rat-infested, subterranean windows into the past.

'Sahib,' said the retainer, cutting off my musings over Ranji's glass eyes. He held out a large manila envelope and handed it to me. 'If you please,' he said and shuffled back into his corner. I opened it and a thick sheaf of letters tumbled onto the desk. I spotted an unopened telegram, but when I was about to open it, the retainer hissed and said that would be out of the question. Nothing was allowed to be altered.

The letters were mostly to do with state business: letters from the Viceroy in Delhi, or the British Resident in Rajkot; thank you letters from various people who had been Ranji's guests at Jamnagar; a few longer letters from Jacques Cartier in London, discussing the history and possible purchase of precious stones. 'Are they of interest, sahib?' whispered the servant. I said they most certainly were.

There was one more sheaf to go through, a thick wad of papers, bound by a silk Cambridge blue ribbon. I carefully untied the ribbon. The first paper was dated 1921, written in Jamnagar and addressed to 'My Dear Charlo'. The writing was in Ranji's own elegant, sloping hand. But if it was written by Ranji himself, what was it doing here? Could it be that he never sent the letter? Judging by the different density of the ink, sometimes thick, sometimes thin and watery, the document was written over a period of several weeks, perhaps longer. For the letter was immensely long. A cursory reading suggested that it was a rambling account of Ranji's life. And Charlo had to be Ranji's great friend, C. B. Fry, who played cricket for Sussex and England. Clearly, I had to have the letter, or at least read it, for no biography, however excellent and exhaustive, would give as good an account of Ranji as his own story. The account might be false, of course, but even a man's lies offer invaluable insights into his character. Would I get permission? Would Binkie be able to give it?

After two days, spent wandering around aimlessly through the streets and crescents of Ranji's town, I managed to secure another appointment at Binkie's boat. It was dark by the time I got there and about half the fairy lights round the deck were on. Binkie was in his usual place, immobile on his cushions, nursing a whisky and soda.

'Well, well, well, so you're still here, old man? What is it you want this time, eh? I'm frightfully busy, as you can see, frightfully busy. They're after me, you know. The bloodhounds have been unleashed.' That said, he shifted his legs a fraction, yawned loudly and closed his eyes. His bluish lips disappeared into the valley of his chins. 'Ahm, Your Highness . . . ' I tried, but he seemed fast asleep. 'So tired . . . ' he blubbered, 'the hounds . . . All over . . . So very, very tired . . . ' Then, a great shudder went through his frame: 'Yes, yes, what is it you want?'

I explained about the letters. First one eye opened, fixing me in its gaze, then the other. 'Take them, take them all!' he cried hoarsely. 'They're taking everything anyway, so you might as well feed off the same carcass . . . So tired, so very tired . . . ' Once again, he fell fast asleep.

I took this to be his permission to borrow the letters. And so I left as quickly as I could, lest he change his mind. You never knew what flights of whimsy lurked in that sleepy head, whose moods changed as swiftly as the August rains. The next day I set off once more to the old palace, where I had an appointment with the ancient retainer, who was to hand over the documents. He seemed positively lively compared to the first time we met. When I left the palace, he shook my hand, and said with something akin to enthusiasm: 'His Highness was a very fine gentleman.'

II

' . . . forgery was a crime which perhaps seems closest to Wilde's presentation of himself.'

Richard Ellmann on Oscar Wilde

Jamnagar
February 1921

My dear Charlo,

I hope this letter finds you in good cheer and good health. As far as my own health is concerned, I am quite all right, apart from my habitual bronchial trouble. The season so far has been most enjoyable. I wish you could have been with me on my last trip to Kashmir, where, as usual, we played cricket against the Maharaja's team. I do believe you have met His Highness?

It is not however with His Highness that I am concerned at present. The reason for this letter is to express my intense disappointment about a most unfortunate event. I am referring to the last minute alteration in the schedule of HRH the Prince of Wales, whose visit to India is, as you know, imminent. I had expected him to visit my State, which, unless I am very much mistaken, was also HRH's wish. We had gone to some considerable trouble to provide HRH with the very best we have to offer in our part of the world, which may not be as good as the best houses in England, but is nevertheless a match for any other princely state in India.

Consequently, my dear Charlo, it was with infinite regret that I learnt that Jamnagar was no longer to be on HRH's itinerary. This has hurt me deeply, for I love the English people – a love which I believe has been reciprocated on many an occasion. You know very well how much store I have always set by the greatness of the British Empire, symbolised, nay, more than that, guaranteed by the affectionate and almost familial ties between the princes of India and our Sovereign, the King-Emperor. I have always tried to express my love and appreciation of Great Britain with every means at my disposal.

So where, my friend, have I gone wrong to deserve this treatment? I do not for one second doubt HRH's friendly disposition towards myself, nor do I believe that he can have had a personal hand in the change of plans. Indeed, I have reason to suspect that rumours have been spread to the effect that there is malaria in my State which could endanger HRH's health. Such scurrilous talk can have had only one source, the very same that has been the cause of so much trouble out here of late: the native politicians. They insist on stirring people up against us – this despite the fact that most of us (I cannot, alas, say all) regard our people with the affection and solicitude that parents reserve for their children. The politicians are looking to upset ancient traditions without the foggiest idea what to put in their place once they have succeeded. I still believe India has much to contribute to the common ideals of our Empire, but not if agitators succeed in sowing ill will against those of us best equipped to understand and indeed further those ideals for the benefit of all. I foresee nothing but chaos and destruction if untutored minds are inflamed by the irresponsible politics propagated by men who are motivated by personal greed and ambition rather than a willingness to work and sacrifice for the common good.

Of course, the native agitators would not get very far were it not for the lack of calibre of the men who are sent out to administer our Empire. There is, it must be said (and I say it with infinite regret), a mean club spirit abroad. The British counterpart to the native politician is the petty functionary, the Jack-in-office who lords it over millions, not because he believes in any higher ideal, but simply because he gets paid to do his job. And after his day's work is done, he retires to his club, to bask in the narrow company of his salaried fellows.

I realise only too well that we still need Great Britain's strong hand to lead and support us in spite of our advance in civilisation, but we can only progress if our guides are men of character and vision. Therefore I deplore the presence of these small-minded fellows who presume, like the native politicians, to meddle in the affairs of princes who have ruled here for centuries.

My dear Charlo, we have been friends for many years now, on the field and off, so I do hope you won't mind my importunity. I ask nothing less of you than to be my judge. Tell me what I have done to be subjected to the cold shoulder of a country I love as much as my own. I shall try my best to plead my case by presenting you with the story of my life, much of which you know already, of course. Nonetheless, I hope you can bear with me. It is not my intention to write a memoir, for I have no literary ambitions. These notes – they are no more than that – are not meant for publication, or for any eyes but yours. Who else, in my hour of despair, can I turn to, my dear friend? So please accept this as my private testimony submitted for your judgement, which, I feel sure, will be suffused with the wisdom and reason imparted by your classical education and your British common sense.

Please convey my best wishes to Madame, your dear wife.

Ever yours,
Ranji

Charles Burgess Fry, classics scholar, sportsman, failed politician and would-be King of Albania, was, to say the least, an odd judge. And common sense is perhaps not the first thing that comes to mind when reviewing his many virtues.

But he did look marvellous. With his wavy, golden hair, his immense height, his blue eyes, his hawk's nose, he could have 'stepped straight out of the frieze of the Parthenon', as an Oxford contemporary put it. Or, for that matter, out of one of those Chester Barrie ads for tweed suits that fascinated me as a child. They were like images in a dream then. I would leaf through back numbers of *Punch* magazine with a feeling almost of reverence, as my eyes caressed the pictures of cavalry twill trousers,

Jermyn Street shirts, Viyella, Oxford cloth, houndstooth, herring-bone, Prince of Wales, three-button, double-breasted, club tie. And the models in these dreams: long legs, white moustaches, blond, tanned faces with a hint of a smile, denoting complete, effortless superiority. When, later on, I saw these images come to life, speaking hearty banalities, I was keenly disappointed. And yet the dream remained. And the image was that of C. B. Fry: an English god, an icon of good sportsmanship, a late-Victorian caricature of the *Boy's Own* hero, one of the last of a dying caste.

Fry was born on 25 April 1872, in Croydon, Surrey, and claimed to be of 'ancient Saxon stock', his ancestry, so he said with pride, going back to the weald men of the Forest Ridge of Sussex. Among the many qualities this generous critic praised in other cricketers was the 'pleasant Nordic ease' with which they played the game.

Fry was a man of many interests, but he had a lifelong obsession with discipline, particularly where it concerned what he called 'boy-training'. This may have had something to do with his early school experiences at an establishment called Hornbrook House in Chislehurst. The school was run by a bearded patriarch called 'Old Cribber' and Mrs Humphrey, his six-foot-tall wife, whose appetite for meting out punishments was insatiable. The day would begin with hymn-singing, led by Old Cribber, followed by a breakfast of porridge, which disgusted Fry and gave him boils. This displeased Mrs Humphrey, who forced him to eat more porridge.

At Repton, Fry gained a reputation as a sportsman and an actor. His performance in Aristophanes' *The Frogs* was considered especially fine. On the cricket field he 'Keeps his bat straight and is a hard wicket to get' and he won prizes for Latin and Greek verse. The sportsman and classics scholar was such a success at Oxford that he was addressed as 'Almighty' and, occasionally, as 'Lord Oxford'.

It was while teaching at Charterhouse that Fry gave more thought to his boy-training theories. English Public Schools, though excellent institutions, could be so much better, he believed, if they were run more along the lines of the Royal Naval College. The problem with schools was that the masters were 'not officers who carry out the duty of officers'. Fry, as he later put it, 'disbelieved in any form of training for boys unless that training contains a real foundation of discipline'. Enter Charles Hoare, the banker, and his boy-training ship, *Mercury*.

The good ship *Mercury* had been a tea-clipper, made of teak, used in the China trade. She was bought by Hoare, a devout Catholic and well-known Master of Fox Hounds, and converted into a training ship for working-class boys destined for the Royal Navy or Merchant Service. Hoare was particularly concerned about the boys' spiritual needs, to which end he built a church – to worship 'Good Friday's Hero' – and a theatre modelled after the Wagner Theatre at Bayreuth.

He had a mistress called Beatrice, with whom he had children. This was a rather scandalous state of affairs, but since he was a Catholic, there was no question of getting a divorce to marry her. Fry liked to play cricket, but had insufficient means to play it full time. Since Hoare wished to secure Beatrice's future, a deal was struck: Fry and Beatrice, eight years his senior, got married, they took over the *Mercury*, Fry could develop his ideas on discipline and devote the rest of his time to cricket.

Mrs Fry, always referred to by her husband as Madame, was as formidable as Mrs Humphrey. She dressed up in a uniform, complete with tie, hat and socks, which often didn't match. She believed in discipline, too. Her favourite time for punishment was before breakfast, when the weather was crisp and the boys tender with sleep. She would have them strapped to a vaulting horse and whipped until their bare backs turned a greenish-blue. More serious transgressions were punished by making the culprits swim round the *Mercury* before dawn of a winter's day, when the water was close to freezing. In the summer boys were made to walk barefoot on the gravel paths. 'Look at that boy,' she remarked to a visiting dignitary, 'he's come a mile barefooted, and he likes it.'

The Prince of Wales – the one who failed to turn up in Jamnagar and later abdicated as King Edward VIII – visited the

Mercury in 1927, and by all accounts was much impressed. (He was, it must be said, an admirer of discipline and strong-willed women himself.) It is unlikely that a punishment was especially arranged for his inspection, but he did enjoy a performance at the Wagner Theatre of the prelude to *Parsifal*, followed by a three-act symbolic play, written by one of the Frys' sons, entitled *The Everlasting Choice*. The play was accompanied by Wagnerian music, and symbolised the travails of the Soul eternally faced with two roads: that of selfishness and ease, and that of high endeavour and self-sacrifice until the end.

In 1934 Fry travelled to Germany, curious to see the achievements of the Hitler Youth movement. He had been singled out by the HY representative in London as just the man to forge friendly links between the German movement and the British Boy Scouts. Fry very much liked what he saw: 'Everyone knew his allotted place and went there when called.' He liked Rudolf Hess, 'spare and powerful, with close-cropped, wavy black hair, attractive blue eyes, clean-cut features, and charm of manner.' He met Herr Rust, Minister of Kultur, Baldur von Schirach, leader of the HY, and Joachim von Ribbentrop, who struck him as 'a keen, wide awake and resolute man'. Fry's aesthetic sense was quickened by meeting the Countess Bernsdorff, 'tall and slim, with a real Anglo-Saxon complexion, white with a glow of red blood underneath. She has quiet blue eyes and a beautifully poised head. Her yellow hair was long enough to make a plaited Grecian bandeau . . . '

The Countess came to stay with the Frys in England and showed an almost maniacal fondness for Grenadier Guards, who, Fry observes, proved to be 'too much for her Prussian ancestral blood'.

Berlin in 1934 left Fry with 'the feeling of a world swept clean by a fresh wind which had left it stimulated, energetic, and ready to work without losing its capacity to enjoy itself'. He had an audience with Hitler at the Reich Chancellery. Hitler, sitting in his favourite Louis XVI chair, looked fresh and fit and impressed Fry by his courtesy, alertness and clarity of mind. He explained the aims of the Hitler Youth movement, and pointed out the twin dangers of Jews and Communism. The Jews, said Hitler, had obtained a stranglehold on finance, medicine, law, and all the learned professions; they were an imperium in imperio, clearly an intolerable situation.

Hitler's ideas struck Fry as sensible. Sure, one might dispute about political and social forms, but 'we cannot dispute the German theory that it is the character of the men who make and administer these forms that really counts'. And it was in the training of character that Germans were superior to Britons. For 'whether we like it or not, we do not enhance our national virtues, however great, by inserting a national ostrich head into a national sand in order to pretend that random voluntariness can obtain the same results as organised discipline'.

Strength through joy, Ranji and Fry: who will ever forget them, delighting the crowds at Hove Cricket Ground, a salty tang in the air, the deckchairs filled with happy spectators. In the immortal words of Neville Cardus: 'East and West twain for hours, the occult and the rational.'

I was born in Sarodar on 10th September 1872. I cannot remember the event, of course, but I have been told that my dear Mama did not have an easy time of it. She never mentioned this to me, but then she never did anything that might cause me distress.

I suppose my birth, as the eldest son, was greeted with the usual pomp and circumstance, which was considerably less elaborate in our village than it would have been in the capital of our State. Drums were no doubt banged, and a goat kid was rotated over our heads to ward off evil, before being buried alive. If I had been born in the palace in Jamnagar, naturally there would have been more to it, as I would have been the heir to the Gaddi from birth. But as it happened, the heir was a boy called Kalobha, son of Dhanbai, the Jam Saheb's Muslim concubine. This was considered a scandal in my family, and I was told later that there had been talk of having the woman cursed. After all, it already would have been considered a blot on the escutcheon of a Rajput prince if he had as much as

47

obeyed an imperial demand from Delhi to offer his daughter as wife to the Mohammedan Emperor! It came as no surprise therefore when we learnt that Kalobha had attempted to poison the Jam Saheb. The boy was duly banished.

My earliest memories of Sarodar are mostly of Mama, who, I rather fear, spoilt me too much for my own good. I was a frail boy and had few opportunities to play games with the other children, so I would watch the village boys from my window and wonder what it would be like to splash around naked in the muddy pond, as they did. Then my mind would drift, as I gazed at the dry, tawny plains beyond the village, where great battles were fought by my ancestors. Soon I would fall asleep, to wake up hours later, conscious of the sweet scent of Mama, who lay beside me stroking my hair. Sometimes I try to recapture this smell in my mind: a mixture of coconut oil and incense.

It was she, I believe, who first told me the stories of my ancestry, in which I was taught to take pride. We belonged to the race of the moon, known as the Chandravanshis, descended from Krishna. This, an Englishman once observed quite correctly, makes us older than the children of Israel, for Krishna ruled more than three thousand years ago. Mama loved talking about Krishna. She was especially fond of stories about him as a mischievous little boy, playing the flute. I do believe she sometimes called me her little Krishna.

She was, in all truth, a superb story-teller. She spoke in a soft voice which drew me into her tales until they seemed so real that for a moment I thought I could actually see the characters she described. I can still recall, for instance, the story of Krishna and Putana. I shall retell it here, for I am sure that such tales, heard in our earliest years, have a profound effect on us, and since it is my intention to have you sit in judgement of my character, this might furnish you with some useful information.

Krishna was born to rid the world of the wicked King Kamsa. The King had been told that the eighth child of his uncle's daughter would one day come and slay him. To prevent this from happening, the King confined his cousin and her husband to a dungeon in his palace and killed off all their children at birth. However, loyal friends of the poor couple somehow contrived to smuggle the eighth child out of the prison. This child was Krishna. The King, ignorant of his foe's whereabouts, ordered the demoness Putana to kill all the boys born in the Kingdom at the time of Krishna's birth. She set about her task by turning into a beautiful woman, but instead of milk her breasts contained a deadly poison, which boys, being greedy, would imbibe at the first opportunity.

At this point in the story I would tremble and Mama would pull me closer. I must confess that my fear was on occasion deliberately exaggerated. But let me continue.

One day Putana reached a remote place called Gokula, where Krishna was in hiding. When she spotted Krishna she pretended to love him and offered him her breast. Krishna sucked harder and harder until not a drop of milk was left and Putana was drained, not only of her poison but of life. She swooned with Krishna's mouth still at her breast and turned back into her demonic self.

I asked Mama what happened to Krishna. She reassured me that he had been saved, for otherwise we, who are among his descendants, would not be here to tell the tale. Indeed, she said, Krishna once appeared in the dream of our most famous ancestor, Jam Rawal, who had led our people from Sind. Krishna revealed that Jam Rawal's people had a great future in the south, where they would make peace with a race of giants and rule forever. Jam Rawal took Krishna's advice and moved down from Cutch to Jamnagar, where he founded our family. The giants, I was told, were the British, to whom we have been loyal friends ever since.

My mother was of course not the only one to tell me stories in Sarodar. Life, in fact, was like an endless round of stories, mostly about bravery in battle. We were always being told that Rajputs never turned their backs in war. Other races might give up and hope to come back and fight another day, but if our men returned in such a cowardly fashion, the women would slam the doors in their faces.

I must have been about four years old when my father told me the famous story of Raysinhji. Whenever this great man did battle with the Mogul armies, he was accompanied by a standard-bearer, whose instructions were to dip his flag in the event his lord was killed. The women would watch the battle from a distance, for in a desperate situation they would gird themselves to join the men. As it happened, the standard-bearer dipped his flag and Raysinhji's eight wives believed that he had fallen. Seven of them joined their husband in death by drowning themselves in a well. The eighth declined to commit suttee.

However, when the fighting was over, much to everyone's astonishment, Raysinhji appeared victorious and alive. It turned out the standard-bearer had left his flag to relieve himself. Raysinhji grieved for his seven wives, but was furious that the eighth had shirked her duty. She was urged to jump to her death as was proper, and, in due course, she did. Since then we have never married another member of her clan.

When my father had finished his story he would always look me in the eyes and recite the three principles of kingship – purity, duty and sacrifice. And I was made to recite the battles in which our ancestors were victorious. Since I never recalled all their names, I would be forced to stand in the courtyard without moving until I did remember or until my father saw fit to release me. I would stand there in the hot sun, staring at the carving of Raysinhji in the wall, imagining that he was witness to my shame. No doubt my father meant well, and these lessons had their use, but this sort of thing did not fill me with affection for him.

I was far closer to Mama, and since I was, as I said, a frail boy I did not find it easy to imagine myself as a warrior. The Rajput worships his horse, his sword and the sun. As a young boy I found it hard to worship any of those things. I was, when all is said and done, clearly a keen disappointment to my father who wished to give me a more manly education. Whilst the other boys strengthened their bodies by wrestling with pigs and other such rough and tumble, I preferred to listen to stories. I was, I must confess, a frightful cry-baby, which enraged my father, for we were taught from our earliest years that we must cry with shut mouths. Then we were duly praised. But if we opened our mouths and roared, we were soundly smacked into the bargain.

Of the Jam Saheb in Jamnagar I heard little. Affairs of the capital were discussed by my father in hushed tones, as though they contained terrible secrets, but I do recall hearing about my uncle's sudden death, though I was never quite sure how it happened. I knew that he was the heir to the Jam Saheb and that his sad fate had something to do with the person my parents kept referring to as 'that Mohammedan woman'.

It must have been around that time – I was about seven – that I had one of my most vivid experiences. We were celebrating our Spring feast of Hooley, in honour of Krishna. I'm not sure why we call it Hooley, but I have heard it said that Hooley was the name of a warrior who fought the giants in Sind. Anyhow, it is, as you know, quite a boisterous feast.

I watched from the roof how the village boys kicked up dust from the road and threw sandals at one another. The idea of joining them was terrifying and thrilling at the same time. When the outside gate was opened and a horde of boys ran up to me shouting 'Hooley! Hooley!', I was so frightened that I turned back, only to find my father blocking my path, grinning like a demon. I felt a splash of cold water on my back, smelling of cow dung. I turned round and was drenched with another bucketful. Then I realised that it was perfectly pointless to resist and shouting 'Hooley!' as hard as I could, I joined the boys in search of other victims. We rolled in the dust, frightened older people, splashed in the tank, and ran away from the frenzied women who pursued us with buckets of cow piss.

There was also much dancing and singing and the Hijarahs, our hermaphrodites, performed bawdy theatricals, which rather baffled me at the time: Krishna, I seem to recall, was doing rude things to the milkmaids, by chasing them with a long pole, which they mounted. I can still hear their hysterical screeching, the nature of which obviously escaped me. As you can tell from such goings-on, we were a rustic people, living rather close to the natural state of things. At any rate, I have never forgotten the occasion, for I do believe I was happier than I had ever been.

Soon thereafter, however, I realised something important was afoot. A group of people, including a large bearded Britisher, arrived from the Palace in Jamnagar. Although I had been taught to speak some English I had never seen a Britisher before and was, I must confess, somewhat astonished by the sight: the large, red face peeping through the curry-coloured beard; and the smell! – that of sweat mixed with sweet tobacco. He seemed, nonetheless, a friendly man, for he winked at me, whilst the Indians in his entourage, moustachioed figures with daggers and red turbans, looked straight ahead without saying a word. I was sent to Mama, whilst the men talked for what seemed an eternity. All the while Mama stroked my hair, as though to reassure me that there was nothing to worry about. I remember her exact words: It is nothing, my little Krishna, nothing at all, and I fell asleep in her arms.

The following day I was summoned by a bearer to come in and see my father. This always filled me with apprehension, since I seldom saw him except to receive a dressing down or, at the very least, a lecture. My spirits hardly rose when I was ushered into my father's room, for there were the Britisher and the Indians, all of whom watched me sternly, although I fancied I saw a twinkle in the Englishman's eye. I greeted them respectfully and was told to sit down. A great blessing had befallen our house, said my father. A great responsibility, a great and noble burden was to rest on my young shoulders. Self-sacrifice and hard work would be my lot. I was to be an example to my people. In short, and here my father scraped his throat and the men cast meaningful glances at one another, I was to be the next heir to the Gaddi of Nawanagar, and to that purpose was to be adopted by the Jam Saheb as his son.

This meant that I should bid farewell to Sarodar and set off for Jamnagar forthwith. Then he told me to stand to attention as he spoke the words he always did on these important occasions: *Yatha Raja, jatha praja!* As the King is, so are the people!

I was, as you might imagine, utterly bewildered. So great was my shock, indeed, that the memory still pains me. The thought of leaving with the Englishman, who, when we were introduced, almost crushed my hand, was too much to bear. It was no use crying over spilt milk, however, for my father smacked me and reminded me of my duty and the singular honour accorded to myself and our family. I rushed up to see Mama in the vain hope that she might intervene and let me stay. But even she could offer me no solace, beyond the promise that I could come back and visit her from time to time. She repeated my father's words about doing my duty, being an example to my people, and following in the illustrious footsteps of my forebears. I now recognise these fine sentiments for what they are, but must admit that at the time they sounded absolutely hateful to me. Indeed, I felt so miserable that I had difficulty breathing. It was as if someone were standing on my chest with heavy boots on.

We set off early the next morning. Nothing much was said to me on the way. Colonel Berthon (that was the Englishman's name) spoke to my father about the affairs of the State. Only once did the Englishman address me directly, asking me what my sport was. When I told him I had no sport, he said that I soon would. 'Must have a sport,' he said, 'must have a sport.'

I was glad when we arrived at the palace, for the town had seemed very unprepossessing: the streets were filthy, as were, it seemed to me, most of the people living in them. The palace, however, was the most magnificent thing I had ever seen: like a great white jewel shimmering over the pestilential streets. I remember the sound of horns playing, as we were led into the Jam Saheb's quarters. The men bowed as we went by, my father urging me on, saying there was little time to lose. I remember seeing great glass chandeliers suspended from the ceiling, and for the first time I saw sporting prints of Englishmen riding horses. But my father pressed me to make haste. We entered a room filled with beams of coloured light reflected through the stained-glass windows. And there, on his embroidered silk throne, saᵗ the Jam Saheb.

I placed my hands together in greeting and he looked at me, not unkindly. He had a peculiar tic: every so often his entire face would twitch uncontrollably and his chins would quiver like jelly pudding. It terrified and fascinated me, so that I could not help staring at him, waiting for the next convulsion. He asked his courtiers sitting in rows on either side of his throne whether everything was prepared. They said that everything was and the Jam Saheb made to leave.

We rushed down a long staircase and the Jam Saheb began to twitch and quiver again. 'The women's quarters,' whispered my father and pushed me on. I was helped into a closed carriage, normally reserved for ladies in purdah. 'This way we cannot be seen,' said the Jam Saheb in the dark, as the carriage began to roll. He seemed very apprehensive. I felt his heavy hand clutch my knee and he asked me whether I was all right. I felt him twitching in the pitch dark: it was like being locked up with a great beast: one never knew when it was going to pounce. I didn't dare ask him why we could not be seen. I was too confused to say anything at all.

It was only much later that I had the courage to ask Colonel Berthon why the whole thing had been so rushed and what all the secrecy had been about. He remained silent for some time, looking at me intently, but then explained that it was all to keep me out of harm's way. I had been adopted by the Jam Saheb, he said, because his late son, my uncle Raysinhji, had come to rather a sticky end. Those were the words he used: 'rather a sticky end'.

After a journey of about one hour, our closed carriage suddenly came to a halt. The door opened and instantly I was blinded by the sun. Once I got used to the light I discerned a large water tank next to a temple with men lined up to receive us. I was bidden to go down and bathe in the holy water, not a very pleasing prospect, but I did as I was told. The stagnant water might have been holy, but it felt cold and had an unpleasant odour. I could hear chanting from the temple and smell the incense burnt therein. Someone handed me a garland of flowers as an offering and the chanting grew louder as I was ushered inside.

My memory of what ensued is quite hazy, but I do recall seeing a man sacrificing a goat, his hands glistening with fresh blood. It was dark inside. I was pushed forward by unseen hands towards a stone image of a large reclining figure with a lotus flower protruding from its navel. Somebody whispered in my ear that this was Padmanabha, our family deity. I could barely make out its features and the smell of incense almost took my breath away. I was told to kneel and pray to the deity, and after completing my puja, was led outside to where my father was waiting with the Jam Saheb, who then placed his hand on my forehead. He called me his son, which felt distinctly odd in the presence of my real father, and told me I should leave for Rajkot with Colonel Berthon and receive a proper education. It was the last I ever saw of my new father, the Jam Saheb of Nawanagar.

Inder and I were discussing the English, one of our favourite topics. The argument this time was about their passion for biography. 'It's their sense of theatre,' he said, and jammed his glasses up his nose. Yes? I said, goading him on (not that Inder ever needed to be goaded).

'The English, you see, think of life as a performance – an attitude one might expect in such a ritualised society. People act out the roles that go with their class – or, indeed, the class to which they aspire, which is even more theatrical. My dear, England is a huge piece of theatre, a continuous performance that goes on day and night. I must say I rather enjoy it. But then I don't have to play a role.'

I let that pass and took a different tack. Yes, I said, but how does that differ from India, perhaps the most ritualised society between Britain and Japan?

Inder snorted and said: 'India is of course quite different.'
Why so?
'We don't have class, we have caste, a world of difference. We don't act out roles to which we are not assigned. It would be quite pointless, don't you see?'

Wishing to avoid another discussion on the merits of caste, I said nothing. But Inder was only just getting started.

'And besides, we have a completely different concept of dramatic time. There is no psychology in Indian drama, no development of character. The Bombay musical takes place in a timeless universe.'

So the difference is, I offered, one between a historical approach and a mythical one?

'Quite so,' said Inder. 'History, after all, is the accumulation of human decisions, while myth, being timeless, is an endless cycle of events, which men are ultimately powerless to stop or change – like caste, by the way. Of course, this doesn't prove the superiority of European rationalism over Indian mythology at all. Quite the contrary, really, it shows the arrogant naïveté of Western thought in assuming that we have power over the universe. Indeed,' (and here Inder's snorts seemed to be getting rapidly out of his control) 'in transcending time and accepting a larger cosmic order the cheapest Bombay musical conveys more wisdom than the most sophisticated London play.'

Inder peered at me triumphantly, as I tried to square this figure in front of me, in his striped shirt and his Cambridge accent, talking like a saffron-robed guru.

'True knowledge', Inder went on, 'is knowing that nothing can be known.'

I couldn't let this pass. Surely, I said, knowledge can only arrive once we have freed ourselves from myth. To do that we can't accept an unchanging cosmic order or a tragic view of life, for only by believing in the possibility of change can we free our minds sufficiently to find the truth and positively affect our fate. Biography and the novel are the arts of a secular society: they express the victory of man over fate, or God, or whatever you wish to call it.

'Ah,' said Inder, his glasses all askew, 'you say we have to believe in the possibility of change, so you admit it's a question of faith. Just as you believe in science and in bloody progress. Why should we accept a belief which could blow up the world in the name of progress?'

The bomb – I knew it had to enter the conversation at some point; it always does. It is the original sin of the scientific West, forever threatening to wipe out the spiritual East. Not that India is not secretly proud of its own bomb. Indeed, Indians rather worship power, the power to build as well as the power to destroy, both of which lie in the hands of the same goddess. It is, however, the idea that such power can be rationally controlled by man that offends, for our fate can be transcended but never controlled.

But Inder and I were not yet through. What about truth in Indian drama, I asked. Is it not true that in the stage setting of the Ramayana, Evil sits on one side, personified by Ravana, while on the opposite side sits Truth, in the shape of Rama? In other words, if nothing can be known, as you say, how can there be truth? It seems to . . .

'You see, you see,' said Inder, the pitch of his voice betraying high excitement. 'What concerns us in India is a moral truth. Rama is victorious to save the moral universe from chaos. Truth, to us, is synonymous with the cosmic order, and that can never change.'

The idea of a fixed moral universe, where every man knows his place, where Good and Evil are balanced in complementary struggle, where fate is decided by gods whom we can try to appease but never control, is perhaps a comforting one. That is why the tragic hero, who challenges fate but is ultimately brought to heel, is a comforting hero; he defines the limits beyond which we cannot go. He points to a divine truth and as a result divinity often rubs off on him. Perhaps that is why I kept on seeing pictures of Napoleon in Indian houses: the ultimate tragic hero turned into an idol of worship.

I wanted to ask Inder about that. The opportunity came about a week after our theatrical argument. We were having tea in his study in New Delhi. 'Elementary, my dear chap,' he said. 'Napoleon was small, he was powerful and he fought the British – all very admirable qualities, don't you agree?'

I didn't know quite what to say to that. So I looked round the room instead. I knew it quite well by now: the modern Indian oil painting of a dancer, the etching of Shelley, the Afghan rug on the floor, the books stacked high along the wall, books in English, in Hindi, in French. Then I spotted something that must have been there all the time, but had never struck me before: a little white bust, on the shelf right above the word processor – a little white bust of Napoleon, which suddenly seemed the most conspicuous object in the room, gleaming like a phosphorescent light in the dark. I see, I said, trying not to sound supercilious, that you count yourself among the Napoleon-worshippers. It was one of the few times I ever saw Inder blush. 'Absolute nonsense, I just picked it up somewhere, it means nothing to me, absolutely nothing whatsoever.' And he poured me another cup of tea.

I shall always associate my memories of school with the cry of the black ibis. The plaintive call of that graceful bird still evokes in me a feeling of sweet melancholy, akin to thinking of distant friends. I used to climb up to the roof after games, at sunset, especially to hear the ibis cry. I felt sad and alone, and at the same time, totally at rest, as though the world had stopped turning for a bit. It was there, on the roof, that I sought solace, listening alone to the ibis, after I had been told of the Jam Saheb's decision to disinherit me. But I am digressing. Let me turn back to my day of arrival at school.

It was hot and humid when we entered Rajkot – we, being Colonel Berthon, myself and a retinue of seventeen men. At the school gate, the Colonel called for the chokeydar, who at first did not seem to pay heed. The Colonel called louder and louder: 'Chokeydar! Chokeydar!' And I was hoping all the while that no one would come, so we could return to Sarodar. Finally, however, the chokeydar did appear and he told the men where to unpack my belongings. After a short rest, we were shown to the office of the school Principal, my dear teacher and friend, Chester Macnaghten, alas, no longer with us now.

I was a bit anxious at first, being led through what seemed like a gauntlet of boys and their fearsome Arab guards. The boys, most of whom were either slight, like myself, or beefy, fell silent as we walked by and inspected me with a distinct air of hostility.

Mr Macnaghten had a long beard, blue eyes, and, like Colonel Berthon, smelled of pipe tobacco. And despite the good services of a punkah-wallah, he seemed to suffer dreadfully from the heat, for he was short of breath and always mopping his red face with a large white handkerchief. I don't think he thought much of our climate, and I can't say I blame him. I distinctly remember his first words to me: 'Are you getting enough exercise?' he asked, fingering my arms, which were, I must admit, decidedly puny. I must have mumbled something vague in answer. 'Well,' he said, 'you soon will and then we'll see the stuff you're made of.' This sounded positively menacing.

But he was absolutely right, of course, to sense a core of weakness in me which had to be knocked into shape. For in truth, our ancestors, great warriors though many of them undoubtedly have been, were educated to be idle. Indulgence and extravagance were held up before their eyes as most sacred duties. It is only in the English schools that we were taught the lessons of *noblesse oblige*. It was there that our characters were formed and our wits sharpened. And for that I can never thank my old teacher enough.

Although comradeship is a cornerstone of every healthy boy's education, it was difficult at first to make friends with the other boys, for suspicion ran deep and this made armed guards indispensable; or so we thought, until Mr Macnaghten showed us the error of our ways. The Arabs, dressed rather splendidly in the uniforms of their masters' houses, greatly outnumbered the boys and were thus the most conspicuous presence at school. The smallest token of disrespect could lead to a serious bout of fisticuffs, or worse. Once, I remember, a great battle took place on the cricket ground between the guards of Dhrangadra and Sihor, the result, I was later told, of a threatening gesture made by Babhutsinhji of Dhrangadra to Ramsinhji of Sihor, a timid boy who, for some reason, was terrified of being poisoned with owls' tongues. The battle took an ugly turn: daggers were drawn and a fearful row ensued, with blood flowing rather copiously. Five strapping fellows, quite badly injured, were carried through the quad on stretchers, amidst much shouting and commotion.

I do not know what happened to those fellows, but the very next day we were all summoned to the Hall, where Mr Macnaghten would address us about the incident. Our guards were ordered to stay outside, which caused a frightful rumpus, for they had been instructed to be with their masters at all times. (Even during the night, they would sleep outside our windows.) However, the Hall inspired an atmosphere of solemn reverence, in which, it must be said, our rowdy Arabs would have been quite out of place, and which, I am sad to say, is rather lacking in our own crumbling temples. Behind Mr Macnaghten's lectern hung a large portrait of the late Queen-Empress, who looked down upon us with an expression that bespoke gravity, but also great kindness.

We were told to rise and Mr Macnaghten entered, wearing a long black gown, which rustled as he walked by. He took his place behind the lectern, waited in silence and proceeded to speak. I shall never forget his words.

One day, he said, many of us would rule over a great number of people. This meant not that we could look forward to a life of licence, but, on the contrary, that we should prepare for a life of duty. One of our duties would be to ensure that our people lived in peace and in order to do so, we should need to contain the violence in our own hearts. One of the great achievements of the British Empire was the way it had restored peace to this great continent, and this had been achieved not through armed force, though firmness was at times needed to contain unruly elements, but through a modern administration, run by men of character.

The purpose of our school was not simply to fill our minds with learning, for there were already enough professors in this world. We were to combine the finest virtues of our ancient heritage with the noblest lessons that modern British education was able to impart.

All this was rather more than my untutored mind could take in at the time, but since I have heard our Principal deliver more or less the same speech on many subsequent occasions, in public and in private, I am able to reproduce it here. I do remember, however, that to me, at that moment, Mr Macnaghten looked like a god: his eyes blazing, his sweet, manly voice penetrating every corner of the Hall. At times he sounded almost as though he were breaking into song: it was all in all a most formidable performance. He then paused and opened a small book, which I learnt to love so well.

It was, of course, *Tom Brown's School Days*. I don't in all honesty remember which part of the book he read to us that day, but venture to guess it was about Tom losing the match with honour against the Lord's men. Lest you have forgotten the scene in question, my dear Charlo, which, I must say, would surprise me greatly, I shall quote Tom's immortal lines here, all the while imagining Mr Macnaghten speaking to us in that Hall so many years ago.

> '"But it's more than a game. It's an institution," said Tom. "Yes," said Arthur, "the birthright of British boys, old and young, as habeas corpus and trial by jury are of British men." "The discipline and reliance on one another which it teaches is so valuable, I think," went on the master, "it ought to be such an unselfish game. It merges the individual in the eleven; he doesn't play that he may win, but that his side may."'

Thinking of our dear Principal today brings tears to my eyes. I still remember the lesson that followed: the nobility of cricket cannot be wholly understood by a scientific approach, he said.

It takes character, judgement, watchfulness, appreciation of the merits of others, and the highest standards of truthfulness and duty. Playing cricket would teach us lessons such as no school instruction could give – the lessons of self-reliance, calmness and courage, and above all, of cooperation and team spirit.

And then he came to the main point: from that day onwards we should discipline our competitive instincts on the playing field only and dispense with sentries and guards, whose presence here had become an affront to the civilised values we all lived, and, if called upon, were prepared to die for.

As you might imagine, an almighty fuss ensued. But Mr Macnaghten stood his ground and never flinched in carrying out what he believed to be right. I cannot speak for the other boys, but to me he was a true hero and stood as a shining example of the virtues of his race which one can only hope are slowly but surely being imbibed by our people.

Nonetheless, and this might surprise you, I cannot honestly claim that I immediately took to games. I was still used to being coddled and the practice of rising at six every morning to run around the field ('eccers' we called this compulsory exercise) I found disagreeable.

As for cricket, there were two important drawbacks: one was the art of fielding, of which, at first, I had no understanding. Indeed, I found it demeaning to run after a ball struck by another man, more the work for bearers than an heir to the Gaddi! How pompous one was! The other problem was fear of being hit by fast balls. The taller boys, proud Rajputs to a man, all wanted to bowl as fast as they could, and looked very fearsome indeed. It was my practice to step out of the way if I sensed a danger of being hit, which more often than not, meant the loss of my wicket.

It was for this reason that our cricket coach, a former sergeant-major called Ridley, took a dislike to me, calling me 'Duchess'. He was a common man who, unlike Mr Macnaghten, had no respect for our country. He was for ever accusing us of what he termed slacking, shirking and sneaking.

'Slacking, shirking and sneaking again, Duchess?' he would say to me, when I had the misfortune of running into him. He delighted in picking me out for fielding practice, when, grinning fiercely, he would throw the ball as hard as he could from a very short distance. 'Can't you take it, Duchess?' he would say, when the ball inevitably struck my chest with a sound thump. I could not understand why Mr Macnaghten ever hired this uncouth fellow.

Ridley did not dislike all 'blacks', as he used to call us, for he had his favourites. One of them was a chap Ridley called 'Bill', the heir to the Gaddi of Bilkha. Bill was tall and strong, and a ferociously fast bowler. Ridley would often call me over for batting practice against him. It was quite terrifying, I can assure you, for he would tear up to the wicket and with a cartwheeling action smack the ball into the ground, where it kicked up the dust like an exploding bomb. It was all I could do to dodge the ball as it hurtled past my ears. I wager he was as fast as Jonah in his prime, when he bowled W. G. Grace through his beard! And all the while Ridley's whining voice rang out: 'Too much for you, Duchess? I thought you Rajputs were supposed to be brave. Where's your warrior spirit?' And so on and so forth. It was more than I could bear. Indeed, the memory of that wretched little red-faced man still makes my blood boil!

And so I plotted my revenge, for it was my wish to humiliate him, reprehensible no doubt, though perhaps, even in hindsight, understandable. It so happened that Colonel Berthon was in Rajkot and I was to report to him on my progress at school. I had come to be fond of 'Colonel' as I called him, and, I do believe, he of me. I felt safe in his company and, what's more, he would bring me precious letters from my Mama. There we were, in the Resident's house, exchanging news. He asked me how I was enjoying school. I'm afraid I lied to him and said that I enjoyed it very much. I then asked him whether he would kindly give me some letter paper, since I should like to write to Mama. 'How could I refuse you anything, my dear boy,' he said and gave me a few sheets of his own letter paper. He then tweaked my cheek – he always did this, and though I found it painful I put up with it since he was such a kindly man – and sent me on my way with my bearer.

That night I set to work. My plan was to forge a letter from Colonel Berthon to Sergeant-Major Ridley, informing him of the Colonel's visit to the school on Thursday and that he, Ridley, was to present himself, dressed in full military uniform. He was to carry a cricket bat with him and wait for the Colonel's arrival in the middle of the quad at noon. It was of course an absurd prank, which would have betrayed its childish author to anyone more astute than Ridley. To get the language right was not an easy task for an Indian schoolboy, and no doubt the letter was clumsy, but it was also very brief and Ridley, I hoped, would be too flustered to notice its linguistic deficiencies.

I had my bearer slip the letter through Ridley's letterbox, and went to sleep in pleasant anticipation of the next day's fun. Thursday arrived: we did our eccers, prepared our lessons, had breakfast, and went to class. From the classroom I had a capital view of the fountain in the centre of the quad, and there, right on time, appeared Ridley in full uniform, wielding a cricket bat quite as though it were his rifle. He stood facing the Hall with his bat at the ready, his face red as a beetroot and pouring with sweat. A quarter of an hour later, as I had anticipated, Mr Macnaghten emerged from the front gate, chatting in a friendly manner with the Colonel. As soon as he saw them coming, Ridley saluted absurdly, his uniform dark with perspiration. I rather thought the man might faint. Mr Macnaghten looked at Ridley as if he had gone mad, and the Colonel cast a questioning glance at Mr Macnaghten.

I can only imagine what followed, for the exact words have escaped my memory, but I trust my reconstruction of the conversation is not too far off the mark:

'All right, Ridley, what's all this about?' said Mr Macnaghten.

'But sir . . . you . . . I was asked . . . '

'Yes, Ridley, what were you asked, spit it out man!'

'To be present sir . . . Colonel Berthon . . . '

'Nonsense, Ridley, I never asked you to do any such thing and nor did Colonel Berthon, did you Colonel?'

The Colonel shook his head.

'Now get on with your work, Ridley.'

This little contretemps had by now elicited the attention of the entire school, with everyone avidly watching Ridley's moment of humiliation. I must say I felt very much tickled with the success of my prank. It gave me intense pleasure to see people behave in precisely the way I had anticipated. Perhaps, my dear Charlo, I should have been a playwright instead of a cricketer!

Unfortunately I had not reckoned with the consequences of my little entertainment. The truth of the matter was soon revealed, when Ridley showed the letter to Mr Macnaghten, for he quickly surmised its provenance. I was summoned to his office, tucked away behind the stairs in the corner of the quad. I knocked. Mr Macnaghten told me to enter. And there, inside the office, on either side of the large desk, were the Principal and the Colonel. Mr Macnaghten wore a deep frown, and the Colonel got up and made to leave. 'A pretty state of affairs,' he said, 'a very pretty state of affairs.' But when he tweaked my cheek I looked up and thought I detected a twinkle of mirth in his eye.

'Well, young man, that was cute, very cute,' said Mr Macnaghten. (Here again, I must rely partly on my imaginative powers, but I believe these were his words, and if my recollection is not always literally precise, let me assure you it is exact in spirit.) He beckoned me to stand before him, so we could talk man to man. I stood virtually touching his knees. He asked whether there was anything I would like to say for myself. I shook my head, for truly I felt no great shame for what I had done.

'Do you realise', he went on, 'that forgery is a very base crime?' He proceeded to explain: if the word of a gentleman could not be trusted, we should be delivered to the savages.

Nothing is higher than the trust between gentlemen, for it was we, the elected few, born and educated to rule the uninstructed masses, who had to stand in the breach for civilisation; it was our sacred duty to protect everything that was noble in man; only by behaving in the manner to which we were born could we serve as examples to the others, less favoured by nature; for nothing stood between us and barbarism. 'Do you follow me, young man, do you follow me?' I indicated that I did.

Mr Macnaghten bade me come closer and proceeded to smooth my hair, affectionately at first, but then he cuffed me hard on the back of my head, before withdrawing his hand, which was trembling. This was rather a shocker, I must admit, for the Principal was a gentle man, who rarely resorted to physical punishment.

There followed an awkward silence. Then, all of a sudden, Mr Macnaghten took my hand into his, which was still shaking, and without letting go, he asked me whether I knew the two most beautiful achievements of man? Much confused and still dazed by the unexpected cuff, I confessed that I did not. He then told me what they were: the friezes of the Parthenon and gentlemen playing cricket. The reason, if I remember well, was as follows: in the ancient sculpture and the noble English game we see the apotheosis of classical form, both, in their ways, perfect: the expressions of two great civilisations, where logic and beauty are one, where society is ruled by harmony and tradition, whose continuity is ensured by noble men, distinguished from the common herd by their selfless devotion to duty. Now, one cannot deny that men can be rivals, but the brute hostility of competition must be nullified by good manners and gentlemanly conduct, and, above all, trust, so that we all play the game fairly. The point of cricket is not to judge our respective merits by so crude a measure as who wins and who loses, for we, who play the game nobly, are all superior men. Indeed, there is greater beauty in losing elegantly than in winning without grace. This, then, is what the modern English gentleman has in common with the noble citizens of Ancient Greece. One could call it form. But if one of us lets the side down, so to speak, the harmony is destroyed, the form unbalanced, and civilisation delivered to the barbarians.

I looked into Mr Macnaghten's eyes, which shone with emotion and, I like to think, affection for me, and I thought of my father, telling me stories about Rajput heroes, and my mother, soothing me with her tales of Krishna. It is hard to express this adequately, but Mr Macnaghten had a queer effect on me: he combined the natural authority of my father with the tenderness of Mama. His words affected me more than I can say and from that day onwards I can truly say I loved him, and I should do everything in my power to please him.

Mr Macnaghten let go of my hand, drew himself up and announced that, unfortunately, the time had come now to attend to the unpleasant part of his teacherly task. I was told to bend over his desk and lower my trousers, like a true gentleman. 'Duty, my boy, is a rod to guide the erring,' he said, and I heard the swish of his cane and felt its sting six times. Mr Macnaghten was breathing heavily. Indeed, it seemed the exertion had quite taken his breath away. He slumped in his chair and silently dismissed me with a wave of his trembling hand. Rarely have I seen a man look so ghastly: a ghostly pallor had come over his normally florid features, his beard hung down in matted strands, his eyes looked at me beseechingly. Clearly, he had suffered more punishment than I.

I, too, had trouble breathing that night: my chest felt as though it were constricted by a steel hoop. And as I lay awake until the early hours, Mr Macnaghten's words turned round and round in my mind. I intended never again to let the side down. No matter how fiercely Bilkha hurled his thunderbolts, I should face them without flinching.

Every year come December the school Eleven played the Rajkot team, and I had decided that by hook or by crook I should be chosen to play. Henceforth every minute of my spare time was spent on batting practice. I was scientific in my

67

methods, and asked the boys to bowl short or long, or on the off or the leg side, in order for me to perfect every stroke in the game. When Bill or one of the other boys got tired I even got my poor bearer to throw the ball at me, which turned out to be a somewhat risky enterprise, as the fellow's aim tended to be erratic. Slowly but surely my batting began to improve. I began to hit the ball more and more cleanly, and I fancied I saw Mr Macnaghten watching from a distance, nodding his head in approval. Even Ridley could no longer accuse me of slacking, shirking and sneaking, though our relations were by no means perfect. We were soon to see the last of him, however, but more about that anon.

Thank God my exertions paid off, for I was duly selected for the match. Mr Macnaghten seemed quite as tickled as I was and he came up to congratulate me, whispering in my ear: 'The nobility, my boy, remember the nobility.'

The day of the match was quite cool, but the wicket was as hard and dusty as ever – the perfect surface for bowling lobs, at which, I was told, the Rajkot captain was a past master. He was the Dewan's son, a Banyan named M. K. Gandhi – yes, my dear Charlo, the very one who is presently causing us so much trouble! He was, like myself, a frail-looking youth, wearing spectacles. I remember him being very soft-spoken and utterly fluent in English. Truly, it was difficult then to imagine the rabble-rouser he was to become.

I have just looked up the statistics of the match in an old school-book to refresh my memory of the occasion. The Rajkot men were first to bat. We were not much afraid of their physical prowess, since most of them were Banyans or Brahmins. But they were clever chaps and by snicking and jabbing the fast, low balls that were our bowlers' stock-in-trade, they got off to a promising start. Indeed, by the time they reached a century and a half they had us seriously worried. Fortunately Bill and a fellow called Gambhirsinhji, known at school as 'Gambo', contrived to dismiss the last of them. Gandhi, not much of a bat, made five.

So there we were, having to chase their total of 168. Ajitsinhji and Kiritsinhji laid a solid foundation of thirty runs, before both were dismissed by a boy called Bhanu. I played cautiously at first, for the slow high lobs from these Banyans could be treacherous. But soon I began to enjoy myself and went forward to crack them prettily around the field. My partners, alas, were not doing so well: Ramsinhji was out for nought, Takhtsinhji went for a mere four, and Shivsinhji, who did at least stay in for some time to keep me company, made fifteen.

Still, by then I had compiled about four score runs and there were four more wickets to go. It was clear that my most dangerous adversary was Gandhi, for his slow balls had a way of breaking back from leg, and since the surface of the wicket was highly irregular one never quite knew where the ball would end up. So I treated his bowling with great respect, even as I punished the other chaps. When I reached a century, my first, a loud cheer went up from the pavilion, and Mr Macnaghten, who was one of the umpires, beamed like the Cheshire cat. I do believe it was the first time since I arrived at school that I could honestly say I was popular.

Two wickets fell in quick succession and we had another fifteen runs to go. Baubha, facing Gandhi, lifted his bat high – he was a strong, tall, clean-limbed boy – and attempted to smite the breaking ball clear out of the ground, beyond the Maidan. The ball went higher and higher and then descended with ever greater speed, smack into the hands of a fielder. In came Bilkha and I knew it was all up to me now. I felt a little like Tom Brown, trying to stave off defeat against the Lord's men. I told Bill to block his stumps and not to try anything reckless. This he contrived to do, much to my relief, as I slowly accumulated the runs, a two here, a single there, always trying to shield Bill from the bowlers.

With two more runs to win, Bill was facing Gandhi. Hoping for a quick run, I started up the pitch as Gandhi came in to bowl. Quite abruptly, Gandhi stopped at the wicket and flicked off the bails. He appealed to the umpire and with a sad expression on his face Mr Macnaghten judged me out. I was dumbfounded, for I had never seen such a trick before. I looked to Mr Macnaghten to see if he might change his mind. He told me in no uncertain terms to walk, as Gandhi had acted quite within the laws of cricket. I could see Gandhi smirk as I turned smartly towards the pavilion. I thought him an absolutely loathsome fellow, for though his act may have been within the laws, it surely was not within the spirit of the game.

Since I already mentioned Ridley's premature departure, I might as well describe how this was effected – on second thoughts, perhaps effected is not quite the right way to put it, for it was not anybody's doing but his own. This is what occurred: Ridley had the commendable habit of running with us every morning for eccers. This took considerable effort on his part, and we were young and fit, whereas he was getting on in age and was rather stout. It was the hot season before the rains and eccers, even in the early morning, began to take its toll. Then, one particularly hot day, it became too much for Ridley. He lagged behind the rest of us, puffing and panting, getting redder and redder all the while. A few of us – I am sorry to say I was not of the party – took pity on the wretched fellow and asked him to rest, but he wouldn't hear of it and pressed on, albeit by now at a much reduced pace, until at last he crumpled to the ground.

We crowded round him, fanning his crimson face. One man took off his shirt and turned it into a makeshift pillow. Ridley's eyes were closed and his panting made way for an odd wheezing sound. Several times he tried to tell us something. It was hard to make out what it was: Bilkha even got down and put his ear close to the coach's mouth. But we shall never know his last words, for the wheezing only got louder and with a last gurgling breath, poor Ridley passed away.

I was almost as keen on the theatre as I was on cricket. My first performance was a recital of Sir Walter Scott's 'Young Lochinvar'. It was an excellent exercise in English-speaking, to be sure, and the words were very fine, but it was more than that, for theatricals were the closest approximation of English life available to us; the theatre was, so to speak, a window affording at least a glimpse of a civilisation which was, after all, still alien. Naturally our own culture was not neglected, since Mr Macnaghten wished us to take pride in our heritage. I remember singing 'Praise of Queen Victoria the Good' in Gujerati, and acting the part of Arjuna in a scene from the *Mahabharata*.

The Indian plays were written by Englishmen, who contrived, successfully I think, to combine the best of both worlds: the modern skill of the West and the spiritual beauty of the East. I thought it a good method, since English writers knew how to translate ancient ideas into modern terms in a way that was yet beyond the reach of the native mind.

One such play, entitled *Raja's Last Stand*, was written, I seem to recall, by Major Henry Stokes. I played the Raja of Jodhpur who fought a tragic battle against the invading Marathas. Even though his men were falling left and right, the Raja stood firm, until he was the last Rajput still fighting his ground. It took one thousand Maratha men to cut him down and henceforth the British decreed that the rajas of Jodhpur were to be maharajas. The play ended with a long speech, which I had a devilish time committing to memory, describing the Raja's noble sentiments before his certain death. Although I cannot imagine that my performance was much good, I was told it brought tears to Mr Macnaghten's eyes.

I enjoyed these theatrical performances hugely. There is a joy in acting which cannot be well accounted for by one who is not a professional psychologist or hypnotist. The power to move one's fellow creatures, whether to laughter or to tears, is one that gives the actor a mysterious sense of power and elation. Whether the elation comes of admiration excited in the breasts of the audience or from the feeling that you are bringing happiness to others, is a matter of some question. Perhaps there is yet another, less lofty reason for the keen sense of joy I experienced in performing on stage, which has to do with my weakness for dressing up. In this I am a true Indian: the love for fine cloth, colourful hues, precious jewels, this comes naturally to me. But I am also a great believer in the British maxim that 'clothes maketh man', for one's costume determines, to such a large degree, one's bearing, one's manners, in short, one's public character. To this I attach the utmost importance, for it is through the display of one's character – as distinct from one's private thoughts – that one is accorded the respect of one's fellows.

By that same token I enjoyed dressing in my black Sherwani for dinner with the Principal. Mr Macnaghten insisted on this, and I believe quite rightly so. Some of the boys found it irksome, but in my view it bound us all in mutual respect. Mr Macnaghten himself always dressed like a gentleman, and he took equal care over our dressing habits. Indeed, it was the Principal himself who designed our cavalry uniforms in which we took such immense pride.

Only nineteen boys, of whom I was pleased to be one, were accorded the honour of being chosen for the Mounted Volunteers. Our uniform consisted of a pale blue turban adorned with a gilt aigrette, a long black cavalry coat with a red Kummerbund, white Bedford cord breeches and black riding boots with spurs. I must say we looked very fine fellows. Just imagine us, if you will, my dear Charlo, riding through town after practising cavalry manoeuvres on the polo ground. Mr Macnaghten never seemed to tire of drilling us, after first subjecting us to a thorough inspection. An unpolished button, a lace untied, shoulders not properly held straight, would invite his instant censure. One chap – I shan't mention his name – who was a bit of a slacker, once earned himself six of the best, administered by the Principal in our full view, because of poor posture. Posture is character, Mr Macnaghten used to say. So you can imagine that henceforth the rest of us were keen as knives!

I am not sure whether it was my Rajput heritage, or Mr Macnaghten's inspiration, but I found that the martial life agreed with me to such an extent that I have often wondered since if I shouldn't have been happiest as a soldier. It was not to be, however. And the closest I got to soldiering, apart from a thoroughly unsatisfactory career in the Great War, was the display of our skills for the benefit of visitors to the school.

Our guests ranged in importance from political agents to the Viceroy himself. Certainly the most memorable visit during my time at school was that of the Duke and Duchess of Connaught. For me personally, it was also nearly a disaster. Let me explain. Mounted on greys, we trotted off to meet the Duke's party a few miles beyond the town border, whence we escorted them to school. Mr Macnaghten rode with us, of course, adding to the splendour of our little cavalcade. The Duke looked very grand, his white moustache curled and waxed under the hawkish nose of a true nobleman, and the Duchess, with her blonde hair and blue eyes, was quite the most beautiful woman I had ever seen.

The near disaster did not occur until later, however, when we had gathered in the Hall to hear the Principal and the Duke speak, after which some of us were to recite our pieces for the entertainment of our guests. I had swotted hard to learn 'Mark Antony's speech' and Sir Walter Scott's 'The Cavalier'. I was sitting on the Duke's right side, awaiting my turn, and I thought I should be sick with nerves. The Duke, I recall, made some remarks about a boy from a great Rajput house, who was convinced his ancestors had sprung from an alligator. Now this same boy was a diligent scholar, a gentleman and a cricketer. Considering the transition from an alligator to a cricketer, the Duke predicted rapid improvement in our ranks.

Then Mr Macnaghten rose to speak. My heart was, by then, in my mouth, as it were, and I had great trouble breathing, a predicament made worse by the fact that I dared not show it, so that I ended up gasping in silence. I cannot for the life of me remember the Principal's words. Doubtless they were very fine, but I was fighting for breath.

I tried to listen to my fellows recite their stuff, probably the usual chestnuts: 'After Blenheim' or 'Ye Mariners of England'. There must have been more, but I cannot remember. It was all

I could do, when my name was announced, to stumble blindly to the rostrum.

'Friends, Romans, countrymen, lend me your ears . . . ' I began, and suddenly I saw the Duke tapping his foot, as though impatient for me to finish my piece. The Duchess peered at me through her opera glasses, and dear Mr Macnaghten kindly urged me to go on. But I could not. It was a perfectly horrifying moment, for the speech I had taken so much care to learn had simply evaporated from my memory and I was left, quite literally, speechless. Mr Macnaghten whispered something to me, but I might as well have been deaf, for I could not hear a word. For a moment I thought I might flee from the Hall, but thought better of it. I could hear a rush of whispering voices and feet scraping the floor. The magic that is so enthralling when one holds an audience in one's spell was gone, seemingly broken for ever. I felt as though I no longer had any control over my own actions, let alone over my audience. It was almost as if I could see myself in the distance, like a lifeless puppet, frozen in horror. Just then I looked up to the portrait of our dear Queen-Empress and she looked at me so kindly that she might well have been there in spirit to save me from my humiliation – I do believe such things are possible. Perhaps such occurrences, which are beyond the bounds of scientific inquiry, are more readily perceived by the Asiatic mind. Thank goodness, I was finally able to repeat what Mr Macnaghten had been whispering all the while: I come to bury . . . and so on. After that, 'The Cavalier'* was a piece of cake.

* The poem referred to by Ranji goes as follows:

While the dawn on the mountain was misty and grey,
My true love has mounted his steed and away,
Over hill, over valley, o'er dale, and o'er down;
Heaven shield the brave Gallant that fights for the Crown!

For the rights of fair England that broadsword he draws,
Her King is his leader, her Church is his cause;
His watchword is honour, his pay is renown,
God strike with the Gallant that strikes for the Crown.

I have been asked on many occasions by Englishmen what English poetry or history could have meant to us, who had never left India. Were the stories we were taught to recite not strange and devoid of meaning to the Indian mind? Such comments are no doubt well meant. And it is true that descriptions of the English landscape, the valleys, dales and downs so fondly evoked by the poets, taxed our young imaginations, and that the great British cities were as yet unexplored and, from the perspective of Rajkot, remote. But my answer is always this: is Shakespeare's Verona less alien to the average English schoolboy than it was to us? And what of the Bible stories, set in the ancient land of the Israelites, where conditions were closer to our own in India than to those in the advanced nations of Europe?

Indeed, English literature was a kind of Bible to us. It spoke of a wondrous land where men could still be heroes. In our minds Tom Brown was a kind of saint, no less impressive than the gentlemen of the New Testament, in some ways more, for he was a modern saint and not some greybeard roaming the desert. Tom was a hero to look up to, for he represented an ideal, a noble ideal combining virtue and a manly spirit. It was an ideal one did not have to be English to appreciate, though I believe it to have been polished to its brightest sheen in England. England was our Promised Land because of its ideals, and because it offered the chance of adventure and progress. If only our native politicians could see that our only hope for advance lies not in fighting our masters but in following their example. But I am digressing again. I shall carry on with my story.

I was beginning to enjoy a very smooth ride at school, for I was scoring plenty of runs, I was popular and I was chosen as second headboy. The school discipline, so irksome and unfamiliar at first, I now underwent gladly as a bracing, indeed uplifting influence on our young lives. No longer the fragile flower I was when I arrived, I had been transformed into a healthy youth full of high spirits. However, if I have learnt any lesson from getting older, it is this: precisely when one feels that life is a bed of roses, disaster strikes like a bolt out of the blue.

I knew something was up when the Colonel arrived to see the Principal, for his general demeanour suggested worry and fatigue. What is more, I had heard the crows cry at night, which is always a bad omen. I rather feared it had something to do with Mama. Moreover, the Colonel was in the Principal's office so much longer than was his wont, that when I was summoned to come in, I was filled with dread.

Both men were looking very grave; it was the Colonel who spoke first. As I had feared, he had come with bad news, but when I realised it had nothing to do with Mama, I was much relieved. However, what the Colonel had to communicate was serious enough: the Jam Saheb had chosen another heir for the Gaddi of Nawanagar. One of his concubines, it seemed, had had a son called Jaswantsinhji and she had convinced the Jam Saheb to choose him as his successor.

My dear Charlo, you could have knocked me down with a feather: it meant I was dispossessed. What I didn't know at the time – for the Colonel was discreet on that score – was that the government in Bombay had judged against this turn of events, but that their ruling had subsequently been overturned by the Viceroy himself. I know Lord Ripon to have been a most honourable man, so I can only surmise that he was kept ignorant of our private affairs and thus helpless to affect their course. This one can readily understand, for if our own men are defeated by the intrigues of women, how can an Englishman, unused to the ways of the zenana, be expected to come to the rescue?

I was assured by the Colonel that the Rajkot Agency would bear the costs of my education, but, though I do not wish to dwell on the matter, I should mention one thing: this disgraceful episode was not only a blot on my honour, but a severe financial setback. Not to put too fine a point on it: I was broke. As though this sudden turn of my fortunes was not sufficiently dramatic, it was further decided that to complete my education I should be sent to England. The not inconsiderable costs would be born by the state coffers. This, the Colonel thought, had the added advantage of keeping me out of harm's way. I need hardly add that he was referring to the plots being hatched behind the thick veil of the women's quarters. After the Colonel took his leave, Mr Macnaghten bade me stay a while in his office.

He could not hide, he said, his misgivings about sending native boys to Britain. For Britain was a land of many temptations which were not only harmful, but also quite alien to the Indian temperament. Much of what is native, which had better be retained, would be sacrificed. No one could wholly admire an occidentalised Oriental and English air had an unhappy tendency to detach Indian minds from their old anchors, some good ones as well as some bad. So, to see to it that we should enjoy the best possible conditions for broadening our minds, he would personally accompany us on our long voyage and act initially as our guardian.

I did not readily know how to respond to this demonstration of kindness, and the shock of the occasion had utterly overwhelmed me: I rushed into Mr Macnaghten's arms, sobbing like an infant (how my father would have disapproved!). He embraced me and I buried my head in his suit, with its familiar smell of sweet tobacco. As he tried to calm me, I could feel him trembling, no doubt prey to strong emotions himself. And he began to speak of God and sin.

His words made a deep impression on me, because they were so entirely unexpected: 'If only we could feel the presence of God,' he said, 'I am sure we should not be so prone to sin.' He let go of me, breathing hard, his eyes shining. I thought for a moment that he was going to cry. 'If only we could feel God's presence!' he repeated, sounding almost desperate. He told me to go down on my knees with him, on the floor of his study. I did as I was told, too shocked to wonder why. 'Think for a moment, my dearest boy! Feel His presence! Could anything be more wonderful and more grand!' Mr Macnaghten seemed absolutely beside himself, and he waved me away, as he had done before after meting out punishments.

I left, feeling confused but also better, for I had quite forgotten my own troubles. It was a moment forever engraved in my memory: my Principal, on his knees, gasping for breath.

I chose this breathless moment to take a rest from Ranji's narrative. My hotel room overlooked one of the busiest streets in Jamnagar, filled with honking Ambassadors and bullock carts. I was happy to be off the streets for a bit. But even here, behind closed windows, one could not entirely escape from the pervasive smell of cow dung, petrol and cooking oil.

I tried to think of the first time I had consciously acted a language – as distinct from just speaking one. This is not quite the same thing as acting a role. I remember doing that quite clearly. I must have been about five, when I imitated my grandfather's mannerisms in the pulpit. He was a Protestant minister of a sober and liberal denomination, which didn't prevent him from enjoying the theatrical side of his task. He affected a stern expression and a quivering voice, both of which I tried to mimic as I mounted my improvised pulpit. The way he prayed before meals was also designed to draw attention, and, which was perhaps the main point, to annoy my grandmother. It was a long drawn-out process which continued until my grandmother got visibly agitated as lunch was getting cold. Only then did he open his eyes, very slowly, eyelids fluttering, as though gradually waking from a deep trance.

I suppose I learnt from him how to use language and gestures purely for effect. Not that his attitude to religion was in any way false; he was, I am sure, a good Christian. But all the same I believe he kept a kind of ironic distance from the rituals of his faith. His studied mannerisms were a way of showing his awareness of a gap between form and content. I don't think that in his mind the two were ever quite the same.

The first time I remember being aware of acting language was when I deliberately pronounced English words with a Dutch accent. I was born in a town on the Dutch coast where to pose as an Englishman was a mark of class. One joined the cricket club, where one made one's appearance on Sundays for the weekly match with a copy of the *Daily Telegraph* or *The Times* in one's blazer pocket. One tuned in to the BBC for the latest Test Match score. At school one wore long gaberdine raincoats and striped college scarves and brogues. These brogues had to be absolutely genuine, that is to say, English. There was the sad case of the boy who had arrived from the provinces. He saw that to be accepted in his new milieu, brogues were indispensable and asked his mother – alas unschooled in these matters – to buy him a pair. They were of Dutch make, a clear imitation, without the requisite number of holes. I don't recall whether anything was said about them to his face, but he did not last long at the school.

I started playing cricket when I was seven. I was given a cricket bat by my English grandmother for Christmas. But since we played on straw matting instead of grass wickets, my bat lacked the little, dark triangle of dried earth on the back of the tip, which English players used to pat and smooth the ground. There was but one way to acquire this subtle but all-important mark and that was to go out into our back garden and tap the grass until eventually the triangle began to form by absorbing the soil. It would have been best of course if the soil had been English, but still, soil was soil, and who could tell the difference? The process was rather like forging an antique bowl: the patina of time achieved in a few days by soaking a brand new object in strong tea. The whole thing would have seemed absurd had I not lived in an Anglophile town. Yet there was an important difference between the other Anglophiles and me, as our aspirations were by no means the same. Their Anglophilia had less to do with England than with class in Holland. The last thing my friends at the cricket club wanted was to be English. The scarves, the ties, the tweeds, the cricket distinguished them from the hoi polloi, who went to vocational schools, wore polyester clothes and didn't play cricket. I wanted to be an Englishman.

The jargon on the cricket field was of course English in origin: 'How's that!', 'Well played!', 'batting', 'bowling', 'fielding', 'leg break', 'silly mid-off', and so on. But to pronounce these English expressions – these forms which to an English ear spell a quintessential Englishness – in an English accent would have subjected me to ridicule. And so I pronounced them the way my friends did, carefully turning every 'th' into a 'd'. Obviously neither an Englishman saying 'How's that', nor a Dutchman saying 'Howsdet', would feel like an actor. But I, mispronouncing the words in Holland, and saying them correctly in England, passing as a native in both countries, felt theatrical. I felt the ironic gap between words and their associations. To this day I cannot use such expressions as 'a nice cup of tea' without, as it were, placing quotation marks.

Long after I stopped playing cricket I was attracted to Japan. There was a reason for this, beyond the obvious lure of the exotic: in Japan the idea of a unique culture that grows naturally from the native soil is pushed to its extreme. A Japanese, so Japanese like to think, behaves in the way he does, that is to say, naturally, because he is a Japanese. Culture, in Japan, is not something that can be acquired; it is something one is born with, a biological fact, a matter of genes.

It is perfectly logical, then, that foreigners who learn to speak Japanese are seen as impersonators, actors, trained seals, imposters. For to some extent they are: if you speak a foreign language well enough, you give expression to attitudes and manners (the 'nice cup of tea') which are not your own; they are studied, acted. Of course, form and content diverge in the case of the Japanese, too, but then, saying one thing and thinking another is still part of 'Japanese' behaviour. What is lacking, in the case of a native speaker, is the self-conscious act of watching yourself perform.

Language to many Japanese has taken the place of a national religion: it is imbued with a unique spiritual force, accessible only to the native born. Japanese, and only Japanese, can express this mystical concept of Japaneseness, as natural as it is inexplicable. So the Japanese language is pregnant with something which it is beyond words to convey. It follows, naturally, that foreigners can mimic the language, but never really speak it. It also follows that the Japanese have a natural difficulty with other languages, for to speak an alien language too well is to run the risk of losing the core of one's identity, to lose the spirit behind the mask. It is for this reason that, perhaps unconsciously, many Japanese deliberately speak other languages badly. It was for the same reason that Japan often reminded me of my British grandfather, the son of German Jews, who, I believe quite consciously, mispronounced his French. It made him feel British.

I approached the delicate matter of speaking Japanese in various ways. First there was the Method school of acting: I would try to internalise the forms I was expressing: in effect, I would try to be Japanese. The embarrassed giggle, the hiss through the teeth, the exaggerated expressions of agreement or personal humbleness: I would try to forget that these forms did not come naturally; I pretended that they did, to the extent that the hisses, the half bows, the giggles, the signs of humility, began to appear even when I spoke Dutch or English.

This can go on for some time and well-meant compliments that 'you are very Japanese' were at first gratefully accepted. It gave me the illusion I was passing, just as I passed in England. But soon the pleasure became a strain. For, of course, I never did pass; the compliments were for my acting skills; and one cannot be on stage all the time; one needs, at least some of the time, the illusion that one is seen by others roughly the way one sees oneself. For many Japanese this has to involve that ineffable core of Japaneseness; as for myself, what? British? Dutch? European? Western? All of the above? How could I express any of this without falseness or irony?

What I could do was to distance myself from my Japanese role, not by deliberate mispronunciation of the language, or by cutting out the mannerisms, but rather by exaggerating them, by stylising the act: Brechtian instead of Method. By showing the act for what it was, a theatrical turn, I created an ironic distance from the role. I bracketed my Japanese with quotation marks. This could be deeply offensive to the Japanese, to whom this form of play-acting smacked, not unreasonably, of sarcasm. But what was I trying to protect? Could it be that atavistic fears of losing the spirit behind the mask are not confined to the Japanese?

I argued the point with Inder, once again taking tea ('taking tea') at his house in Delhi. He showed off a new pair of wide

81

khaki trousers, modelled by his tailor after a pair he had bought at Marks and Spencer in London. Inder was so pleased with them that he had had six pairs made up. From now on, he said, he would wear no other kind of trousers. I asked Inder whether he ever felt like an actor.

He thought for a bit, his tea cup poised in his right hand, his glasses perched almost at the tip of his nose. 'Look,' he said, 'I don't believe in the universality of beauty.'

'Yes, but . . . '

'No, no, let me finish. I was educated in English, I feel comfortable in English clothes. These don't make me feel like an actor, they are part of me. But, deep down, they are insignificant, mere props really. An English poem is beautiful in its context, in England. In India it loses its power, or at least the power to generate other poetry. Perhaps resonance is a better word – it loses its resonance.'

'But I thought you wanted to be a poet.'

'At Cambridge, yes. But I couldn't write English poetry here. To express myself as an Indian, here in India, I must write in Punjabi and draw from the classics. The landscape, the weather, the food, the language, these are all part of the same thing, which cannot be transplanted without losing its meaning. That is why I am here and not in England. This is where I belong, it is the deeper part of me.'

'But still you write in English, which I believe is better than your Punjabi or Hindi.'

Inder laughed, rather loudly, more like a bark: 'Yes, and that is why I stopped writing poetry.'

After leaving Inder's house, I walked through the streets of New Delhi, past the elegant Lutyens bungalows, and thought of Disraeli, who had had such a fine understanding of the theatre of Empire. He would have made an excellent Viceroy of India.

Disraeli was of course a very theatrical man: he liked to use rouge on his cheeks and addressed his male friends as 'Darling'. Perhaps Dizzy acted English more than he spoke it. There were some who thought they saw through Dizzy's performance and were annoyed by the artifice. They felt they were the butts of a private, practical joke.

'There was something', said Colonel Ponsonby, Queen Victoria's secretary, 'in his over-civil expressions about the Queen or "my dear Colonel" which made me think he was playing with me . . . ' On another occasion he remarked: 'I so fully believe that Disraeli really has an admiration for splendour, for duchesses with ropes of pearls, for richness and gorgeousness, mixed, I also think, with a cynical sneer and a burlesque thought about them . . . His speech here on the Palatial Grandeur, the Royal Physician who attended on him, the Royal Footman who answered his beck and nod, the rich plate etc. – all was worked up half really, half comically into an expression of admiration for Royalty and the Queen. Yet there may also have been a sarcasm under it all.'

More like an ironic distance, I should say.

I decided to call on a Bengali writer, whose book on cricket I much admired. What fascinated me was his description of the ways in which Indian traditions were revived or distorted as a kind of native mimicry of British attitudes.

I called him at his home in Delhi. He answered the phone himself and we made an appointment for the next day. Before calling off he said: 'By the way, are you an Indian?' I told him I was not. 'Oh,' he said, 'I thought only an Indian would speak English the way you do.'

Alone on the rooftop of the school, listening to the plaintive cry of the black ibis, watching the sun go down over the yellow-brown plain, I fell prey to conflicting emotions: I was sad about leaving my native land, to be severed by whole continents from Mama, and it was distressing to be sent yet again from pillar to post by the conspirators of Jamnagar, but at the same time the prospect of seeing with my own eyes the greatest nation on earth thrilled me to the bone. At last I would be able to see in their full splendour those places I had only read about in books: Lord's cricket ground, St Paul's Cathedral, Pall Mall, the Vale of White Horse, Rugby College

... It truly seemed as if all the wonders of the world were soon to be mine!

Of the journey to Bombay I remember but little. The cities of Baroda and Ahmedabad did not leave a deep impression, but that, no doubt, was due to the fact that my heart was already set on greater adventures. Mr Macnaghten declared Bombay itself a wicked place with a thousand ways to lead us astray. There was, however, little danger of running into any of them, for the Principal made very sure that we embarked on the *Assam* without delay.

Excepting a few hours of respite here and there, I had few opportunities to enjoy myself on board, as it soon became clear that I was not destined to be a good sailor. A Rajput first and last, I could never find my sea legs, and was overcome much of the time with mal de mer. This, combined with a bad bronchial condition, made life an absolute misery. Perhaps it was just punishment for breaking the rules of my religion which were set against sea voyages. Such, I suppose, is the price we have to pay for progress.

There were nonetheless some memorable moments. Among the passengers was a group of high-spirited young Englishmen who celebrated their passage home by making quite a dent in the ship's supply of whisky. They were none too careful in their language either, especially where it concerned my countrymen. This caused Mr Macnaghten much distress and he tried his hardest to keep us away from them. Nevertheless, repelled though I was by their manners, these young men with their bright red faces, pink legs and curly blond hair, were fascinating specimens, for I had never seen the likes of them before, unless one counts Ridley.

They had contrived a curious entertainment on deck, curious, that is, to one without experience of English entertainments. It was a Nigger Minstrel Show of the kind that is common enough in England, but rather rare, I should say, in Kathiawar. They blackened their faces and reddened their lips to resemble blackamoors and sang bawdy songs in a funny accent, jumping up and down like monkeys. Alas, I saw but little of the show, for as soon as Mr Macnaghten caught wind of it, he ordered us to our cabins. But what I saw made me laugh so much I almost forgot about my wretched sea-sickness. We were still in the tropics and it was a very hot day and the funniest thing was the way their black face-paint melted in the boiling heat and ran down their white shirt-fronts in tiny black rivulets.

Other fellow travellers on board the *Assam* included an elderly Bengalee who drank beer from a champagne glass, a genteel English lady with her daughter who was continuously in tears, and a ruddy-faced vicar who insisted on patting me on the head every time we met. His wife addressed me as Maharaja, which rather pleased me, and I did not venture to correct her mistake. Indeed, my two fellow Kumars pronounced it a capital joke and they pretended to be my brothers. It was a good thing Mr Macnaghten did not catch on to our little deception, for we should no doubt have been severely reprimanded.

It was with a great sense of relief that I caught my first glimpse of England. Not that it was a very prepossessing glimpse, but at least it meant an end to what had become rather an ordeal. Mr Macnaghten was in a state of high excitement and he summoned us on deck. 'There she lies in all her splendour,' he said, 'our modern Babylon, the capital of the world.' It was early yet and we stood there shivering in the chilly morning fog, through which we were barely able to discern the cranes and docks of Tilbury.

My greatest shock on arriving in England was not the cold weather, for which, after all, we had been prepared, or the hurly-burly of the Tilbury docks, which was rather similar to what we had seen in Bombay. No, it was the sight of Britishers engaging in low caste work that came as a surprise. The stevedores, dressed in filthy clothes, shouting in an unintelligible language, seemed very menacing. I asked Mr Macnaghten who they were and he explained that they were Irishmen. I asked whether that meant that they were of a low caste, and Mr Macnaghten answered that they may seem that way, but that even though every man was assigned his task, in the eyes of God there were no castes, which left me none the wiser. I mention this to illustrate what a callow youth I was, so new yet to the ways of my adopted country.

Rain is my overriding memory of that first summer in England: it seemed as though it would never stop. At times it poured down as in an Indian monsoon; sometimes it just spat or merely dribbled, but always it threatened in dark grey clouds that almost turned day into night. We were compelled for much of the summer to watch the world go by through the windows of Mr Macnaghten's house, and there were moments that I must confess I longed for the sunny skies of Kathiawar. I did not much care for the wet streets of London, which smelled perpetually of soot.

The general gloom was relieved, however, by our visits to Mr Macnaghten's tailor in Jermyn Street. He was adamant that our sartorial appearance should be commensurate with our station, something with which I could only whole-heartedly agree. How I loved these visits, my dear friend! It was an opportunity to dress up, and I was much flattered to be addressed by the tailor as Young Prince. We ordered suits, shirts, boots and several fine waistcoats. And as a result we felt like proper English gentlemen.

The shops and outfitters of St James's were the most wonderful thing I had ever seen, for, of course, I had never encountered such opulence: the gorgeous silks and beautifully crafted collar studs, the gun shops and cigar merchants, the hatters and bootmakers and jewellers. I could have spent days just gazing at all the fine things on display in these as yet inaccessible treasure troves. And in truth, even though life has been kind to me since and I have been able to indulge my passion for fine things to the full, the shops of St James's have never lost their magic appeal; every time I walk through those beloved streets, it is still as though I were seeing them for the first time.

For our general education we were taken to see the paintings at the Royal Academy, the Elgin Marbles at the British

Museum and the buildings of Westminster Abbey, and doubtless more that I cannot remember. Mr Macnaghten gave us a
most instructive lecture on the Marbles, the beauty of which
seemed to move him profoundly. He told us to behold the
harmonious genius of the Ancient World, whose spirit still
inspired the leading races of our own time. After finishing his
lecture he stroked my hair, as he did so often as a token of his
affection for me, and I saw a tear rolling down his cheek.
Truly, he was a man of great sensibility. Naturally, I, too, was
deeply impressed by these relics, and could not avoid compar-
ing them favourably to the gaudy and even salacious artefacts
of India. The Hindu faith has been reduced by latter-day
Brahmins to a collection of grotesque fancies and super-
stitions. It was of course not always thus. If only we could
clear away the rot and decay of our present civilisation and
return to its ancient origins, when Indian art and culture
were no less harmonious and beautiful than those of the
Greek Marbles. It is perhaps, more than anything, a matter
of disciplining the mind, for real religiousness lies in right
principles, upright character, and a pure soul.

Another artefact that gave me pause for thought was something called the Tiger-Man-Organ, displayed at the Victoria
and Albert Museum. It represented an Indian tiger in the act of
eating an Englishman, the beast making a ferocious noise and
the sahib evincing his agony through a strange gurgling sound,
all of which was set in motion by a mechanical device. It was
extraordinary and a little shocking, for this object had
belonged to Tippoo, the Sultan of Mysore, who was hardly the
sort of figure to inspire Indians with pride in their race. For
one thing, Tippoo had been a fearful nuisance to the British
who quite rightly saw the Mohammedan ruler as an obstacle
to progress in India. I am pleased to say that my own ancestors
had played their part in finally bringing the perfidious sultan to
heel. After fighting all his life on the side of the French, for
whom he had a mysterious liking, he was defeated by a
combined force of Indian and British troops, and he died
without honour during the siege of his capital in 1799. But

despite my misgivings about this unlikely hero, I could not help laughing, for it was a rather pretty joke. What a strange people the English were! – to watch one of their own men being eaten by an Asiatic beast and being entertained by the spectacle to boot. Such a thing would never be tolerated in India, to be sure, but I dare say it whetted the Englishman's appetite for Eastern adventure.

Perhaps, though, there was more to it than that: for I remarked upon another English phenomenon, not unrelated to the mechanical man-eater, namely the popular taste, fed by the press, for spectacular and gruesome violence. Indeed the first thing I heard upon disembarking at Tilbury was the cry of newspaper vendors announcing the latest murder story. They catered, I realised even then, to a plebeian audience, but one still wondered how to reconcile this vicarious cruelty to the gentle temperament of the English race. It was not as though I was unused to violence or tales of bloodshed; these were, after all, part of our own heritage too. But there appeared to be a singular lack of nobility and a surfeit of rather unpleasant prurience in the stories dished up for the readers of the popular press. Was it that civilised values had not yet permeated among the common men of England? I found this very hard to believe, and do not believe it yet, for I have found the English working man to be, on the whole, perfectly decent and well-mannered, and I have endeavoured always to treat him with the respect that is his due.

I cannot very well continue my story without mentioning my first visit to Lord's, since those hallowed grounds were to be of such moment in my life. Luckily, Mr Macnaghten was a member of the MCC and he kindly consented to take me to see the Australians play the English Eleven, whose captain was of course none other than W. G. Grace. Not even in my wildest dreams did I imagine that one day I should play in his team myself. That summer I felt like an artist going to Italy to pay homage to Great Masters, or a pilgrim visiting Jerusalem to worship at a shrine. Pleased as Punch and dressed in my best summer suit I set forth, proud to be in the charge of

Mr Macnaghten, who sported the famous egg and tomato tie.

The only fly in the ointment of that otherwise perfect occasion was the fact that we were to meet M. K. Gandhi, of whom my memories were none too fond, but to whom social obligation decreed that one displayed good manners. He was, it seemed, virtually alone in London, and it would have been churlish to avoid him altogether. And so we had arranged to meet outside the main gate, whence we would make our way to the public stand. Even though, as I said, Mr Macnaghten was an MCC member, he judged it imprudent to take us into the pavilion; not because, so far as I know, there were rules against the presence of Indian guests, but because it would have been highly irregular and he wished to avoid unpleasantness.

Rather to my relief, Gandhi was not at the assigned spot when we arrived, and after a decent wait, we left instructions at the gate where we could be found. Dr Grace was batting in England's second innings, and what a fine specimen he was! I had seen illustrations of the great bearded hero, but watching him here, in the flesh, was like seeing a god come to life among mortals. Dr Grace's partner at the other end was, I seem to recall, W. Barnes, who soon got out to a rash shot. He was replaced by Mr W. W. Read, and just then a man came over and discreetly tapped Mr Macnaghten on the shoulder. He said there was a young native chap outside who was most insistent on seeing us – clearly the confounded Gandhi. We went down to the gate and sure enough there he was, his spectacles glinting in the sun, standing amidst several agitated stewards, as though he had every right in the world to be there. He was dressed rather foppishly, I thought, in white trousers and a loud striped coat, more appropriate to boating than to attending a cricket match. Mr Macnaghten got him in, of course, for which Gandhi showed a singular lack of gratitude. Indeed, his behaviour struck one as being decidedly gauche.

One tried to be cordial all the same. And I suppose we

should have got on all right were it not for his annoying conviction that he always knew everything better than the next man. Whenever I commented on a fine off-break, he would claim that, on the contrary, it had been a leg-break. When a shout for Leg Before Wicket was turned down by the umpire and I pronounced it a fair decision, he would claim it had been plumb. His pedantry became truly insufferable when he was plainly wrong. He insisted for example that Mr W. W. Read was a professional Player, whilst it was plain he was a Gentleman.

Our exchange had begun to attract unwelcome attention, which prompted Mr Macnaghten to enlighten us on the subject. He confirmed what I knew perfectly well, that Mr Read was indeed a Gentleman of the finest kind. However, he said, the distinction between Gentlemen and Players went beyond dressing-rooms and titles. It was not so much a matter of time spent on playing the game as of the spirit in which it is played. The Players included many sterling men who adhered to the highest principles, but to play for the sheer joy of the game, and in so doing refining one's character, is playing for higher stakes than mere material gain, and therein lay the difference between Gentlemen and Players. It was a difference in spirit, of which the social distinction between titles and initials, or separate dressing-rooms, were mere tokens.

His final words on the subject were a salutary lesson to me, and I have never forgotten them. Indeed I have repeated them on many an occasion when I detected the kind of snobbery to which I myself was prone as a callow and inexperienced youth: 'If only the viscounts and barons of France had deigned to play cricket with their peasants, their châteaux would never have been burnt.'

These profoundly civilised sentiments were received by Gandhi with a self-satisfied smirk, which ensured that henceforth I should despise him as the petty Banyan that he was and always would be. I fear for the fate of India if it should ever be decided by small men such as he.

*

In his celebration of cricket, *Cricket Country*, published in 1944, Edmund Blunden described the national cult in flowery but nonetheless exact terms. His 'dream country' was village cricket, where the blacksmith bowls at the squire, and, of course, vice versa. To describe the spirit of such games, Blunden hit upon the word 'degree', as in:

> Take but degree away, untune that string,
> And mark what discord follows.

It was war and Blunden was apprehensive about the future of England. Would the harmony of English life be destroyed by conflict? 'Perhaps', he worried, '"degree" will be taken away without all that harsh consequence. Yet in our country life hitherto, the much execrated principle of grades of society, walks of life has been maintained not by compulsion but by inclination, and the keeping up of distinctions and of separate worlds in little has been done not just by those at the supposed top but by those, quite as much, who accept fortune and know a thing or two at the other end of the scale . . . '

The war did change much of that, of course, but not as much as it did on the continent of Europe. It was precisely because the world of Gentlemen and Players still survived in England – though formally only for a couple of decades more – that the gentlemen of Holland turned to Anglophilia and cricket. France had long since lost its aristocratic allure for the élites of smaller countries in its periphery, and Germany was naturally quite beyond the pale. But England remained, a model of degree and good manners, and so the gentlemen of Holland made their way every summer Sunday, if the weather was fine, through the pleasant tree-lined streets, past the pleasant water-sprinkled gardens, to the pleasant green fields of their cricket clubs, where the First Eleven would be playing against other gentlemen, from Haarlem or Wassenaar, or, on special occasions, against true Englishmen on tour. It seemed, in the turmoil of *après guerre* Europe, as though there would always be an England, a cricket country, a dream country, where one could still live in a state of grace, 'through an afternoon of warm delicate rain, with feathery woodlands fencing us in from the world of worry . . . '

Perhaps to keep me off the beer and skittles, Mr Macnaghten had arranged for me to spend my first year at Cambridge with Revd Louis Borissow, Chaplain of Trinity, and his charming family. Not that I suffered from his decision; not in the least; quite the contrary in fact: I had remarkably little trouble adjusting to their English ways, with the exception of their fondness for roast beef, which of course my religion forbade me to eat. Indeed, I decided from the beginning that it would be best if I did in Rome as the Romans do, and since the atmosphere of the house was overwhelmingly religious I judged it only right that I should take part in the proceedings. You might well ask whether the Christian faith is compatible with my own ancestral beliefs and my answer would be an unequivocal yes. It is my firm conviction that we can live happily with any number of faiths, for, despite their different ways of going about it, all men worship more or less the same God. This, at least, I hold to be true so far as higher civilisations are concerned; the similarities between us and the ways of savage races are indeed more difficult to discern, that is, of course, if they exist at all.

But, as I said, I had few problems falling in with the customs of the Borissows. I got on especially well with the Reverend's young daughters, in whose games and pranks I took part with considerable gusto. Many a time I would play elephant, with the two of them mounting my back like practised mahouts! It is an odd thing, but I have always found the company of young girls delightful, for it appears to me that members of the female sex are most charming when still in the stage of childish innocence, before being worn down by the trials and tribulations of womanhood.

I dare say the Reverend thought me a bit of a dunderhead for I spent all my time playing cricket instead of swotting away at books. But I consoled myself with Mr Macnaghten's oft-stated opinion that there lives more soul in honest play than in half the hymn books. Not that I ventured to express such sentiments to my good host, for they hardly would have squared with the Reverend's sound church notions. However, I tried to make up for my academic deficiencies by composing a prayer for the girls, which we would recite each night after I had read them passages from the Bible or, more likely, played hunt the slipper around the dining-room table. I took some pride in my accomplishment and you can imagine how tickled I was when many years later a revised edition of my prayer found its way into British school-books: I, a mere 'heathen' from the East, preaching to the children of England! If it had not concerned such a serious matter, I should have considered it rather a lark.*

My first year at Cambridge, the kind hospitality of my hosts notwithstanding, was nevertheless not altogether an easy one, for it was somewhat lacking in cheerful companionship. This, I felt, was due to the fact that I was unable to entertain, and under those circumstances could not expect others very well to offer me their friendship.

I was not entirely bereft of company, of course, for I played cricket for St Faith's and billiards at the Liberal Club. But especially at the latter establishment I tended to attract rather odd fellows. A man, whose name I can no longer recall, persuaded me to attend a lecture at something called the Society for Psychical Research. There, a retired colonel proceeded to demonstrate how a mahatma of his acquaintance had suddenly dematerialised through a closed door, leaving behind only his headgear. With a look of triumph the Colonel produced a grubby turban as evidence of his tale. Then, much to my discomfort, the Colonel turned to me and asked me whether as a native of the East I did not have similar stories.

* The text of Ranji's prayer is as follows: O Powers that be, make me observe and keep the rules of the game. Help me not to cry for the moon. Help me neither to offer nor to welcome cheap praise. Give me always to be a good comrade. Help me to win, if I may win, but – and this, O Powers, especially – if I may not win, make me a good loser. Amen.

93

For a second I thought I might try to pull his leg, but since I couldn't think of a likely tale to tell off the top of my head, I declared that I had not and made to leave instantly, for I was rather afraid that people would mistake me for a magician!

Another friend suggested I might enjoy visiting a menagerie that had come to town from Worcester. We set forth in the evening and at the tent made our way through a gauntlet of Jews attempting to sell us trinkets. Inside the brightly-lit tent the noise was quite deafening, what with townsmen and gownsmen trying to outdo the screeching and howling of the caged birds and beasts. The keeper tried valiantly to instruct us about the more interesting details of his animal family, whilst men and boys were doing their hardest to provoke the beasts. One man tweaked the tail of a panther, which proceeded to howl with rage, and a group of town boys tormented a poor ape by tossing him lighted cigars.

Perhaps my state of mind during this introduction to Cambridge life is best expressed by quoting from a letter I sent to Mama. This is how I commenced:

My Dearest Mama,

I hope this letter finds you in good spirits and good health. Thank you so much for your last letter, which, as always, did much to brighten my day. India seems so very far from here, and the days seem so very dark, but I am well taken care of and try to keep up my spirits as best I can.

Perhaps it is for the best that I am far away, for my treatment at the hands of those conspirators in Jamnagar still fills me with a bitter rage. Oh, if only you were here, my dear Mama, to talk to me, for I am alone with my thoughts. The English people are friendly, to be sure, but the affairs of Jamnagar are far removed from their lives and attempts to interest my good friends at the Liberal Club – about which I believe I reported in my last letter – in my case, have, alas, fallen on deaf ears.

It is a curious thing indeed how the people living here in the centre of our great Empire seem so oblivious of their overseas

94

possessions. Whilst we are here to learn about the progress of the modern world to drag our people from their present state of degradation, the English are interested in our part of the world only insofar as it appears exotic and strange to them. India to the average citizen of Great Britain is a place of wild beasts, displayed in cages for his entertainment, and magicians who disappear into thin air at the drop of a hat. I have no idea how the common Englishman views me, but I rather suspect it is as a combination of wild animal and fakir!

My dear Mama, let me not fatigue you any further with my problems, which must seem trivial in the extreme. There are many wonderful things I have seen in this great country. Cambridge is a most beautiful town, full of splendour, and I am settling very well into the English way of life, which is, however, not yet without surprises . . .

And so on, and so forth. I was, as I said, not entirely lacking in new friends, but they were rarely men of my kidney. For example, I struck up a brief acquaintance with a sickly fellow at King's called Ross. He was what was known as an aesthete (you remember, of course, the lady aesthetes in their absurd loose robes and their dreamlike demeanour). He wore his hair exceedingly long and dressed extravagantly in velvet suits. I was, however, rather taken by his pleasant manner, and most particularly by his genuine interest in my plight as the rightful heir to the Gaddi. He had the courtesy to call me Prince, which, though strictly speaking inaccurate at that time, still cheered me up no end.

Ross was keen on poetry, which he would read to me in a most beautiful voice. He was also wont to publicise his rather trenchant opinions in such periodicals as *Granta*, which tended to get him into hot water – or cold water, in fact, since one of his articles earned him a ducking in the Fountain of the Front Court by some irate swells. He was much shaken by this event, but since I judged him to have been imprudent, I found it difficult to offer him my sympathy and our relationship fizzled out. Of course, we never had much in common to begin with. For one thing, Ross expressed a deep disinterest in games, which I believe is always a sign of sickliness in a man, a sickliness of the spirit most likely.

I shall always remember Ross, nonetheless, for it was through him that I met the notorious pederast, Oscar Wilde. I had no idea of his perverted habits at the time, of course, and found him rather amusing. He was physically exceedingly unprepossessing, large and pallid, with protruding teeth of a most unattractive colour, and he dressed most oddly. Shaking his hand was like holding a clammy fish and he giggled like a woman, hiding his mouth behind his great white hand. Not at all my type, and I could not follow half of what he said, but he had a captivating manner, and I found myself laughing at his jokes. He showed great interest in my country and promised that one day he would write a story, or rather a thousand and one stories – that is the way he put it – about me and my fabulous kingdom. It was all stuff and nonsense, of course, but, I must admit, rather enjoyable nonsense.

I saw him just once and the most memorable thing about the occasion was the manner of his farewell. We had taken luncheon at Ross's rooms and repaired to the station to see Wilde off. Ross and I were not the only ones there, for Wilde had quite a following, mainly of effete young aesthetes, for whom I did not care at all. They were like our Hijarah dancers in India, neither men nor women, who might bring one luck on auspicious days but are hardly the sort to carry on with socially. Surrounded by these creatures, Wilde boarded his train to London. He leant out of the window, dangling a cigarette in his right hand, spewing forth an endless stream of witticisms which elicited gales of laughter from his doting followers. Only when the train began to pull out of the station did Wilde sit down, but then something very odd happened: the train came to a halt and backed into the station again, where we were still standing, waving him off. This time, however, Wilde did not even deign to acknowledge our presence. His performance was over, his window firmly shut, and his attention was now entirely riveted to his newspaper. What an extraordinary fellow he was. Nothing I read about him since surprised me much. No doubt he got his just deserts, but my feeling is that it was those effete young minions that got him into mischief. They were very far from being gentlemen.

The Bengali writer in Delhi, whose book I had admired, and whose name, by the way, was Subhas Chakravorty, had arranged to meet me at the Maidens Hotel, which had been recently restored to a semblance of its former glory. Subhas thought I would enjoy its 'Raj ambience'. We had tea on the terrace. Indian families were sprinkled round the lawn, the men dressed smartly in blue blazers and club ties. The women, dressed in saris, were chirping away like elegant birds in a mixture of English and various Indian languages. I overheard one plump gentleman observing to another that it was 'really most important, most important indeed, to take milk with one's tea, not boil it in milk, mind you, which spoils the whole damn thing, but to take it with the tea'.

'Look here,' said Subhas, speaking very fast, his right hand tracing graceful patterns in the air, 'Ranji reminded the Britishers of what Michel Foucault called heroic ambivalence. You see, cricket in Victorian England was in a peculiar state of transition – a discourse, so to speak, between pre-industrial, playful, aristocratic values and puritanic, industrial, masculine, scientific, professional ones – the texts, as it were, of tradition versus modernity. The Gentlemen represented the former, the Players, the latter. And in order for the Gentlemen to enjoy the fruits of modernity, without the alienation, in the Marxian sense, of industry, the Players did the professional labour, while the Gentlemen talked about fair play. The professionals later turned middle-class, of course, taking on the personality type Erich Fromm calls the market orientation, a type which allows the person to present and sell himself as a commodity. But now we are talking about a period Ranji didn't live to see.'

He paused only for a quick intake of breath, frowned, and carried on.

'You see, what I am driving at here, is that India, which was

97

pagan, aristocratic, androgynous, still retained the values of the society that existed before Arnold introduced masculine Christianity and all that, before . . . '

Yes, I said, trying to edge my way into Subhas's torrential discourse, but Ranji, surely, would have identified with the martial tradition of his caste. He was hardly androgynous . . .

'Quite true, quite true, point taken. But Indian Kshatriyahood, which is what I believe you are referring to, was the native response to masculine Christianity. Now, Indians needed their counterpart to the aggressive Victorian imperialist, so they repressed their androgynous nature. But it could not be totally repressed, you see. Our gods remained androgynous and by extension, so did our secular heroes.'

We fell silent, listening to the tinkle of teaspoons stirring, and the plock-plock of tennis balls on the adjacent courts. Subhas looked at me askance, past his fleshy nose, with a roguish twinkle in his eye, and resumed the discourse: 'I'm willing to bet that it was Ranji's feminine side that appealed to C. B. Fry, and, I would say, Fry's attraction for Ranji was precisely the opposite. And that . . . ' here Subhas's hands went for his rather ample stomach, which began to quiver with silent laughter, ' . . . and that is how you fellows managed to rape us for hundreds of years.'

You might well wonder, my dear Charlo, whatever became of my fellow Kumars in England. In fact, I hardly ever saw them, for, if the truth be told, I did not greatly care for them, especially not for Swaroopsinhji. No doubt this will sound uncharitable of me, but he truly seemed to exemplify the cunning that is, alas, so typical of our race. I may not yet have been acquainted at that early stage with every nook and cranny of English life, but some differences between the British character and our native soul were apparent to me even then. Let me explain, for I do believe that my conclusions at the time might shed light on some of my subsequent actions, which would otherwise remain a mystery to you.

We are from an ancient civilisation, which has in the course of time created great religions, very fine arts and many noble and wise rulers, but it has also, in the natural process of selection, left a propensity in our people for treachery and cunning, necessary to survive in a hot and often barren land. Our native soul is deep, devious and melancholy, forever closed to the outsider, who is soon befuddled by its secrets. Those who are foolhardy enough to seek to penetrate the hidden depths of the East will emerge utterly bewildered and, I fear, much the worse for having tried to enter an area that should remain out of bounds. You, Charlo, have often complained of being cheated by blacks. How right you were. For no son of the tropics will ever be honest with a white man; trickery is too deeply embedded in his soul.

How different is the character of the Englishman! So open, so light where the native soul is dark. The English character is childlike almost in its eternal optimism and its belief in progress, whereas the Indian mind remains chained to its morbid belief in fate. Of course I recognise that there are bad apples in every basket, but the bad Englishman rarely starts out bad; the rot comes from the outside, from the putrefying heat of foreign climes, from the corruption of peoples whose torpitude and deceit is the residue of ages. For England is so young and India so old. Our only hope is to be saved by a more vigorous nation from the decrepitude of our ancient past. And let us pray that one day we will regain our youth and enjoy the light of progress.

Swaroop, I am sorry to say, was a corrupt and corrupting soul. He led a dissolute life at Cambridge, surrounding himself with disreputable men. The only game he knew how to play was whist, which, I grant, he played with a certain degree of skill. But the stakes were high and he was soon without funds and would come to me to tide him over. I quickly tired of this and elected to have nothing more to do with the wretched duffer. From then on, strange tales began to circulate about me, most of which I do not care to repeat. One rumour had it that I was a bogus prince, who didn't have the authority to carry a title. The point of the exercise was to blacken me with the same tar that stuck to my fellow Kumar, the tar, that is, of deceit. It still pains me to think of it. Thank God it was not long before the fellow sank back into the obscurity whence he came. But enough of these complaints about nonentities. I shall let bygones be bygones and resume my story.

It was after I had basked for several years in the hospitality of the Borissows – a kindness I shall never be able to repay – that I decided to stand on my own legs and set up house at 22 Sydney Street. I was very happy there, and well looked after. And I was able to indulge my taste for beautiful objects of ivory and silver – precious stones were as yet beyond my capacity to afford, jewellers being notoriously tight on credit. I also acquired some comfortable English furniture and Persian rugs and soon I deemed my rooms fit for entertaining. Although continuously strapped for cash, I was not wholly penniless, and a gentleman was still accorded the privilege of living on credit in those days, when human bonds of trust still had greater weight than the rules and strictures of our more business-like age.

I had passed into Trinity, of course – an easy enough task since no examination was required – but soon concluded that I was unlikely to be taken at all seriously as a scholar, since cleverness was never a quality I could claim as my own. Instead, I decided to draw the bow up to the ear and make my mark as a cricketer. This was, as you well know, easier said than done, for those were vintage years for Cambridge cricket, what with such fine specimens as C. M. Wells, F. S. Jackson and D. L. A. Jephson. With such gentlemen around it was almost impossible to be noticed.

Consequently, it seemed a good idea to engage for my instruction the best coaches available in Cambridge: Richardson and Lockwood, two very fine professionals. I had trouble with my right leg at the time, which I did not seem able to keep still, so I pegged it down, whilst having my coaches aim at the leg stump, keeping the ball well up to me. In this manner I worked at perfecting my back-foot strokes, which, I am afraid, still left much to be desired. For hours and hours I practised, cuts, pulls and drives, over and over again, until my technique improved by leaps and bounds. It was my practice to place a sovereign on my leg stump, to be presented to the first man to knock it down, an occurrence, I am glad to say, of decreasing frequency, for otherwise I should have been in penury.

It has been suggested by some learned observers that there was a degree of wizardry in my game, but, in all conscience, that was wholly untrue. Excellence, in any endeavour, is a combination of native ability, science and application. As far as the first is concerned, swiftness of eye is a gift of the people of my race. Englishmen know when the ball is coming and get into position for the shot when the ball is over halfway in its flight towards them. I know, though, when the ball has accomplished but a third of its journey towards me. Moreover, the message from the eye to the brain, and from thence to the muscles is flashed with a rapidity that has no equal among Englishmen. This, then, is a natural advantage. But to turn the gifts of nature into technical perfection demands scientific study, an area in which Englishmen are yet to be surpassed. Only by theory, steadfastly applied, can one improve on the physical tools bestowed by God. In the case of a single man this takes self-discipline, in the case of guiding others, as yet ignorant of theory, strong leadership.

My own gifts, I can state without false modesty, soon attracted attention at Parker's Piece, where I kept the crowds well entertained. On one occasion I scored three centuries in a day – in three different games! The tale has been told so often, in so many versions, that you might as well have it from the horse's mouth, so to speak. The first hundred was for my own Cassandra Club, a feat that was easily accomplished well before luncheon. I then wandered over to another game in progress, which I was promptly invited to join. 'Smith,' – I was known in those days to my sporting friends as Smith, affectionately, to be sure – 'Smith,' they said, 'have a slog.' And slog is precisely what I did: over a hundred runs in little more than one hour. I had begun to attract quite a crowd by then and was greatly amused by their comments as I returned from the wicket. 'Do you think he speaks English?' said one curious yokel to another. ''Course he does,' was the wise reply, 'he's called Smith, ain't he.' I could barely suppress my mirth.

Since my club was still batting at that hour, I decided to have some more sport and much to the delight of the crowd, which had grown almost as big as that at the menagerie, I went to bat for yet another side, called, I believe, the Harlequins. The bowling posed few problems and I despatched the ball to all sides of the wicket, until I reached my third century of the day and retired from the game. The crowd was delighted with my performance and I was paraded round the ground, whilst people threw their hats up in the air and cried: 'Three cheers for Smith!' One chap tried to spoil the festive spirit by shouting: 'Three groans for the nigger!' But he was swiftly reprimanded with cries of 'Shame! Three groans for you, sir!' I was deeply moved by this display of friendship.

To celebrate the occasion I organised a supper party in my rooms, to which I invited all the Cassandra men. The food and the claret were, I believe, much to their taste. And to commemorate the occasion I gave each man a set of silver cuff-links, with which they declared themselves very pleased. It was but a small token of my affection and, truly, it is a greater pleasure to give than to receive, and there is no greater pleasure than to receive in return the friendship of one's fellows.

My dear Charlo, at this point in my story I must relate how I came to meet my greatest and truest friend (excepting your good self, of course), my dearest Popsey. It was a fortuitous meeting, since, if the truth be told, my life in Cambridge was still rather a lonely one, notwithstanding my recent popularity amongst the crowds at Parker's Piece. I spent much time playing billiards and the men at the Liberal Club were cordial enough, to be sure, as were my shooting chums. Nevertheless, I often found myself alone in my rooms, thinking of India and Mama – melancholy thoughts which I could not possibly share with my friends, for they would not have understood. Such moods were not good for my constitution, for I had trouble sleeping, a condition made far worse by my asthma. And though I found some good cheer in running up a bill at my tailor's, where many a happy hour was spent selecting shirt materials or having new suits made up, these expeditions never succeeded entirely in dispelling my gloom. What I needed, in brief, was a more intimate companion.

As you know, there was a bakery below my rooms which belonged to George Barnes, the landlord. Around the back was a pleasant little public house where we would repair for drinks: ginger ale for me, and Bitter and Swipes for Barnes. The first time I noticed Popsey, I did not actually see her. I heard her, and what I heard was remarkable enough, for she cursed like a trooper! (I believe she had kept the company of a sailor before.) Nonetheless, when I first laid eyes on the dear thing, I knew I wanted her for myself. It was, as the saying goes, love at first sight. She was green all over except for a red patch on the back of her dear head (gone quite bald now, I'm afraid), and despite her purple phrases she was really quite sweet-tempered. As it happened, the publican was happy to get rid of her and I paid him a fair price.

At the time I acquired dear Popsey I was renting a shoot in Norfolk, where I had some excellent sport. Ignorant people sometimes wonder how a keen sportsman, such as myself, who enjoys nothing so much as bagging a brace of partridges or a handsome stag, can claim to love animals. Such an opinion is founded on a deep misunderstanding of human and indeed, I believe, of animal nature. For let no one say that I don't love animals: in fact, I think the pleasure of shooting is by no means incompatible with affection for one's quarry: on the contrary, the pleasure is all the keener for one's love of nature and its denizens. Those that hunt or shoot out of hatred are killers not sportsmen. I should say that the greatest joy is afforded the instant one has the animal in one's sights, for at no moment do man and beast feel a closer bond than when one has the power of life and death over the other. To pick the exact moment of another creature's death is not an act of hatred, but more an act of charity, of sacrifice, indeed of love.

God forbid that I should ever wish to take dear Popsey's life, for she is far too precious a companion. Even as I am writing, the presence of my dear bird gives me solace, for she can offer me something that no human can: absolute loyalty. No creature is as pure, as devoid of any deceit as my sweet parrot, whose language was once so foul. Actually, in a way, the profit was in her ability to curse, for it made people laugh, which is perhaps the greatest gift that nature can bestow, for it offers far greater protection than any weapons yet devised by man.

At times, when I got tired of reading, I would turn to photographs of Ranji, in the hope that by scrutinising his face long enough, something unexpected or new would be revealed, some hidden clue that words could not express. I once met a Japanese man who had been a secret police agent in Shanghai during the war, in charge of interrogating captured partisans. He spoke neither English nor Chinese, but he was an expert at physiognomy and had made a good living before the war by reading palms at temple fairs. All he needed to do to impress his clients was to look at their faces and give them a vague insight into their characters. After the war, the old interrogator returned to the fairgrounds to resume his former trade.

Physiognomy is an interesting idea, but is there anything in the bland features of Heinrich Himmler, say, that shows the evil nature of a mass murderer? I have looked and looked and still cannot see what that puffy, piggy-eyed face reveals apart from the soft, smug mediocrity of a ruthless office politician.

And yet, what makes a certain face (Anthony Eden's) look so English, or another (De Gaulle's or Mitterrand's) so French? Language, perhaps? Mouths appear to be especially revealing: they seem to be shaped by the words that pass through the lips – tightly drawn lips in the case of an upper-class Englishman, protruding ones, like the mouthpiece of a trumpet, in the case of a Frenchman. The face of Ranji, however, remained a mystery.

He had been, since his Cambridge days, a very keen photographer. He loved taking pictures as much as he enjoyed posing for them. But it was difficult, if not impossible, to tell what kind of man he was from pictures, for he seemed to have had only one expression: a bland half-smile, rather like the idealised portraits of gods and politicians in modern Indian posters, ageless and devoid of character, a bit like middle-aged cherubs.

Not that Ranji wasn't vain: after he lost his eye in a shooting accident, he would always turn his head sideways to hide his injury. Yes, he was vain all right. It was just that he gave nothing away. At least, that was true of his private character. About his public persona he was by no means so coy. Pictures of Ranji were a bit like Japanese woodblock prints: the face was stylised, bare of detail, but the clothes were a different matter.

At the palace in Jamnagar, I examined stacks of dusty pictures, laid out for my inspection by the old retainer. There he was: Ranji, the young cricketer at Cambridge, with his light blue cap, which seemed a bit too small, his bat dangling crosswise by his side, his right hand stuck casually in his blue blazer pocket, all perfectly studied; and there was Ranji, in cricket whites, posing at the crease at Hove, smiling blandly as he takes his block; and there, sitting on a wall, in a striped blazer, next to C. B. Fry, in a relaxed holiday pose; there, sitting in his chowdah on top of a richly bedecked elephant, on his way to his installation as Jam Saheb; or in his British Army uniform during World War I; or crouching in tweed plus-fours beside a slain tiger; or, resplendent in silk and jewels, posing at a maharaja's palace – a picture, a pose and a uniform for every occasion.

Why this passion for photography? Is photography a form of collecting, of hunting and gathering? Perhaps choosing the moment to fix images is rather like catching butterflies or shooting wild animals, collecting their heads, to be displayed on the wall, mementoes of power over life. The hunter choosing his decisive moment.

'Of course photography cannot at all be called an art.'

I knew that Inder would say that. He rebelled ostentatiously against technology, even as he enjoyed the comforts it provided.

He wrote in longhand – 'You can't write poetry on a word processor.' He refused to learn how to drive. He never watched television.

'Photography is not an art, my dear. All it can do is reproduce reality or, not even that, really, for a photograph is not real – more like a form of mimicry, and mimicry by definition can't be art.'

Yes, I said, but why did so many of the maharajas have a passion for photography?

'Ah, well, you see,' said Inder, 'that is because they had no poetry left in their souls. They were hybrids, created by the British. Going here and there and back again, their roots were in their suitcases. How could they express themselves? All they could do was record their mimicry.'

Deep inside Inder there was still a stubborn and primitive belief that technology and thus, of course, photography, robbed people of their souls. And Inder, though a brilliant mimic himself, hated mimicry without irony, which he thought was merely ersatz. He believed in poetry of the soul, which was as real as the blood in our veins. And the test of its reality was the impossibility to fake it; it could not be acquired or learnt or collected, for it could only grow, like a beautiful flower, out of its native soil.

Social life in Sydney Street soon picked up speed, quite literally so, for I had acquired a very fine four-seater, single-cylinder Peugeot – the first to appear in the streets of Cambridge! It would take years to pay for it, but since I invariably invited my creditor to shoots and since he was a capital fellow, credit was gladly given. It is often said that a similar vehicle belonging to C. S. Rolls – the chap who went on to manufacture motor cars himself – was the first, but that is a mistake, for I bought mine four years before he did. I must say we cut quite a dash, scattering the crowds in Petty Curry like so many pigeons. Truly, I felt like a god among mortals, motoring along at a speed hitherto unknown to man. It was also a rather useful way to please the various tradesmen to whom I had outstanding debts, for I would offer them rides with their wives, if they were not too fearful. And afterwards I invited them all back to my rooms for a slap-up dinner – the victuals often supplied by the very same guests!

However, life was not all a bed of roses. My main ambition, to get my Blue, continued to elude me. This was becoming a source of intense anguish, for if truth be told, at times I felt that no matter how my game progressed I should never get my chance to play for the University, simply by dint of my native provenance. I had no clear evidence to show for this feeling. But I did find it tiresome that many people in Cambridge regarded my game more as an amusing demonstration of Oriental wizardry than as anything that merited more serious consideration.

Then, one day, as I strolled past the Cam, just behind Trinity – and good gracious, how malodorous the Cam still was in those days! – I had a premonition. It was in every respect an unremarkable summer's day. I stopped at the bridge, looked down at the river, where pieces of soiled paper floated by like little crumpled boats, providing food for the rats under the bridge, and I had the strangest sensation: everything looked the same as always and yet completely different, as though I were no longer part of my surroundings. Perhaps it was only my imagination, though I do not think so, but I distinctly heard a voice telling me in my native language to hasten home, for a messenger bearing good news would soon come. I confess I could make head nor tail of it. Was this the voice of my own mind? I looked round to see who could have spoken. But there was no one, except for an unremarkable man, sitting on a bench, dressed in a grey suit, bearing a slight resemblance to Mr Macnaghten. He was eating a roll, smiled at me and said nothing. I tried to pull myself together and concentrated my attention on the Cam, flowing peacefully under the bridge. But when I looked in the man's direction again, he was gone. It really was most extraordinary. Was this an answer from the gods to whom I had been praying? To this day I believe that it must have been. But who was the man on the bench? I shall never know, of course, but I should add that our native gods are masters of disguise.

After I had returned, I could not stop thinking about what had passed. But if further proof was needed that it had been more than a trick played by my imagination, a messenger did indeed arrive presently, with a letter from F. S. Jackson, captain of Trinity and Cambridge, asking me to visit him in his rooms.

He was living in college, and I felt dreadfully anxious, as I walked up the stairs to see him. I barely dared to knock on his door, and had to pluck up considerable courage to go through with it. But go through with it I did, and there, in his rooms, sprawled on various sofas and chairs, was the *crème de la crème* of Cambridge cricket: P. H. Latham of Malvern, blond and lithe, a god of a man, H. E. Bromley-Davenport, a marvellous specimen with broad shoulders and brown curls, F. S. Jackson himself, former captain of Harrow, the very embodiment of a patrician Englishman. (How could I have dreamt then, my dear Charlo, that Jacker would one day be one of our dearest friends?) They were drinking mulled port and Bromley-Davenport blew cigar smoke in elegant rings and took my measure with his trusty brown eyes. Truly I felt I had ascended Mount Olympus, there to converse with the gods.

The conversation, as far as I can recall, went something like this:

Bromley-Davenport: 'I trust you understand English well enough?'

I assured him that I did.

'Yes, you chaps all seem to. Do you know Patiala?'

I said that I had of course heard of the Maharaja of Patiala, but did not as yet have the honour of his acquaintance.

'What about old Sir Pratab Singh?'

I said that he was my uncle.

F. S. Jackson: 'Splendid chap. Gave us some excellent cricket when we were over in your part of the world. But that's by the bye. We think you might be a useful bat.'

I said that I had had some good innings.

P. H. Latham: 'Yes, we observed some of those. Style a little unorthodox, though. Lot of chaps that can make runs, but it's the chap who can make runs when they are most needed that we're looking for. Character, that's the thing. You seem a bit wild to me. Can you discipline yourself for the good of the team, that's what we want to know.'

I said that it would be such a singular honour to be in the team, that I could but try my best.

F. S. Jackson: 'That's the spirit. Be at the ground on Saturday morning. Playing the Gentlemen of England.'

After that business was concluded. I was offered a cheroot and some port. By God, I was happy! Jackson, Latham, Bromley-Davenport – to be able to count myself amongst their peers! How I relished the opportunity to show that I was worthy of their trust, that I could be one of the team. I should rather have died than let them down. Indeed, when I repaired to my lodgings, I felt so tickled – and a trifle tipsy, too – that I wanted to sing and dance all the way home. But that would have proved a little awkward, sitting in the back of the motor car. So I tipped my driver a sovereign instead.

Since there was nobody around with whom to celebrate my good fortune, I had to make do with the delightful company of Popsey. And when I retired to bed that night, I heard her squawk with pleasure. At least, I believe it was pleasure, for I do not recall quite what it was she said, but I rather think it was 'Good show!' This, in itself, was a minor victory, for I had spent months trying to teach her those words.

It was hot on the day of my début and the grass was freshly cut, emitting the fragrance I treasure above all perfumes: the smell of English summer. The ground was full, since there were some capital players in the Gentlemen's team: Dr W. G. Grace and Lord Harris, of course, and yourself, Charlo, picked, as I recall, for your bowling abilities. This was, of course, before you were recognised for what you were: the quintessential English hero – to wit, a batsman, and not just a batsman, but the greatest of your generation.

I was sent in at number six and was nervous as a cat. Our side had not done awfully well, as both Jacker and J. W. H. T. Douglas had been dismissed rather cheaply. I remember being patted on the back by several men in the pavilion, who wished me good luck. I felt that a great responsibility rested on my shoulders, for how could I let down the honour of my race, as well as the expectations of these good people?

When I took my block at the crease, I overheard one of the slip fielders say to another – whosoever it was, I do not wish to remember – 'Let's see how the little black man likes a taste of English mustard!' It was said, of course, in jest, but it made me all the keener to succeed. You, my dear boy, were the bowler, graceful as a Greek athlete in full flight, hurling your thunder-bolts like Zeus himself. The first ball hit me painfully in the ribs. I must have gasped a little, for the same fielder remarked: 'I don't know what he speaks, but it ain't English.' This elicited great mirth, and I decided I should have my sport with the gentlemen, so I remained silent. You, I was glad to see, were not among those who laughed at my expense, which endeared you to me from the start. Your bowling was none-theless ferocious: The next ball was fearfully fast and broke back. The stumps behind me crashed like skittles, and I knew I was out for a duck's egg.

'You're out, old chap,' said one of the men, as though I had not realised. 'Perhaps he really doesn't understand,' said another. As I walked back to the pavilion, there was a terrible silence all round. I knew I had let everybody down. And much as I tried to tell myself that I ought to take it on the chin, be a good loser, live to fight another day, and so on, I could not suppress my feeling of bitter disappointment. The men in the dressing-room muttered 'Bad luck, Smith' and left me alone in my misery. The only good thing was that Mr Macnaghten was not there to witness my humiliation.

Thank goodness I was given another chance in our second innings. This was after we had feasted on a brilliant perform-ance by the Doctor. What style he had! What power! I do believe that he revolutionised cricket, for he turned it from an accomplishment into a science; he had made utility the criterion of style. The elegance of his batting was like that of a complex mathematical problem: everything fitted; there were no loose ends or fripperies; he moved like a new and well-oiled machine, a run-making machine, and splendid it was to behold. He was, quite frankly, an impossible act to follow. Still, all one could do was one's best and again I strolled out to the wicket with great apprehension and again I bore the friendly taunts from your lot in silence. I decided a classical, scientific defence was best designed to keep me out of trouble and so I played forward, very straight, keeping my right leg quite still, and to make runs, I turned my bat towards short leg at the last possible moment, so as to make maximum use of the ball's velocity. I had practised this shot for months in the nets and I must say it paid handsome dividends, for I was soon in double figures.

Some of the Gentlemen did not much like it at all. I think it was Lord Harris who called it 'a damned Indian rope trick' and declared it 'not cricket'. I shall be eternally grateful to the good Doctor for later springing to my defence in the inimitable way of that biggest of men: 'If that ain't cricket,' he said, 'I'm a bloody Hindu!' And a Hindu he most definitely was not. At any rate, I managed to hit two score runs, before I was caught in the gully, and all in all, it was not too discreditable a performance.

You will recall that the day was concluded with a capital supper, during which many toasts were exchanged. I remained silent and listened to the speeches, which seemed to scale ever greater heights of eloquence. At one point I was startled to hear a reference to myself, when one of the speakers kindly welcomed 'our dark young friend sprung from the jewel in Her Majesty's Crown'. This elicited requests for a speech from me – the very opportunity I had been waiting for.

I rose and summoned all my rhetorical powers, honed on the whetstone of Shakespeare and Scott, to deliver a speech on the human bonds that hold together our great Empire, enriched by the spirit that reigns over the playing fields of

England. My words, I believe, were well enough received, but there were quite a few red faces around the table when the Gentlemen heard me speak perfectly well in their native tongue. And let me assure you, I relished the moment, for the joke was now on them.

I do confess to enjoying such pranks as much, if not more than the next man. If truth be told, this was not the first, nor would it be the last time that I disguised my ability to speak English in order to startle my company. People were as yet unused to meeting Indians, and they did not know what to expect, so I hope I shall be forgiven for once in a while giving in to the irresistible urge to have some fun at their expense.

One of the more memorable pranks of this nature was the visit of the King of Zanzibar. The King was of course myself, suitably done up by a first rate costumier's in London. We had made sure that the Mayor of Cambridge received a message on the previous day to the effect that the King of Zanzibar would arrive on an official visit and would much appreciate making the Mayor's acquaintance. And, sure enough, when I arrived, dressed in a resplendent silk robe, surrounded by my friends, got up in blue velvet liveries, there was the Mayor, accompanied by several local notables, to meet us. He, too, was in full regalia, with the chains of his office round his neck, and the poor man was effusive in his greetings. Everything went swimmingly at the luncheon, where I had my own pot of hash, served by my courtiers, since, as we explained, I kept to a strict diet of monkey brains. People really are remarkably gullible, don't you agree? Afterwards speeches were exchanged expressing a variety of noble sentiments, and we were shown around some of the more celebrated local spots – causing moments of acute anxiety, lest we be recognised by fellows we knew.

But everything was perfectly fine, until it was time to take our leave. This presented a problem, for whilst we had no intention of returning to London, the Mayor insisted on escorting us back to the train station. There was but one thing for it: I decided I should visit the public convenience and insisted on having my courtiers accompany me on this errand, doubtless an odd thing to do, but monarchs are after all entitled to their whims. Once inside, we made sure we were unobserved, climbed through the back window, and ran as fast as we could to my rooms, where we laughed until we were ruddier than David!

But that was not the end of the story. The good Mayor was, it turned out, a keen follower of local cricket, and a regular visitor to Fenner's. The inevitable happened: as I trotted out to bat for Cambridge against the MCC, who should I run into on the pavilion steps but the Mayor himself. I saw his jaw drop, but I pretended that nothing was amiss. Since he could not very well risk making a fool of himself, the Mayor took his seat and shook his head in disbelief.

About one week after this unexpected encounter I had a rather handsome cigarette case delivered to his office, engraved with an expression of gratitude for his gracious hospitality, from HRH the King of Zanzibar. I am glad to say that the Mayor had a superb sense of humour, for he sent me a note in return, thanking me for the precious gift and wishing me the best of British on the cricket field!

W. H. Auden, writing about the character of Iago, described the typical practical joker: ' . . . though his jokes may be harmless in themselves, and extremely funny, there is something slightly sinister about every practical joker, for they betray him as someone who likes to play God behind the scenes. Unlike the ordinary ambitious man who strives for a dominant position in public and enjoys giving orders and seeing others obey them, the practical joker desires to make others obey him without being aware of his existence until the moment of his theophany when he says: "Behold the God whose puppets you have been and behold, he does not look like a god but is a human being just like yourselves."'

Iago's self-description is 'I am not what I am.' Who or what was Ranji? An English cricketer and an Indian prince was his self-description. So far as one knows, he said this without irony.

It is as good a description as any. But others saw him as something more complicated than that: as an English cricketer he behaved like an Indian prince, and as an Indian prince like an English cricketer.

One of the things that fascinated me most about Inder was the central enigma of his personality: he was always performing, but it was impossible to say which was more contrived, his English or his Indian persona. More than once I tried to draw him out on this, but never with much success: he would always slip away, ending the enquiry with an elegant quip. The problem was he could laugh at his Englishness, which he liked to present as artifice, but not at his Indian side, which was a serious business.

There was a very old Indian writer, much admired by Inder and myself, called Nayan Dasgupta. Every time I visited him at his house in Oxford, he issued the same warning: 'An Indian will never tell the truth to a foreigner. You will never find out what Indians outside a tiny minority think. You don't know the languages and Indians will never speak the truth to you. They talk and talk, but not as I do, to express the truth, but to express falsehoods.'

Dasgupta was a tiny man, usually dressed in an immaculate dhoti, though when he still lived in India he favoured well-cut English suits. He was a connoisseur of literature, music, Indian and European philosophy, French wine, military history, garden flowers, anything, really, as long as it was associated with high civilisation. We had tea and Indian sweets in his study. The walls were lined with bookcases, and where there was space between the books, he had put up some fine eighteenth and nineteenth century prints: of Benares, Calcutta, Oxford and Napoleon.

Despite the fact that he was well into his nineties, Dasgupta had a habit of jumping on tables and chairs to reach for books to illustrate his points. When I asked him about Ranji, he instantly hopped on to a rickety-looking stool to grab a large picture book from the top shelf.

'Look here,' he said, 'I'll show you.' He sat next to me,

wagging his head in anticipation of the pleasure to come. He found the picture he was looking for: a family portrait of Indian princes, taken in 1910.

'Just look at those wretches,' he said. 'Look at that deformed creature, like a damned monkey.' He squealed with delight. 'Now can you see why we felt complete contempt for those wretched princes.'

Were they all philistines?

'Not philistines; they were barbarians. Despite their hunting dogs, their Venetian glass and all that, their innate barbarianism never disappeared.'

Dasgupta paused to take a bite from his cake. I looked at the prints of Napoleon. He resumed his discourse.

'They affected many things, of course. You see, I never wore English clothes in my life . . . '

I didn't wish to tell him I had heard different. Nor did I remind him of what he had said when, on a later visit, he proudly displayed a handsome houndstooth tweed jacket he had ordered from the finest tailor in Oxford.

' . . . But I am Anglicised inside. They were only half Anglicised. Let me show you . . . '

He hopped on to another small table, agile as a sparrow, to take down yet another book.

'Let me see now . . . ' He wagged his head and restlessly leafed through the book. 'Ah, here it is, look here.' It was a letter from Sir Pratab Singh, the Maharaja of Idar, Ranji's uncle. There was a photograph of Sir Pratab, standing with Ranji. Ranji looked bland as usual, while Sir Pratab looked ferocious: left hand planted in the waist of his half-English, half-Indian style military tunic, his head adorned with a Kaiser Bill moustache, held proudly aloft.

'This man', said Dasgupta, 'wanted to go to Calcutta to personally spear a Bengali babu. Fortunately, one of his advisers managed to talk him out of it.'

Practically choking with mirth, Dasgupta read Sir Pratab's letter to a friend in England. The English was that of a barely literate schoolboy.

'Of course the British loved him. You see, the British despised Indians who spoke good English. Kipling, who was the best British writer on India, likened the Bengali babus to monkeys. They were the Bandar Log in his incomparable *Jungle Book*. The Indian masses – not Neolithic men, quite, but certainly Bronze Age men – the British could cope with. But Indians with minds – those they absolutely detested.'

Dasgupta leapt up from the sofa, where I sat with a pile of open books on my lap. 'Let me show you something.' He fished out a file of newspaper clippings from a desk drawer. They were articles by Dasgupta in the *Daily Telegraph* about the decadence of modern Britain, full of footnotes and references to classical writers, some in Italian and French, left deliberately untranslated.

'Look,' he said, returning to his place next to me, 'British editors ask me, an Indian, no, a Bengali, to write these articles, for British writers can't make the connections any more. Tocqueville, Macaulay, Gibbon, Bacon, they don't know – I, a babu, whose accent was laughed at by the British in my youth, I have to teach them about their own literature and history.'

He chuckled and clutched my knee hard with his bony hand: 'You know, I came to England as an act of revenge.' He fell silent for a few seconds, still holding my knee. Then his eyes fell on a book, sitting on an antique side-table. This filled him with new excitement.

'I must show you something very amusing.' The book was in Bengali. 'It is about the decline of Bengali intellectual life. And in it I have written the greatest joke in modern Bengali literature. Look, look at this . . . ' He pointed out a footnote and slapped his thigh with glee. 'What language is this?'

Greek, I said. Dasgupta shrieked with laughter.

'That is why they hate me in India. It's my puckishness. I don't do these things to show off my knowledge. I just love being frivolous.'

I laughed and looked at his wizened features. A tear of mirth was rolling down his cheek.

*

I came down from Trinity in 1894, after what had been, I think, a creditable innings. Unlike your good self, I did not add a distinguished notch to the annals of British scholarship – I admit it freely – but my efforts at Cambridge, may, nonetheless, have helped to preserve the standards in other spheres. I was singularly honoured to be elected to the Hawks Club, something that was surely worth more than perusing a million dusty tomes. Which is to say that my getting on was not simply a matter of personal pride and gratification, though I cannot deny that such existed, but of a far higher purpose; nothing less, indeed, than the future of our great Empire.

Such was my affection for Cambridge that I kept my rooms in Sydney Street, even when dear Popsey and I moved down to Brighton for the cricket season. Although I had been kindly invited to play for Surrey, I decided to join Sussex. The reasons were twofold, or perhaps I should say threefold: my real affection for Brighton, which I shall explain presently; the great tradition of Sussex cricket; and the fact that you, my beloved friend, were a Sussex man yourself, which promised some happy innings together – a promise which, I am delighted to say, was never disappointed.

Sussex, with its rolling Downs and its ancient traditions, is where I believe the heart of England beats most truly. Quite frankly, I never cared greatly for London, as much as I love Lord's, noble and murmurous with history. The capital, to me, always seemed a rather soulless place, more suited to commerce and industry, both excellent endeavours in their ways, but since I was not born to be a businessman, not really suited to my temperament.

Brighton, on the other hand, was perfect for a man of my kidney. I loved the sea and the smell of fish at the West Pier, the splendid hotels, and the theatres, where I spent so many a happy hour. The great Dan Leno, Eugene Stratton, G. H. Chirgwin: how can I ever forget those marvellous performers. The first time I saw Stratton do his Dandy-coloured Coon I thought I should die with laughter! I do miss such entertainments dearly out here. (I have tried to arrange a minstrel show in Jamnagar, but, alas, it never caught on.) The cricket ground at Brighton was everything a man could wish for – and that is saying something, for those were the days of dull, concrete wickets, which made draws more or less a foregone conclusion. There was no concrete in the wickets of Sussex: they were as natural and true as the soil itself and the men that sprang from its bosom. Indeed, Sussex seemed to grow great cricketers, whose natural gifts came to full flower in the beauty of her incomparable landscape.

Finally, there was the Pavilion, which, though criticised by some as being gaudy, I have always thought splendid. It seems to me that 'Prinny' got it absolutely right: the spirit of the Orient presented in the most modern fashion – ornate but not vulgar, impressive but not ostentatious. Brighton, perhaps more than London, represented for me the pinnacle of imperial achievement, for there, common men as well as princes enjoyed a rest from their labours. In Brighton the Empire was at play. There every native-born Englishman was able to feel that he, too, was fit to be King.

Alas, however, my first year at Sussex did not begin auspiciously, for it was the year of the Jam Saheb's death, which rather left me in straitened circumstances, since the State of Nawanagar could no longer guarantee me an income. I was compelled to fall back on a modest stipend provided by Colonel Berthon and other well-wishers, whom I hoped to be able to repay fully for their kindness once things took a turn for the better. This was of course terribly unfair, as I was the late Jam Saheb's adopted son and heir, but once again black intrigues in the zenana prevented me from inheriting what was rightfully mine. Instead the young Jassaji, son of a concubine, took my place on the Gaddi, a most unsatisfactory state of affairs. Nevertheless, one had to carry on one's social obligations, and I was very fortunate to have been blessed with understanding creditors, whose indulgence still allowed me to live in a suitable manner.

But, rather than tax my memory even further, let me turn once again to my correspondence with Mama, for it furnishes,

I think, the most accurate impression of my state of mind in those days:

Norfolk Hotel, Brighton
June 1895

My Dearest Mama,
I hope this letter finds you in good spirit and good health. Thank you very much for your letter, which did so much to brighten up my day, which was still somewhat darkened by the sad news about the late Jam Saheb. I must confess I had had some hope of being reinstated to the position to which I am entitled, but Colonel Berthon has already communicated to me the hopelessness of that notion, at least for the time being. I shall never give up hope, of course, for if I have learnt anything in this great country, it is that one must stand up for one's natural rights. It is not for glory or material gain, but for the principle of the thing.

Otherwise, my dear Mama, I am having a splendid time, what with some capital shooting in the winter and wonderful cricket this summer. I have had some decent innings for Sussex and MCC: 94 against Cambridge at Lord's, 146 Not Out against a South African Eleven, and 137 Not Out against a team of Dutchmen, who played a very creditable game, for foreigners.

The British press has been very kind to me – my achievements on the field occasionally gaining even more attention than the trials of Oscar Wilde! I must say, however, that the press cannot always be trusted to report the truth. Indeed, I have got credit for saying things I have not said, and I have not had the opportunity of correcting the mis-statements. This is especially unfortunate, since such distortions get me in hot water with some of the gentlemen who select the All England Eleven. To be selected is of course one of the highest honours this country has to bestow. As it is, one of the selectors has already branded me as a bird of passage, not worthy of inclusion.

*My dear Mama, I am in good health, so please stop worry-
ing on my behalf. It is true that I have trouble breathing once
in a while, but that is my usual affliction, which I shall simply
have to put up with. It is during those sleepless nights that I
turn again and again to your letters, which are like a balm to
my soul, for they make me feel almost as though you were
there with me in my room, as the rain lashes the windows and
the wind howls along the Esplanade . . .*

I cannot claim that I was ever happier than during those
Golden Years at Sussex, and much of this was thanks to you,
my dear Charlo. The wonderful shoots at Duxford, when,
between shooting partridges, Admiral Walker would argue
with you about Aristotle's *Ethics*; the grand bait and float-
fishing – as you know I was a late convert to fly-fishing – and
the motoring trips. My dear friend, I shall never forget these
pleasures as long as I live.

Of all sports, I suppose fishing is the most like cricket: one
waits for the decisive moment and seizes it, for there are no
second chances. There is no thrill in life to compare with that
split second when one knows the ball is going to be struck, or
the bird shot, or the fish hooked. For it is then, and only then,
that action and thought are perfectly matched, without the
one superseding the other: one instant's hesitation means the
moment is lost forever.

Shooting, fishing and cricket have something more in
common: the sense of solitude amongst one's fellows. What I
mean is that even though one has company, one has to act
alone, for concentration, without which there can be no
success, is the fruit of a struggle, not with one's opponent, but
with oneself. This is not a question of morbid introspection,
but of complete harmony between brain and muscle, that is,
between action and thought.

The sense of pleasure is, of course, all the keener for the
comradeship that is so much part of the game. When I think
back to the innings we have shared for Sussex and England, I
recall with the greatest joy the feeling of hitting the ball cleanly

and then running briskly to the other side, meeting you half way, gazing into your frank, blue eyes, so full of youth and fun and vigour. It was almost like a union of souls, as though we had merged into one.

The summer of 1896 was perhaps the highest point of that Golden Age. I shan't bore you with statistics, most of which I'm sure you are perfectly familiar with anyway, and what after all is the significance of mere numbers? It should suffice to say that I surpassed the record of the Old Man himself. However, the greatest honour to come my way, indeed an honour whose magnitude never can be expressed in mere records or numbers, was the invitation to play for England. Since you were teaching at Charterhouse at the time, let me take this opportunity to record the circumstances of the long awaited call.

I had been turned down for the Lord's match against the Australians, a top-notch team, led by the redoubtable G. H. S. Trott. It was, of course, a keen disappointment, but the reason for my exclusion was explained to me by Mr Perkins of MCC in a kind and perfectly reasonable letter: it would have been highly irregular, he said, for an Indian to represent England. In time, no doubt, people would get used to the idea, but there was no point in forcing the matter. All change, and he was in no doubt that change would eventually come, should be a gradual process and not the result of helter-skelter decisions that fly in the face of prevailing conventions.

Nonetheless, change came sooner than Mr Perkins or I could have foreseen. And this was due to the broad-minded attitude of the Lancashire committee, who were so kind as to include me in the match against the Australians at Old Trafford. I insisted, however, that the Australian team be consulted first. This kind of gentlemanly gesture always goes down well, I think, without costing one undue inconvenience. It helps to convey upon one the princely dignity people come to expect. Given the generosity of spirit that is habitual amongst our colonial friends I was elated though not wholly surprised to hear of their wholehearted approval. And so it was that I came to represent the country that I love as much as would a native son, and whose colours I will proudly bear as long as I am able.

You may not recall the details of the match that I still regard as my finest, so, with the help of an old scorecard which I have kept as a memento, let me take a brief trip down memory lane. We did not get off to a good start, as two of our best bowlers, to wit, Lohmann and Mold, were too unwell for cricket. And the Australians had in the shape of E. Jones a formidably fast bowler. I thought Jonah was a grand fellow, but I suspected him of being a 'chucker' then, and was convinced of it later, when we faced him in Australia. So dangerous was his bowling, that some of our best men, fearing for their health, deliberately threw their wickets away. This was unfortunate, since the Australians had contrived a considerable score and we were forced to follow on: neither the Old Man, nor Jacker, nor even Archie MacLaren, that paragon of Harrovian correctitude, managed a significant score in the first innings. The headlines in the newspapers lamented our failure and predicted a national disaster.

The situation worsened considerably when we lost four wickets in quick succession in our second innings. I was standing in the breach with J. T. Brown, when we resumed play on Saturday morning. Even the weather, damp and windy, seemed to spell imminent gloom. But I must have been favoured by the Gods that day, for I managed to hang on, flicking Jonah's bullets off my face, not infrequently as far as the boundary. I was joined for a spell by Archie, who played with the immaculate elegance born of his patrician breeding, but, alas, he hit too rashly at a ball from Trumble and was caught by Jonah.

Such mishaps notwithstanding, I was beginning to have fun, knocking Giffen's bowling about a bit, while A. A. Lilley held the fort at the other end. He was caught by Trott after scoring a very respectable nineteen runs, but Briggs and Hearne held their ends up well enough for me to complete my century. By the time we were all out, I had made an undefeated 154, leaving the Australians to make 125 to win. We had staved off ignominy, and walked off the field with our heads held high, and the entire, wonderful Lancashire crowd rose to its feet to salute our achievement. I confess that I was moved to tears. By God, it was something! To be there, in Manchester, an Indian from Kathiawar, fighting for the honour of All England! We lost the match, but that was of no great moment; for to go down in glorious defeat is far more honourable than a victory easily gained. The memory of that great day is still so vivid that I have to stop here, lest I blur my ink with tears.

This is how I reported the conclusion of that magical season to Mama:

Cambridge
30th September 1896

My Dearest Mama,

I hope this letter finds you in good spirit and good health. I have just woken up from an unforgettable revelry: a grand banquet held at the Guildhall in honour of your very own son! This honour has befallen me because of a certain amount of success with bat and ball. In fact, I have surpassed Dr W. G. Grace's record for the number of runs scored in one season. I realise this is just so much gibberish to you, my dearest Mama, but I can assure you it is a matter of some consequence in this country.

Oh, how I wished my dear teacher, Mr Macnaghten, could have been here to see me in my hour of triumph! But, alas, as you know, he is no longer with us. I did manage to thank him, though, in my speech, which was only right and proper, since it was he who taught me how to play the game.

Three hundred people attended the dinner, including all my cricketing friends, as well as the Mayor, the Lord Lieutenant, the High Sheriff, Members of Parliament, Dr Butler, the Master of Trinity, my old Cambridge captain, F. S. Jackson, and many, many more. Mama, this must have been the greatest tribute ever paid by Englishmen to an Indian!

123

The Hall was decorated in the colours of my club, and the food was simply capital. You will be amused to know that the main course included lamb 'à la Ranjitsinhji' and the ice cream was 'à la Rajkumar'. I was presented with a cartoon of myself, entitled 'Pride of John Bull'. And my Cambridge friends cried: 'Three cheers for Smith!' (my old nickname when I was up). It was all most flattering and jolly. The champagne flowed copiously, and many a good man left rather the worse for wear.

Mama, you should have heard some of the speeches! I was called a star from the East, a lithe, well-built dusky hero, who stepped from the tent, gracefully and languidly dragging his bat. My batting, I was told, was graceful as a panther in action and my wrists supple and tough as a creeper of the Indian jungle. I was said to have adopted cricket and turned it into an Oriental poem of action. My God, Mama, what an exotic animal you have given birth to! Still, it is a fine thing to be so greatly appreciated by one's fellows and for this I am deeply grateful. I only wish you could be here to share my moment in the sun and no doubt do your level best to bring back to more modest proportions my hugely swollen head.

I am in good health and getting plenty of fresh air and exercise. So please do not worry on my behalf. It is true I am disturbed at nights, for the English weather is making me frightfully bronchial. What makes these sleepless spells such an ordeal is that they afford me too much time for morbid thoughts. My mind turns to Jamnagar and that son of a concubine on the Gaddi, whilst I am here, so far away. I do believe the English people love me as much as I love them; indeed, this country has been most kind to me, but, in all conscience, I am not one of them. Yet I feel there will be no place for me in India, as long as the present situation in Jamnagar persists. It makes me feel so dashed useless, but what is one to do, my dear Mama?

My friend, one does not wish to make too much of a fuss about one's private travails, but I promised I should give an honest account, and this must needs contain the darker as well as the lighter side of my existence. But rather than dwell upon my problems, let me recall happier times.

It was you, of course, who suggested we embark on a tour of the Continent, since the damp English weather was having an adverse effect on my asthma. Our first stop was Paris, where we were so royally entertained by Baron Pierre de Coubertin, through whose sterling efforts the first modern Olympic Games had been staged in Athens. And it was you, I think, who was most anxious to meet the great Frenchman, since you shared a deep interest in Ancient Greece. I am afraid your quotations from the classics were usually lost on your simple Rajput friend, so it must have been a great pleasure to meet a kindred soul.

I must say the Baron's banquet surpassed, in sheer lavishness and gastronomical excellence, anything I had experienced hitherto in England. And the quality of the food and wines was more than matched by the vividness of the conversation. The Baron, whose fine aristocratic features spoke of his long and noble lineage, told me about his enthusiasm for England, and especially for what he called her 'sporting spirit'. He had, he informed me, attended the Anglo-Saxon Olympiad (of the existence of which I had to confess my ignorance) in Shropshire. The pageantry at this event had moved him deeply and with expansive Gallic gestures he impressed upon me that since the Ancient Greeks, the Anglo-Saxon race has been the only one fully to appreciate the moral influence of physical culture.

I was not about to disagree, but where, I wondered, did he place me in the human ranks? An honorary Anglo-Saxon perhaps? Incidentally, I could not help noticing how he looked at you, almost incessantly, with something I can only describe as an expression of rapture, even worship. Clearly, if I was an honorary member of your race, you were the true coin.

I fear I might have made a faux pas when I asked the Baron about the possibilities of shooting in his country, for he expressed no interest whatsoever in the subject. Indeed, the mere mention of blood sports provoked a glum silence.

However, when the awkwardness had passed, he was eager to have my thoughts on the 'Arnoldian system'. I didn't immediately grasp the meaning of his question, but when he mentioned the name Tom Brown several times, the penny dropped.

'*Tom Brown's School Days*,' he said. 'It is my bible.'

I agreed that it was indeed a fine book and told him I had read it at school.

'It is not only a fine book,' he said, 'it is the finest, an incomparable work.'

He told me of his pilgrimage to Rugby, where he had prayed at Dr Arnold's tomb. There, he confided, alone in the great chapel, his eyes fixed on the funeral slab on which the great name of Thomas Arnold was inscribed, he dreamt that he saw before him the cornerstone of the British Empire.

Then a curious dialogue ensued. He turned towards me, taking his worshipful eyes off you for a moment, and said: 'Flashman!' He appeared to be waiting for an answer, so in an effort to match his move in this flight of whimsy, I replied: 'East.' Whereupon he cried: 'Slogger Williams.' Hoping to vary this delightful conversation I then said: 'Football.' Quick as a flash he replied: 'Cricket,' or, as he pronounced it, 'craickette.' 'Craickette! Craickette!' he shouted and clapped his hands, happy as a young pup.

This prompted a remark which I must say startled me by the vehemence of its delivery: 'Craickette, mon cher Prince, will save the world!'

I did not have a ready answer to that. Happily, he did not seem to expect one, for he carried on himself. His point appeared to be that cricket, like the athletics of antiquity, is a religion, a cult, an impassioned soaring which is capable of rising from play to heroism. To be a hero for one's country is not only noble, it is patriotic. Olympia, he said, is consecrated to a task strictly human and material in form, but purified and elevated by the idea of patriotism. And that, he concluded, was why he wanted cricket to be part of the Olympic Games. As he held forth in this manner, his eyes shone in a way I can only describe as fanatical.

I agreed with his sentiments, of course, but I found his zeal a trifle unsettling. When I mentioned this to you, back at our hotel, you declared that, on the contrary, you had found his enthusiasm entirely commendable. No doubt you were quite right. Nevertheless something about his manner went against my grain. Perhaps I was simply too unused to the florid ways of Continentals, for odd though this may seem to you, Baron de Coubertin made me feel English. Cricket was an English game, and I was an English cricketer. Could something that was so peculiar to the English soil become a universal game without losing its character? What about America, you might ask, where we had such a marvellous reception? And what about Australia? Or, indeed, my own native land? These are good and valid questions. But the natives of Philadelphia and Sydney belong to the same family; they are members of a great Empire, subjects of the same Monarch, speakers of the same language. In my view, where the English language remains unspoken, there can be no cricket worthy of the name.

As for India, it is a somewhat special case: she, too, is a member of the family, to be sure, but it is true I cannot envisage myself ever playing for an Indian team against England. (For one thing, my dear Charlo, given present conditions, England could hardly afford to lose such a contest.) Cricket in India will always remain the preserve of a privileged few who have had the good fortune to enjoy the benefits of an English education. For in our country, too, the English language remains and always will remain largely unspoken.

And yet, the Baron has a point. For is it not a fact that all men would live in peace, if only they were infused with the civilising values of the English game? Is this not a goal worth pursuing? Pax Britannica has brought benefits to millions across the world, and long may it continue to do so. I know you do not care greatly for the Jews, but you must admit that Lord Palmerston's defence of Don Pacifico, the Jew from Gibraltar, who was the victim of Greek maleficence, was an example of British greatness. The Jew may not have spoken the Queen's English, but still he was able to say with pride: Civis Romanus Sum!

It would, nonetheless, be quite naïve to assume that every Tom, Dick and Harry, regardless of his provenance, could become an Englishman, or even adopt English manners. Nor would it be at all desirable. Different peoples have different customs, some good, some bad, but all of them natural to those who were raised to abide by them. This we must respect. For traditional customs are the bonds that unify men and anchor them in their communities, even when they live with strangers under one imperial roof. Without such natural moorings, rich with the patina of ages, as much a part of us as our arms and legs, men become mere savages and brigands, cut loose from everything we regard as civilised. It is up to us, leaders of men, to make sure this never comes to pass. It is, however, not sufficient simply to preserve the past; we must show the way to a better future, and advance by following the example of more progressive peoples, who have forged further ahead on the road to justice and peace. This, for what it is worth, is my ideal of leadership, one which I know that you, a progressive man, must heartily endorse.

King George of Greece, our host in Athens, was a fine example of a progressive monarch and I took to him at first sight. His fine blond hair and blue eyes, which spoke of his Viking ancestry, were equally redolent of the athletes of Ancient Greece, which must have enhanced his value as a king of their descendants. I was fascinated to hear the King expound in the most perfect English his plans to revive the greatness of Greece. The great events of the Olympic Games held in the previous year were so vividly recalled, that I wished I had been there. The ancient monuments of Athens, illuminated with coloured lights; the great banquets attended by a myriad of foreign dignitaries; the Greek tragedies performed in their ancient sites; the processions and flags and anthems; and finally the great victory of Spiridon Louis, the humble son of pure Greek soil, who won the marathon, accompanied during his last lap in the stadium by the King's sons: what drama! What perfect unity between the ruler and his people!

This appealed to my imagination far more than the rather

tedious expositions by various ministers on what they called the Great Idea, the unification of all Greeks under one king, a noble and just cause, no doubt, but hardly one to be left in the dubious hands of oily politicians, whose wont it is to divide instead of unite the people under their charge. Meeting some of these characters, I was inclined to have some sympathy for the Ottoman Sultans, who, though perhaps harsh in their methods, were more concerned about the welfare of their subjects than the politicians whose motives, veiled behind their high-flown rhetoric, were, in my view, entirely selfish. I have no proof of this, but as soon as shifty-eyed men start speaking of democracy, I smell skulduggery close under the surface.

My regard for the Greek politicians was not in any way heightened by their appalling gluttony. The way they fell upon the food at the British Consul's dinner! They were like pigs at a trough. If it weren't for their remarkable girth, one would have suspected that these poor wretches had been starved for months. I shall not forget easily the sight of one such personage, holding forth about the Great Idea with his mouth full of Russian caviar, black juice dribbling down his chin and wine soaking his shirt with a crimson stain.

The Great Idea was leading up to a great war and how eager you were, my dear Charlo, to be witness to the fray. There you stood, all dressed up, like Byron, in your Greek costume, which, I admit, showed you off most admirably. In truth, the Great Idea seemed to strike your fancy in a most remarkable manner. Please don't misunderstand me: I had no doubt about the justness of the ideal, but felt more dubious about its feasibility. Where you saw the descendants of Pericles, I saw greedy politicians and shiftless peasants in beggars' rags; where you saw great temples and theatres, I saw shabby ruins; where you heard the sweet language of Homer, I heard unintelligible and, to my untutored ears, savage sounds. There is, I repeat, a certain grandeur to the ideal of restoring greatness to the Greeks, but I wonder whether it can be done without the firm hand of a more vigorous race. This is where I keenly felt the sad limitation of Pax Britannica. In all honesty, my dear Charlo, could even you seriously imagine playing cricket against these men?

Meeting Louis, the great runner, was of course entirely a different kettle of fish. I was longing to find out what drove this rude shepherd to his remarkable feat, what force of nature or man had turned him into a great national hero, celebrated wherever Greek was spoken. His victory was all the more extraordinary, since, so far as I knew, he had received no education whatsoever. I had heard from Baron de Coubertin how the shepherd had prepared himself for the race by passing the preceding night in prayer before candle-lit icons, and how he pledged to his childhood sweetheart, a beautiful maiden resembling the Virgin Mary, that he would win or die, upon which she presented him with a small Greek flag, which she kissed before sewing it on to his jersey.

I should confess immediately that I, too, have prayed to my gods for strength before doing battle on the field, though I still believe that prowess is part courage, part native talent, part luck, and part scientific application. One cannot, of course, measure these various aspects mathematically, and the true nature of one's gifts must remain a mystery. Why, for example, had I, a Rajput from Sarodar, been chosen to beat the averages of W. G. Grace? It was certainly not, as some American newspapers had it during our tour in that remarkable country, because my 'royal father' was in the habit of sacrificing slaves in gratitude for my victories! Was I born with my gift or had I been simply fortunate in my teachers? How much of one's talent, such as it is, is predestined and how much acquired? Although these questions have exercised me for a long time, I cannot claim to have arrived at a satisfactory conclusion. I was delighted, therefore, that my curiosity about Louis, whom fate had plucked, like myself, from obscurity, was to be satisfied. The King was only too pleased to arrange our meeting.

Louis was a small, dark man, dressed in the costume of his

people: a white skirt, a colourful waistcoat and a smart little hat, perched on his head like a plum pudding. It was hard to believe that this tiny, moustachioed figure was the toast of his nation. We shook hands, but he was evidently shy and said nothing, waiting for me to speak. A British diplomat and several Greek officials were at hand to translate. I asked him what had been the most gratifying aspect of his victory. His eyes darted to the officials and after their translation, he replied without hesitation: 'Enosis.'

'He means to say', an official kindly related, 'that his victory was a great step towards the unification of Greece.'

What, I essayed, had prompted him to run? Again the answer was 'Enosis.' Was that, I ventured once more, the only reason? 'Enosis,' he repeated. I then asked him about his future plans, which he answered again with that single, increasingly irksome little phrase.

The conversation, to which I had looked forward so keenly, was proving to be a disappointment. We all fell silent, Louis waiting, politely, for my next question. I could think of nothing more to say. The interview seemed to be over, but then Louis suddenly glanced at me with a sparkle in his shrewd peasant eyes, and asked me a question. He wished to know why I played my game. I answered that in all truth I played cricket because I enjoyed it. This was translated and Louis thought for a while, then shook his head, and for the first time spoke at some length: 'No,' he said, 'you play because you want to win, because you earn respect, because you can be a man.' He then produced an olive branch from his embroidered bag and presented it to me. This, he said, had been plucked especially from the sacred grove at Olympia. He wished to present it to me as one man to another.

I rarely discussed religion with Inder. At least not directly. He was a Hindu, of course, but many of his friends were Muslims, something in which he took some pride. He neither drank, nor ate meat. Instead he took endless cups of sweet tea and ate a kind of rice gruel mixed with vegetables, which he called his 'hash'.

He didn't mind if others drank or had beef, for he regarded his habits as a purely personal affair.

He was, however, fastidious in these matters to an extent one would not have expected in a man so generally lacking in discipline. This was entirely due to the influence of Inder's guru, a middle-aged man called Charu Baba. Inder believed in miracles, and his guru encouraged this belief by claiming to perform them. Inder was firmly convinced, for example, that by sheer force of concentration, his guru was able to be in several places at the same time. He swore to me that one night, after a bad attack of asthma, he had spoken to Charu Baba, while knowing that he was at least a thousand miles away. Naturally, his asthma was much better the next morning. Inder kept with him a photograph of Charu Baba – a plump, smug, smiling face protruding from a garland of flowers – at all times and the first thing he did when staying anywhere was tack this image on the wall, go down on his knees and burn a stick of incense. Twice a year Inder would visit his guru's ashram for several weeks to worship in the company of his fellow believers.

But perhaps the strangest story concerned Inder's so-called cousin. Basu had, so the story goes, suddenly appeared at Inder's family house in Delhi. Nobody knows where he came from or why he chose Inder's household; one day he was simply there and, invoking the name of Charu Baba, he insisted he was Inder's cousin. Since any mention of the guru's name was like casting a magic spell in Inder's house, Basu was accepted without question.

I met Basu only once. He spoke no English, only a lower-class Hindi, and he was dressed in a purple shirt and fawn, bell-bottomed trousers. He looked about seventeen, but may well have been older. He was idle as a pasha, for he didn't have a job and Inder, as well as his mother, whom Inder had converted to the teachings of his guru, served the boy hand and foot. Basu watched television most of the time, sitting on Inder's mother's bed, munching Swiss chocolates, for which he had a craving. There had to be an endless supply on hand, for when Basu's craving was not indulged, he became impossible. First he would sulk, then throw a tantrum, and finally break something: a piece of furniture, a porcelain bowl, a glass.

I couldn't understand how Inder or his mother put up with this. But Inder grew testy when I asked him about it. All he would say was that Basu performed miracles. When I asked for an example of his powers, Inder mumbled something about how I would never understand.

Months later I heard that Basu had gone off to England on a whim, his expenses covered by Inder's mother, of course. He was going to find himself a wife, he said, and sure enough, he did eventually return with a woman in tow, a heavily made-up creature with a thick Bradford accent and a smattering of Hindi. Henceforth she was also part of the household; the young couple took over the mother's bedroom and the door remained firmly locked for most of the day. Only the sound of Bombay soap operas and the girl's high-pitched giggles could be heard. This development, which would have driven most people quite mad, simply strengthened Inder's firm belief in his cousin's mysterious powers, for had he not predicted that he would find a wife?

Cricket had been kind to me during the latter years of the century. The tour of Australia, where we were entertained so superbly by our colonial hosts, was quite simply marvellous. I was lucky enough to make some runs to boot, this notwithstanding my attacks of breathlessness and the intolerable mosquitoes whose continual visitations gave our faces the appearance of prickly pears. I had some good sport, too, bagging a respectable number of snipe at Kalimna, and it gave me some considerable satisfaction to encounter the friendliness of the ordinary Australians, amongst whom, it appeared, I had gained a certain degree of popularity. I had certainly not enjoyed the experience before of seeing myself depicted on such articles as matchboxes and chocolate wrappers!

The only false note of the tour was a trick played upon me at the Randwick races. It was put about that I had been absurdly gullible and did not know my business. Let me put the record straight on this score. What occurred was actually as follows: I had backed an outsider at considerable odds, as a lark, and, much to my own surprise, I won. This prompted me to invite the jockey, who was responsible for my good fortune, to visit me in my rooms to collect a token of my esteem. A fellow turned up, claiming to represent the jockey, who was, it appeared, indisposed. He seemed a charming boy with the honest, open face so often encountered amongst the common people of Australia. In sum, I trusted him totally and handed over the reward with a letter to the jockey. Alas, as it turned out, I had been duped by an imposter. One has to keep one's sense of humour about such things, of course, and I shrugged off the event. However, I was pained to learn that my generosity, even though misguided in this particular instance, was presented as stupidity by certain people who did not wish me well, most probably for political reasons. Still, let me not dwell upon a sordid little affair best forgotten.

Cricket and sport, as well as the splendid entertainment accorded me by so many friends in England, were of course all very well, but there were times, I must say, when I longed to visit my native land. Staying away for too long clearly would not improve my chances of ascending the Gaddi, for as you well know, my friend, no one is so swiftly forgotten as a sportsman. For what, after all, is a cricketer in the eyes of the world, if not just another flannelled fool?

I felt, in short, that more was required in life than scoring runs. My heart was set on doing good for my people, no matter how much I should have to sacrifice in terms of personal pleasure. I loved England well, let there be no doubt about that, but I felt increasingly useless there, and, whilst I was apprehensive about returning to the heat and dust of India, I felt I had an important role to play, whereas in Britain I should remain forever a colourful appendage.

It was with this very much in mind that I set off with Popsey in 1898, ten years after I had first left for England. I was most fortunate to have had as my travel companion that delightful man, Arthur Priestly, MP for Grantham, whose keen interest in cricket was more than matched by his prowess with the gun – prowess which, I might add, he was able to demonstrate many times during our trip.

Priestly was greatly impressed, as was I, with the lush tropical beauty of Ceylon, our first stop. In all truth, it is no less a green and pleasant isle than England. And he was moved by our visit to Rutlam, where my Rajput ancestors, led by the great Jaswant Rao Rathor, had defeated the armies of Aurangzeb. Here was an example of sacrifice and valour that could not fail to stir an English, as much as a Rajput heart. For in their battle against the Mohammedan invaders, thousands of brave men had fallen. We were entertained by the Maharaja and managed to get in some splendid shooting. Priestly bagged two handsome tigers and we managed to bring down 4000 birds in a morning.

For me personally, two events stood out and hence are worth recording: our stay with the Maharaja of Patiala and my meeting with Pundit Hareshwar, the joshi whose predictions would prove to be so astonishingly accurate.

We were invited to stay in Patiala and Simla, where the Maharaja retired from the summer heat. His Highness was a keen cricketer, which put me in his good graces, something that was not unwelcome, since his friendship could prove of considerable worth in my efforts to receive what was rightfully mine. I thought I had seen a thing or two in some country houses in England, which it would be hardly improper to compare to Heaven as places for healthy and innocent enjoyment, but Patiala far surpassed in grandeur and opulence anything I had ever experienced before. The bathrooms in the Moti Bargh Palace were as large as ballrooms, the staff as numerous as a small army, and His Highness's collection of art and jewellery would have done a top-notch European museum proud. The furniture was of the purest crystal and the plates of solid gold. His Highness had a fine eye for ladies, too, and his zenana must have been the largest in India, containing, as he liked to put it, flowers of many hues. Certainly, I never learnt to tell the numerous children apart, except for Michael, Dicky and Roger, who spent much of their time sitting on my knee, listening to tales of great scores at Lord's. Perhaps these were a welcome change to the traditional stories of Rajput valour, to which they were subjected until they were thoroughly bored.

His Highness himself was a fine figure of a man, who bore himself proudly and dressed impeccably. For daily wear he favoured English clothes – I can picture him now, rifle in hand, in his Rankin plus-fours – but on special occasions, when he received important guests, which, quite naturally, was very often, he wore fine silks, adorned with ropes of black pearls, exquisite emerald necklaces and a breastplate studded with the finest diamonds, cut in Antwerp. It was, incidentally, His Highness who introduced me to my good friend, Jacques Cartier.

His hospitality was of course legendary. Knowing my fondness for sport, he took us out on most days in his Dion Bouton to shoot duck at a lake nearby, especially built for His Highness by a British engineer. In the lake, on several artificial islands, we were asked to wait in our butts for the bugle call that signalled the beginning of the day's sport. We used handsome Purdey twelve-bores, most suited to this kind of thing. The bugle sounded and the sky blackened with game. His Highness was able to drop many birds in one flight by switching from one gun to another, handed to him by his bearer. We continued to shoot until the bugle call announced a halt. This heralded a spell of perfect peace, disturbed only by the thrashing about in the water of wounded ducks and the distant squawks of geese. Gradually a new wave of ducks settled on the water, upon which the bugle called us to action once more. Again the sky was filled and again we raked the flying ducks with our guns, and soon the large, fluttering birds dropped upon the lake like giant raindrops. My God, it was a sight to behold! We continued shooting until dusk, with a short pause for a picnic luncheon of duck, grouse and brandy. After sundown, if the moon was out, His Highness would shoot bar-headed geese with his rifle. The bursts of fire were followed by the splash-bang of geese hitting the water. By the end of a good day we would have bagged at least ten thousand ducks and hundreds of geese, which the bearers then piled up neatly at our feet to enable us to record the occasion with a snap.

There are few men, apart from you, my dear Charlo, whom I have held in greater esteem than the Maharaja of Patiala. Indeed, my admiration for his courage and wisdom knew no bounds. He was highly respected by the British too, of course, and close relations with the British Crown were a venerable Patiala tradition. (You might not be aware that His Highness's grandfather fought with the British in the Anglo-Sikh war of the 1840s and the Patialas helped the British cause greatly during the Mutiny.)

I was deeply honoured, therefore, that some of my high esteem for His Highness seems to have been reciprocated and was immensely flattered to be made His Highness's honorary ADC. I was enrolled in the Patiala Lancers and I wore their distinguished maroon and saffron colours with pride and joy. My first duty as ADC was to receive the Viceroy, Lord Elgin, on his visit to Simla. The visit was a particular pleasure as in the Viceroy's retinue was a man whose book on pig-sticking I had much admired: Colonel Baden-Powell, the very same, of course, who was to distinguish himself a few years hence at Mafeking.

We spoke about pig-sticking, but also, you might be interested to hear, about you, for Baden-Powell had seen you play for Sussex and in the Gentlemen v. Players match at Lord's, and had much admired your style. Indeed, it was in talking about you that we struck up a friendship. It transpired that he had also met your dear wife, whilst out on a hunting party with the Duke of Beaufort, of whose hounds, I believe, she was an honorary whip. He spoke of his deep interest in the training of young boys and how impressed he had been by your dear wife's efforts with the good ship *Mercury*. It seems he had established such a rapport with Madame that he had considered taking up employment there. However, in the end, adventure and the Army had proved a stronger temptation. He asked me whether I thought there might be an opportunity to establish a training school for boys in India along the lines of *Mercury*. I said I honestly didn't know, but that I should have thought a man with Baden-Powell's redoutable gifts would be a boon for our boys, who it must be admitted, often lack sufficient backbone.

Baden-Powell was a handsome young man, with a splendid sense of humour. He liked to be called B-P. 'B-P', he would say, 'is my name and my motto.' And with a mischievous twinkle in his eye, he would invite a new acquaintance to guess what the initials stood for. Then, without waiting for an answer, he would roar: 'Be Prepared, always Be Prepared!'

But under his hearty manners I sensed a certain nervousness, often found in brilliant men. His jokes were invariably accompanied by a high-pitched giggle, rather like the sound of a goat, which I found somewhat disconcerting. It was of a piece with his oddly flaccid handshake, almost as though he were shy of human contact. And yet he was very close to his men, to the point of sharing his bath with his batman, who would scrub B-P's pink back with a hard brush, until it became quite livid. This ritual took place twice a day, mornings and evenings, for he was a stickler for cleanliness, more so, perhaps, than was absolutely warranted.

It must be said, however, that B-P was a marvellous actor and dancer. His performances dressed up in skirts were very popular with the men, who adored to watch their officer kick his legs in a vaudeville show. Some of his fellow officers found this behaviour a trifle rum, but, since B-P's soldiering was beyond reproach and his popularity with the men so evident, they let it pass. B-P's theatrical bent certainly endeared him to His Highness, for, among his many other good qualities, the Maharaja had a genius for the theatre. He was forever inventing new ways to amuse his guests and had a passion for dressing up.

Thus it was that one fine day after breakfast he announced that we should have a game of fancy-dress cricket. The only requirement was to dress up as ladies. Most of us were quite used to His Highness's caprices, so we hardly registered any surprise, but some of the guests were, to put it mildly, in a state of high animation. It was, of course, absolutely up B-P's street and he giggled even more than usual.

The finest dressmakers were summoned from Lahore to make up our costumes. B-P decided to appear as the Queen of Sheba and ordered an elaborately exotic costume with baubles and bangles and silver gauze. I rather fancied myself as Mary Queen of Scots and had a splendid tartan creation made up. A young captain of the Guards, a strapping fellow and a very useful bowler, was kitted out as a demure European bride, and Priestly had chosen to appear as a milkmaid. The *pièce de résistance* was, however, provided by His Highness himself, who fancied himself as a Catholic nun. Truly, it was a shame that our costumes, all designed, fitted and sewn with such care, should be used but once.

The cricket ground, with a view of Simla, whose houses on the hills were like cherries in a rich cake, and the Himalayas stretching as far as the eye could see, was one of the most beautiful in the world. The air was crisp and the smell of hay, fresh grass and mountain flowers exquisite. The surface was a little uneven, it is true, for the field was really a sawn-off mountain top, which meant that we had to play on a wicket made of matting. It was a good thing that the fastest bowler amongst us was restricted in his movements by his bridal gown, for otherwise the ball would have shot off the mat like a bullet.

Our side had a decent innings and I managed to knock the ball about a bit. We got the first few wickets of the side without too much trouble. B-P, not in more conventional circumstances a bad striker of the ball, was tripped up by his long gown and was clean bowled. He returned to the pavilion and kicked up his skirts to reveal a pair of thin, hairy thighs. The crowd roared with pleasure! Then it was the turn of His Highness. In he came, looking rather striking in his nun's habit and his manly black beard. I gave instructions to the bowler, an engineer called Barnes, to go easy on him, since he liked to get a few notches. The first ball went wide of the wicket. The second was a gentle lob, at which His Highness took a mighty swipe and missed. The third, alas, skittled the stumps. But this did not disturb the Maharaja in the very least. He calmly asked the wicketkeeper, a portly major in the Lancers, to restore the bails whence they came and proceeded to take his block. We didn't utter a word of protest, of course. For we all knew perfectly well that the rules applying to common men had nothing whatsoever to do with the Maharaja.

In the end, His Highness scored a few runs, with, it must be said, some little assistance from the fielders who were conspicuously slow in returning the ball after it had come off the royal bat, and with great deftness of limb contrived to kick it over the boundary. Indeed, the Maharaja was having such fun that we never did get him out, or, rather, never had the heart to press the point, and many was the time that shattered stumps were quickly mended and catches clumsily fumbled. Alas, in the end, His Highness ran out of partners, but not quite fast enough from our point of view, for the Maharaja's Eleven won the game by a whisker. His Highness, with an undefeated twelve runs to his illustrious name, was cheered all the way to the pavilion. Elated by his triumph, he ordered Mr De Silva's band to strike up a tune, and the waiters to uncork the champagne. 'Dance, chaps, dance!' he cried, delighted with all the fun, and soon the cricket field was transformed into a great, green ballroom, filled with men in swirling gowns and gorgeous dresses, splotched here and there with patches of grassy mud, dancing in the beautiful Himalayan sunset.

It was also through the kind introduction of His Highness that I was able to arrange a meeting with Pundit Hareshwar, the joshi in Bombay, who was to be of such inestimable worth. His Highness strongly advised me to see the joshi, so as to receive a clearer picture of my future, so that I should know, as it were, where I stood.

I decided – partly as a lark, I must admit – to put the joshi to the test. I dressed up as a servant, and kitted out my favourite bearer, who was more or less of my size, in one of my white tropical suits. We then invited the astrologer to the bungalow where I was staying before embarking on the trip back to Europe. My impeccably dressed bearer was seated in a comfortable chair, as were one or two other chaps, including Priestly and my dear friend, Roland Wild. I was the only one standing, waving the punkah to keep the gentlemen cool. It was all I could do to stop myself from laughing. The joshi was a small man of considerable girth, dressed in a dhoti of the finest cotton. He was reputed to be very old, but his face was as smooth as a young girl's. He had a most singular explanation for this: 'I have no wrinkles inside,' he said, 'so I have no wrinkles outside.' Such statements were utterly typical of the man.

His pronouncements were invariably thus: short and to the point, never a word in excess of what he had to impart. And he spoke with his eyes closed, suggesting deep meditation. He was not one, in other words, to engage in amusing gossip or idle banter.

So we came straight to the point. Which one of the present company, we asked, would one day become a ruler? The joshi said absolutely nothing, then opened his eyes for a fleeting moment and asked for the dates of every man's birth, every man, that is, but me, for I was, after all, a mere punkah-wallah. Once he had received the requisite information, he closed his eyes and sat completely still for what must have been at least a minute. He then requested the gentlemen to let him inspect their hands, which he proceeded to do, tracing the lines with his finger. Another minute of the most profound concentration followed, upon which he declared that none of the men would be rulers.

Since we had little else to ask the pundit, we were about to conclude the interview. But just as the company rose to bid him farewell, he opened his eyes a fraction and cast a glance at me. 'Show me your hand,' he said, and this, with some trepidation, I did. Tracing the lines of my hand, his eyes never left mine. It was as though they were bottomless and I should sink in those dark pits without trace.

'I think I see', he said, 'that you are already a ruler.' I was startled, to say the least. 'In the field of sport, I think . . . But you will be a ruler of men, as well, in, oh, only a few years . . . ' Whereupon, much relieved, we thanked the joshi and he took his leave. Priestly was convinced that I had organised the entire thing as a prank, but that was of course too absurd for words.

We left India two days later, and my heart was filled with hope. Our departure was not a moment too soon, for the dust was having a terrible effect on my ability to breathe. I was, of course, sadly aware of what I was leaving behind, but consoled myself with the thought of an auspicious future. As I stood on the deck of the good ship *Hormuz*, facing the cool breeze with Popsey on my shoulder, I felt almost happy. 'To England!' I cried to my faithful bird. 'Good show!' she squawked. (At least that is what I think she said.)

The summer of 1899 was filled with sadness as well as great fulfilment. You, my dear Charlo, had reached the top of your form as a batsman. Your clean style spoke of the grace of a classical education and the arithmetical precision of a scientific mind. What a pair we made: if the press was to be believed, I matched my heathen scimitar with your Anglo-Saxon sword! Oriental magic and Occidental logic! And how could the press possibly be wrong?

The season did not start well, however, for the damp weather had made me bronchial and I did not really want to play in the first Test Match against the Australians. That I was selected nonetheless turned out to be fortuitous, for I had one of my best innings ever. Since you played a prominent part in the match yourself, I need not give a detailed account of it. Suffice it to say that I was moved to tears, yet again, by the reception I got from the common English man, after my 93 Not Out in the second innings staved off an England defeat. The newspaper headlines that day, 'Ranji Saves England', will be etched in my memory for as long as I live.

Here I would like to take the opportunity to put some thoughts on paper about the man who captained the English side for the last time in his great sporting life: W. G. Grace. I shan't forget his last Test innings ever. He was, if truth be told, long past his prime and had grown far too stout to move with the swiftness that the modern game required. Even his famous black beard, which had in the past put the fear of God in his opponents, had turned as grey as porridge. As we watched him make his way slowly to the wicket, using his bat more as a walking stick than the weapon of assault we had learnt to fear and love, only his massive back still spoke of the great strength he once possessed. The Australians cheered him all the way to the crease, a demonstration, indeed, of good manners, which stood in stark contrast to the disgraceful behaviour of some rowdy elements in the crowd who commented on the slowness of the Old Man's gait.

Jonah's bowling was now beyond the Doctor's powers. Those great arms, which once moved with the speed of lightning, poked fearfully and unsteadily in the general direction of the ball, which by then already had passed through his beard. He didn't last for more than an over and was bowled through his legs. The Old Man blinked, as though he could not quite believe it, then shrugged his broad shoulders and slowly started on his way back to the pavilion, like a great fighting lion in the throes of death. The hero had at last lost his strength. All that was left was the memory of his deeds. As he passed us before entering the dressing-room, his eyes fixed on the ground, his shoulders stooped, he muttered to no one in particular: 'I am finished, it is over, I shan't play again.'

W. G. Grace was not simply the greatest cricketer of his time, or even, perhaps, of all time. He is often called an English institution, but he was more even than that, for W. G., the hero of heroes, was almost divine, an English god, a symbol of all the honest English virtues: pluck, discipline, character. But even that cannot explain entirely the special place occupied by the Doctor in every true Englishman's heart.

For these virtues, and more, are shared by many great English cricketers: MacLaren, Jacker, Barnes, your good self.

Wherein, then, lies the difference? I believe it is this: whereas MacLaren was a fine example of aristocratic grace and Barnes played with the gusto of his solid yeoman stock, W. G. was neither yeoman, nor aristocrat, but somehow stood above such distinctions. He was an amateur and a gentleman, to be sure, but he was as much at ease with common men as he was with the great noblemen of his age. His wide, rugged shoulders formed the great bridge that united all Englishmen, from the loftiest lord to the lowliest working man. He was a true king and after his parting there was not and never will be another one comparable to take his place.

His batting style was not just impeccable; it was inventive. He was, above all, a modern batsman, a paragon of his progressive age. W. G. united in his mighty self all the good points of all the good players and then added a great many that were uniquely his own. He turned the old one-stringed instrument into a many-corded lyre. And, in addition, he made his execution equal his invention. Where a great man has led, many can go afterwards, but the honour is his who found and cut the path. The theory of modern batting is in all essentials the result of W. G.'s thinking and working on the game.

I have tried to live up to the Doctor's standards, and, being a mere mortal, must confess to my failure. This is not to say that W. G. had no human foibles, for, in truth, he was a red-blooded mortal, too. Nay, I am talking about what he stood for, rather than what, in private, he was. (Even kings have their little weaknesses, mercifully hidden from the vulgar gaze.) He stood for what is best in men. Wherever the Doctor appeared, on the village green as much as at Lord's, he rose to the occasion and filled us all with pride; those lucky enough to have played with, or against him, as well as those who cheered him from the sidelines. It would be no exaggeration to say that W. G. was England, and England was W. G. There will never be an England quite like him again.

*

K. C. Lewis lived on the second floor of a corner house in a bleak South London street, which still bore the marks of recent rioting: the wooden ceiling beams of a burnt-down Victorian pub were now mere slabs of charcoal dripping in the rain; video shops were boarded up, as though expecting a violent storm. Young Rastafarians with nowhere to go huddled up against the cold, leaning against the walls of a deserted playground, which was decorated with colourful paintings of Sandinistas and Nelson Mandela. One of the men shouted something, but his words were drowned out by the sound of rap music coming from his ghetto-blaster.

Lewis, I knew from his books, was an expert on Ranji, and what is more, he had seen him bat. A good reason, I thought, to pay the old man a visit.

On the ground floor, beneath Lewis's room, was a printing press for a pamphlet against racism in Britain. The walls were filled with posters for various anti-racist, anti-fascist, anti-Thatcherite causes. One of the paper's editors, a young Jamaican, showed me where Lewis lived.

The most striking feature of the ninety-three-year-old writer from Trinidad, who looked very frail, wrapped up in a plaid blanket, his skin the colour of charcoal, his hair very white, was the colour of his eyes. They were a milky green. It was difficult to tell how much he could see with those emerald eyes, for he was about to have them operated on. I asked him how he first became a cricketer.

He tried to focus his eyes as he spoke, in short bursts: 'I have been interested in cricket since I was two. I was also interested in history and literature very early on. Do you know, as a young boy, I read *Vanity Fair* at least twenty times. Books, magazines – *The Strand Magazine*, *Blackwood's* – I read them all, as well as learning Latin and Greek. Horace, Vergil . . . '

He paused for a while, and I could faintly hear the rap music wafting in from outside. He resumed: 'You see, I'd be looking up an article in Blackwoods on Walter Pater, and find one on county cricket, or, indeed, vice versa. Cricket, history and literature were part of the same thing to me. Moreover, it is most important to understand that cricket was a part of Caribbean history. People were pleased because here was something native – Caribbean cricket, taken up by the Caribbean upper classes. This is most important.'

Lewis spoke with the cultivated accent of an English gentleman, but not with the languid, ironical hesitancy so often adopted by the British upper class. For Lewis seemed self-assured, but not to the extent that he could afford to pretend otherwise. I glanced around the room, which showed the mind of a collector, mainly of books. There were books everywhere, stacked high up to the ceiling; books on European history, a great many on the French Revolution; biographies of Palmerston, Bismarck, Napoleon; books on Italian Renaissance art; on Third World politics; many English novels – Dickens, Thackeray, Sterne; and books on classical music, on Wagner and the German Romantics. In one corner was a high stack of Wisdens, the annual bibles of cricket, from 1925 to 1972; in another, I saw works by Karl Marx, in English and German, Friedrich Engels and Frantz Fanon. On top of this pile was a book called *The Black Jacobins*, and perched on top of that, shining like a precious jewel, was a dark crimson cricket ball.

Lewis resumed his discourse: 'You see, I was already a British intellectual before I was ten, an alien in my own native land. Even in my family I was an oddity. Somehow, from around me I had selected and fastened on to the things that made a whole – clippings about Ranjitsinhji and W. G. Grace, the classic novels – they spoke of another world, grander, more noble, a world of honour, truth, justice . . . a world far away from the rootless place where I was born. This is why cricket was so important to me – cricket is a game of disciplined people with aristocratic tendencies.'

I asked whether he still considered himself a Marxist.

'Oh yes, dear me, yes, yes. A Marxist-Leninist through and through, that's Lewis. But never a Communist Party member, you see, never that. I may be a puritan, but I am not dogmatic.'

How, then, did he square his Marxism with the aristocratic tendencies of cricket?

'Oh, no problem with that at all. I say, could you reach that book up there . . . ' He pointed at a book with a red cover, which I took down from the shelf and handed to him. 'Yes, here it is, let me read you this passage: 'Had Grace been born in Ancient Greece the Iliad would have been a different book. Had he lived in the Middle Ages he would have been a crusader and would now have been lying with his legs crossed in some ancient abbey, having founded a great family. As he was born when the world was older, he was the best known of all Englishmen and the King of that English game least spoilt by any form of vice.'

He closed the book and thought for a bit. 'The point is, you see, that every age has its own heroes. Grace was a Victorian hero who, in an age of commerce and industry, appealed to something older, deeper, more valuable than material gain. Grace inspired an enthusiasm in the English people unknown since the Olympic Champions of Ancient Greece. In Grace's greatness the English people found an unforced sense of community, of the universal merged in an individual. Now to your point about Marxism – it is my belief that only Marxism offers a higher civilisation to strive for in our debased and materialistic age, and you may call that aristocratic, if you like.'

The emerald eyes closed. I thought Lewis had had enough and I was prepared to leave him in peace. It was getting chilly and I closed the window.

'Please don't do that. Must have fresh air. You said you were interested in Ranji. You see, you must realise there is a basic difference between India and the West Indies. The black West Indian has no culture of his own. Indians, Burmese, Chinese, they come to England with their own cultures. Caribbean blacks come here and within hours they are Britishers. They grow up as Britishers with a black skin. They are committed to British civilisation because they regard it as their own. They don't have to learn it in the way Indians or Ceylonese have to.'

'Is this still really true?'

'Oh, most certainly, yes. Caribbean blacks are cricketers, not baseballers. Their literature is Milton and Shakespeare, not Nathaniel Hawthorne. No, they are very much cricketers . . . '

'You insist on saying "they" ... '

'Well, we, we, if you like. You see, the thing is this: British attitudes, behaviour, all that ... We have retained them far better than the British, who are vulgar and commercialised. For us the principles of the game were what distinguished cricketers from the rank and file, a mark of cultivation, if you like. The black middle classes can say to the British – Look, we are the genuine cricketers, we understand the fundamentals of the game, as opposed to the whites, who only want to win and make money ... '

There was another pause and then it really was time to go. The emerald eyes had shut, the head of white hair was slumped forwards on the blanket, which had slipped off one shoulder to reveal a herring-bone tweed jacket. I pulled up the blanket, had a last look at the books, the music scores, the cricket ball, the collected bric-à-brac of a remarkable life, and left.

The press downstairs hissed and spewed out copy after copy of an anti-racist tract. There was a stylised black fist on the cover. It was dark and cold outside. The young Rastas must have left, for the rap music had ceased. There was only the howl of the wind in the playground. And then, very faintly, I heard the sounds of a Haydn string quartet coming from the second-floor window opposite the burnt-down pub.

I remember distinctly the time I heard about our late Queen-Empress's death, for the sad news came after a memorable day's shooting near Cambridge. Hawke was of the party and, as you so well know, his appetite for sport was matched only by his propensity for scoring runs on the cricket field. He had contrived to bag more than his share of partridges, as did Priestly, Jackers and, if I may say, myself. It was, therefore, in considerably high spirits that we repaired to the supper I had laid on in town. I was in an especially good mood since I had succeeded in securing a little loan from an English benefactor, who had taken an interest in my plight. He wished to buy some jewels, which I could procure for him in India, thereby enabling me to repay him and perhaps even improve my own financial state. But enough of these sordid affairs. I was, as I said, in good cheer, and even managed to raise the spirits somewhat higher by playing a little joke on my friends. Dressed up in the uniform of my chauffeur – making sure all the while to hide my face in the folds of a thick muffler – I took my place behind the wheel of my Lanchester, and since my motoring skills were rather limited, proceeded to frighten my unsuspecting passengers half to death! It was with some relish that after a few perilous swerves I turned round to reveal my true identity, which elicited a huge roar of laughter!

This was, I am now ashamed to say, round about the time that our Sovereign died, in the early evening of the 22nd of January. We didn't know about this until we arrived at Cambridge. It was one of the servants who bore the bad news, which cast, at first, a rather sombre spell upon the evening's revelry. I was rather surprised, however, to find that the event seemed to have affected me to a greater degree than my friends, who were, if anything, rather more elated by the prospect of King Edward's reign than by the passing of Queen Victoria's. Without much further ado, Jacker proposed a toast to good King 'Bertie', who, he declared, would make a splendid king, since he sat so well on his horse.

This does not mean that I disapproved of the new King by any means, for I knew him to be a gentleman and a thorough sportsman. But I had my doubts whether he was quite as dedicated to all the peoples of our Empire as his late Mother had shown herself to be. All of this is simply to declare that I had loved our late Queen-Empress dearly, for she had been, as it were, a Mother to us all. Whilst she was alive, I felt that our great imperial family, regardless of race or creed, could march in harmony towards a common destiny feeling secure under her benevolent stewardship. But, truly, with her passing, it seemed as though the keystone had fallen out of the arch of Heaven.

I motored down to London to attend the funeral in the pleasant company of the two Borissow girls, who had blossomed by now into splendid young women. I thought it was most important for their education that they should be witness to a great though melancholy day in our history. We suffered some discomfort, since we had to stop for the night at an inadequate hotel, for London was absolutely crammed.

It was dark and cold on the day of the funeral, but what left a lasting impression on me was the unearthly quiet that hung in the streets of the capital, usually so full of raucousness and hurly-burly. The main thoroughfares, it is true, had been cleared for the cortège, but even off the funeral route, it was as though Londoners, for once, had lost their capacity to speak, except in hushed tones; such, I surmised, was the reverence in which the Queen-Empress was held by the common English people. All one heard that day was the faint sound of muffled drumbeats, which became ever louder as the procession drew near. The drums and the booming guns fired as a final salute sounded ominously like doom approaching, ever nearer. Everyone wore black of course – indeed, I had availed myself of the opportunity to wear my black silk waistcoat with black pearl buttons. I noticed that even the crossing sweepers had tied little black ribbons of crêpe to their brooms.

The late Queen's casket was laid out on a gun-carriage, followed by her son, Edward, who could not help looking rather jolly, marching next to the German Kaiser, who couldn't look jolly even if he tried. As the procession went slowly forward, nothing was heard except the drums, the guns and the marching footsteps of long columns of soldiers in their pitch-black uniforms. Then came the closed carriages, draped in black, carrying the female members of the Royal Family. And still the crowds remained silent. This was broken on just one occasion: when Earl Roberts of Kandahar, who had acquitted himself so bravely at Paardeberg, after that dreadful business at Kimberley, was spotted in the cortège. Only then did the people of London permit themselves a brief burst of enthusiasm.

How extraordinary to think that only four years before we had both attended the Diamond Jubilee! How different the world looked to us then: with the sun shining, the people singing and waving their banners – 'One Race, One Queen', 'The Queen of Earthly Queens'. The procession was enormous, with Indians, Chinamen, Dyaks, Australians, African chiefs, indeed, with men from all corners of our Empire marching together, shoulder to shoulder. Truly, it was the most glorious thing I ever saw. I remember Lord Roberts then, resplendent on his grey Arab, and the redoubtable Lord Wolseley, hero of Tel-el-Kebir. Truly, it was the best of times.

But on that dark day of the Queen-Empress's funeral, I was filled with the deepest melancholy. It was as if time had crept up stealthily and was now leaving me behind. What, in all those years, had I really accomplished to add my notch to the march of Man? I was a cricketer, some were even kind enough to say a great cricketer, but, my dear Charlo, what mark is left behind by a fine late cut or a handsome cover drive, except some dumb cipher on a yellowing scorecard lost in the drawer of an aging lover of the game? When the final tally is counted, can one really say that we were more than athletic buffoons performing our magic tricks for the entertainment of the toiling masses? I should like to think so, my dear friend, but I am not at all sure.

I do apologise for indulging in these morbid meditations, which must be sorely trying your patience. I know you always say there is nothing like a cold bath and exercise to get one out of a funk, but if I am to give an honest account of myself, I cannot ignore my doubts, trivial as they may seem to one blessed with a more rugged constitution. There was much to enjoy, it is perfectly true, yet nothing entirely succeeded in dispelling the feeling that I was a bit of a passenger in life. I did believe, however, that if one was going to be a *flâneur*, one might as well maintain the highest standards, and the lure of St James's never lost its power; the cut of a fine waistcoat or a well contrived pair of boots still filled me with the greatest joy. But of all the fine things in this world nothing afforded me more pleasure than a beautiful gem. I always had an eye for pretty watches, cigarette cases, snuffboxes and other such trinkets, but compared to precious stones, these were mere trifles, to be given away without second thought. My passion for jewels has often been misunderstood by sadly uninformed people, who have praised me for behaving generously, where I was being merely selfish, and for being a spendthrift, where in fact I very much bore the interests of others in mind. Perhaps the love of gems is a princely weakness. No doubt it is. But there is so much more to it than a vulgar desire to show off or, God forbid, the mere pursuit of wealth – for what good is wealth anyway if it is not put to a greater purpose, without which one would be no better than a Jew.

No, the pleasure of collecting fine gems is of quite another order; it has to do with what my great friend Jacques Cartier calls the precious vein of history. When I look at a finely-cut diamond or a beautiful ruby or, especially, a perfect emerald, what I see is not a mere precious stone; what I see is much more than that: it is the history, the magic, if you like, accumulated by so many noble hands that touched it, cherished it, pampered it. And once I have set eyes on such a gem I cannot rest until I have added my link to that long and distinguished chain. When I acquire a perfect diamond that once belonged to the Sultan of Turkey, its history becomes, as it were, my own, just as when I bestow it on another man, his history will be forever linked to mine. You will no doubt remember, my dear Charlo, that the true worth of the black pearl I gave you in Geneva lay not in its size or colour, though both were of a rare quality; no, its real value was the fact that it had once been caressed by the hands of Lucrezia Borgia. What is represented by such treasures is the spiritual power of history, a power, alas, increasingly lost to the Western mind, so preoccupied with mere material gain.

The peculiar fascination which decorative forms and visible emblems of greatness exercise over Oriental minds is however well recognised. This is why ignorant criticism of our princely privileges by petty men is so unsound. Indeed, it is the conferment and preservation of such privileges, so dearly cherished by a Rajput and Indian mind, that render possible sacrifices readily and cheerfully made in the service of the Sovereign in times of need. Precious gems are small things to look at, but they possess a value which is never correctly represented by such figures as rupees or pounds.

How well Cartier realised this! And, to be sure, without his patient guidance I should not have succeeded in building a collection which is, in truth, in no way inferior to that of any prince in India. Not only did he guide me in matters of taste, but he was a great man of the world, who understood that good taste has no price and that if one is blessed with the former, one should not be impeded by the latter. In short, my dear Charlo, he was most generous in allowing me unlimited credit. Business, if one cares to call our little transactions by that name, was always a matter of trust and discretion, as is proper among gentlemen. Happily, our tastes coincided almost perfectly. Indeed, if we differ at all, it is on one matter only: Cartier prefers rubies to be the colour of fresh blood, whilst I favour just a tinge of purple; I find it lends character to the stone.

Now, as to my supposed generosity, it is true, I give away as much as I acquire, often, so it must seem, with a nonchalance that borders on indifference. Whilst it is true that often, once the shooting is done, I am happy to leave the dining to others, it is not true that I am indifferent. Indeed, I choose my little presents with great care. However, this has little to do with generosity, let alone charity, for the pleasure is entirely mine. You see, to me, the sparkle of gratitude in the eyes of a recipient is as radiant as the light reflected from the finest gems of Antwerp.

Alas, my dear Charlo, even though the collecting of stones could offer me a temporary respite from my travails, it could not preserve my good health. Since you were present at the time I needn't recount the occasion of my physical collapse, nor should I be able to, since all I remember was my supper party at the Grosvenor House, where several gentlemen became rather tighter than perhaps was good for them. The room was hot and stuffy and I had trouble breathing. I believe Hawke rose to make a speech, but I haven't the foggiest what he said, for I must have fainted in the middle of it. The next thing I knew I was in bed with a fearful fever. I really thought I should die, for it felt as though I were drowning in a bowl of hot soup, which, I can assure you, was an awfully unpleasant sensation.

Oddly enough, although the occasion of my mishap remains hazy in my mind, I can remember with an almost unbelievable clarity the dream I had that night. I recall going in to bat, at Simla I think it was, although I seemed to enter the ground from the Gentlemen's entrance at Lord's. The wicket seemed frightfully far away and my feet felt as though they were being sucked into the ground, and I distinctly recall the crowd shouting at me to hurry up. When I finally reached the crease I faced the most horrifying thunderbolts I had ever experienced on a cricket field. Indeed, I could hardly see the ball, much less hit it, and one of the demon bowlers was you, looking more than ever like a god, with your golden hair flowing, like an Ancient Greek helmet. Actually I was convinced you were chucking the ball, but the umpire kept absolutely mum about it. (I realise this is a sore point, my dear friend, but it was after all only a dream.) Not only couldn't I see the ball, but I couldn't move my arms at all, with the entirely predictable result that the ball hit my stumps with a crashing sound. Even then I couldn't move and the crowd began to cry louder and louder, calling me 'Smith' and telling me to go home. I tried to indicate to them that I couldn't move, but to no avail, and the row became quite deafening.

Then, all of a sudden, I was swept away by a mysterious force, for which I have no logical explanation. I felt lighter than air, as though an enormous burden had been lifted. The sense of drowning or being sucked into the soil was no longer there. I flew higher and higher towards a sparkling light, like the centre of a huge diamond, more desirable than any stone I had ever seen. It is impossible to express this in words, but I felt quite as though I should dissolve into this light. But something stopped me from doing so, something I could not see. And as the light receded I became aware of someone sitting right beside me. I tried to see who it was but couldn't focus my eyes properly. Then I realised it was Mama, watching over me with a sweet expression on her face, like the Virgin Mary, and I knew I had been drawn back to life. A nurse mopped my brow and told me the crisis was over. I am convinced to this day that I had been saved by a miracle and made up my mind to return to India as soon as I was able, which, in due course, I contrived to do. And here, my dear Charlo, I propose to leap a few years, during which little of note passed in my life. Indeed, I propose to leap to an event than which little was of greater personal importance: my installation in 1906 to the Gaddi of Jamnagar.

To rejoice in the news of another man's death is of course a base thing to do, but I cannot honestly claim that I felt any grief when communication reached me to the effect that my predecessor on the Gaddi had suddenly passed away. Naturally, I felt sorry for the wretched fellow, who, it was said, had suffered greatly from a disease brought on, some believed, by a dose of poison surreptitiously administered to him. Such rumours always flew thick and fast around the Jam Saheb's court but I had no reason to disbelieve it. It was, therefore, with mixed emotions of renewed hope and some apprehension that I received the tidings. Here, at last, was the chance I had spent so long waiting for, to fulfil my destiny as the ruler of my State, and yet I was not absolutely sure any more whether I truly wanted it. I should be less than candid if I denied that I suffered from an acute case of cold feet.

At any rate, my future was entirely in the hands of the Agent to the Governor of Bombay, an old family friend called Percy Seymour Fitzgerald. 'Fitz' was a good man and a true friend, to be sure, but he was also a chap who played everything by the book, whatsoever the circumstances. I thought it might be a good gesture to entertain Fitz during my visit to Rajkot, and, besides, it would help pass the time, whilst the

Government made up its mind about my investiture. Fitz was very keen on hearing me tell stories about cricket. Indeed, he never tired of my account of the match at Nottingham, when I batted for the honour of England, for he was a sentimental man and the story always made him weep. I invited him up to Gir, where I made sure he was able to shoot a panther (as you know, it is not difficult to arrange and it always pleases my guests so). I gave him a small memento after supper, which I thought might amuse him: a silver snuffbox, engraved with the words – For Fitz from K. S. R., the man who saved England. I was pleased to see that he was tickled, but in the event it hardly seemed to speed up my ascent to the Gaddi, which appeared as remote a goal as it always had been.

I retired to Sarodar to be with my dear Mama who was, if anything, even more apprehensive than I about my future. We spent long evenings together, watching the sun sink into the brown and thirsty land, discussing what I should do. I had grown to love the landscape of my youth, for I found its solitude soothing. It is so very different from the English landscape, for in England everything seems to have found its final form; England is a tailored land, every inch showing the hand of man, so perfect, so civilised, so finished, whilst here, in my native country, man seems but an insignificant intruder, whose efforts to tame or cultivate the land are doomed to failure; one might as well try to build castles in the sea, for all the good it will do. And yet, I felt it was worth trying. I dearly wished to recreate at least some of the great works of man that I had seen in Europe, something that would outlast my short life, something that would stand as an example for future generations, as a model of what can be done, even here, in the hot and dusty desert. I should like to build a city here, forever linked to my name.

For weeks I sat in Sarodar imagining the shape of my city. It would be a city of palaces, of broad avenues lined with trees, a city of parks and gardens and fountains and great sculptures. I should have a solarium built, and a zoo, a cricket ground and a grand new railway station which would rival for splendour the

156

one in Bombay. I should commission statues of my ancestors, to be made by the finest European artists, and have palaces built by the ablest architects.

I had plenty of time to dream in Sarodar and I might well have been in the midst of one when the news finally arrived from Rajkot that the coast, so to speak, was clear: I was to ascend the Gaddi as soon as the joshis had selected an auspicious date. Mama was of course delighted for me, but her joy was mingled with apprehension. She touched my face as though to make sure it was still her own son's, despite the dramatic rise in my station, and told me to be careful since there were evil spirits abroad that meant to do me harm. Never have I seen love so pure as when I looked into Mama's eyes that day. Tears of joy and worry had made the kohl run down her cheeks like delicate black veins.

Since you were not there to witness my installation, my dear Charlo, I feel I should record the event in some detail. We had arrived in the early morning, at half past six to be precise, in a special train kindly lent for the occasion by the Nawab of Junagadh. It was a most beautiful train. Imagine, if you will, a saloon modelled after the Blue Train (oh, how sweet the memory of traversing France with you by my side), but entirely furnished according to the Nawab's personal taste: the windows were of Venetian glass, engraved with charming hunting scenes; chandeliers from Paris swung from the ceiling and the floor was covered in the finest Persian carpets. The walls, panelled with dark mahogany, as in a top-notch London club, were decorated with prints of the Nawab's favourite horses, some of whom were Derby winners.

Since we arrived at half past six and the joshi had determined that our arrival should be at seven o'clock sharp, we were compelled to linger longer over our early tea. Outside our window a military band played the same march over and over; a pleasant enough march, to be sure, but it was tiresome to hear the wretched tune repeated so often. Meanwhile a contingent of young ladies had entered the train to welcome me to my city. They paid all the proper respects and hung so many garlands round my neck that my entire head disappeared under these fragrant decorations. I was dressed rather splendidly, if I say so myself, in yellow silk and a salmon pink puggeree, decorated with a rather fine emerald that once belonged to the Jamshed of Persia. I also wore a set of pearls and a collar of diamonds, and round my waist, a golden belt with a clasp of diamonds and pigeon-blood rubies from Mandalay. The hilt of my sword, which had belonged to Raysinhji, one of my greatest ancestors, was encrusted with Ceylonese sapphires set in gold. By the time we finally alighted from our train, we were wading through a thick layer of red and pink flower petals, which stained the Persian carpet a deep crimson, as though we had left a trail of blood.

Our progress through the narrow streets of Jamnagar was slow, as I was compelled by tradition to climb down from my comfortable chowdah every time we passed a temple. We are a spiritual race and I had to acquit myself of all manner of religious duties. An honour guard of Lancers kept the chattering mob of beggars, petitioners and well-wishers away, which was a good thing, since these simple folk were convinced it would bring them good fortune to touch a part of me. Given half a chance, I fear I should have been picked clean by the crowd, as surely as an animal carcass is devoured by vultures. I looked straight ahead of me, for I did not feel altogether at ease with all those beaming faces trying to catch my eye. I could not fail to reflect upon the discipline of British crowds compared to the pushing and shoving that appears, alas, to be the Indian's second nature.

Nor, in all truth, could I avoid being shocked by the altogether shabby appearance of the city now under my charge. No matter how many festive banners and flags were put up for the occasion, they could not hide from my sight the general filth and decrepitude. Nor could the overpowering smell of incense and flowers thrown at our feet disguise a pungent odour of decay that percolated the air. Apart from this, the moral atmosphere seemed to me very noxious, for the place was full of loafers with far too much time on their hands for their own and others' good. Not that I hadn't been prepared for this; indeed, Fitz had warned me about the sorry state in which my sadly neglectful predecessors had left the city – the streets were pestilential and dark, the bazaars were an affront to civilised men and the buildings, if one could use such a word for what were usually little more than rude hovels, seemed to be held up by some miracle. No wonder that people were said to be dying in distressingly large numbers of all manner of diseases. To be sure, these were caused not only by the general state of neglect, but by a most terrible famine; indeed, much of the surrounding country was still prostrate because of the scarcity that had resulted from scanty and unseasonable rain and plagues of locusts and rats.

Pomp and circumstance – what the Indian, with his instinctive feel for the onomatopoeic expression, calls dhoom-dham – is of course of enormous importance in our part of the world. However, it was with some sense of relief that I was able to retreat that night into the more exclusive confine of the palace, where it was my pleasant duty to receive guests. Musicians were playing a fanfare outside, making, if truth be told, a fearful racket, and Brahmins were chanting their mantras all over the city, emanating a monotonous drone that continued until morning. The banquet, I was happy to note, had been pronounced a success, due, it would be less than honest to deny, to the generosity of a number of kind chiefs and fellow princes, who had lent me everything from the silverware to the coaches in the procession. Indeed, the chiefs were fine fellows to a man, and capital company, if only they would desist from their dreadful habit of spewing betelnut juice all over the furniture, a custom I found no less distasteful for the fact that much of the furniture belonged to them.

My dear Charlo, I wonder how you, as an arbiter of sartorial elegance, would have judged my outfit the next day: to perform my religious duties I was dressed up in a saffron robe, rather like that of a monk. It was a simpler robe, but one imbued with great dignity. I was led by Brahmins to the old palace temple, whose dilapidated state suggested strongly that it had not heard the footsteps of man for many a moon. There I was made to sit on a throne of umber wood and covered with a lion skin. One of the priests proceeded to sprinkle water over my head, intoning his mantras the while. It was customary for a priest to wave a burning torch inches from my eyes, during which I was not permitted to register the slightest hint of discomfort, or indeed any sign that I noticed the presence of fire at all, for that would be deemed most inauspicious. Once this was concluded, rather to my relief, another priest came forward to put the holy caste mark on my forehead. He performed the sacred task by cutting his thumb with a pin and anointing me with his blood, which trickled down the side of my nose, the idea being that the flow of the Brahmin's blood would determine the fate of my reign. The blood, I was pleased to note, flowed quite copiously, but instead of carrying on down to my chin, it trickled in through the corners of my mouth. The salty taste made me feel a trifle nauseous.

The next item on the agenda was the worship of the family arms. I was told to ascend a pair of rickety stairs, which seemed a highly perilous undertaking, but one, I am happy to report, that was accomplished without mishap. At the top of the stairs was a dark and musty room, lit only by the refracted shafts of light that came through three coloured windows. I could barely make out the sacred arms laid out for my worship, but the priest pointed out a rusty object, which I recognised as the sword. 'Jam Vibhaji, Wagher Rebellion,' he whispered, and I realised it had belonged to my ancestor who had fought on the British side during the Mutiny. I paid my respects and pressed the weapon to my forehead. The priest then drew my attention to a spear, which stood upright in a corner. 'Ranmalji, Muzaffar,' he whispered in my ear, and I remembered, albeit rather vaguely, the story related to me by my father about the heroic Ranmalji, who had behaved so staunchly in the battle against Akbar by placing himself between his chief and the enemy, whereupon he was cut down by a hundred swords and drowned in his own blood. I made the appropriate gestures towards the spear, as I did towards Jam Rawal's shield and Raysinhji's bow.

Next came the Royal Horse, resplendent in his Royal Jewels, his neck festooned with garlands, his ankles wrapped in gold. Once more I did as I was told by the Brahmins and touched the horse's feet. He was, in all truth, a splendid horse, who would have done us proud at the Derby! To the English mind it might seem to be going a bit far to actually worship a horse, but a Rajput considers his horse to be virtually human and in some ways a nobler creature than man, for when it comes to the finer points of character, such as loyalty, perseverance, or sacrifice, the horse is unsurpassed. Hence, when the old Maharaja of Rewa ordered a state funeral for his horse, this was considered an unusual, but by no means exaggerated homage.

It was late afternoon by the time we finally arrived at the shamiana for the formal investiture. It was a most remarkable sight! Picture, if you will, the elephants standing on one side of the square and the Lancers drawn up on the other, whilst the crowds sat in trees and on rooftops, looking for all the world like a swarm of blackbirds, chattering and squawking away, jolly as could be, despite their scruffy appearance, for truly, the Indian can make do with very little and be happy still. The guards presented arms as I alighted from my elephant and my Muslim Chobdars made sure the way was clear for me to ascend the Gaddi. I was dolled up in my finest gold brocade Durbar dress and wore a necklace of diamonds and emeralds set in gold (platinum, I always think, is a rather vulgar metal). And when I finally took my place on the Gaddi, thirteen-gun salutes went off and the band played the State National Anthem, a rather impressive tune, composed during my grandfather's time by Colonel Frank Nicholson, a most talented musician. It was inspired, I believe, by the 'March of the Grenadier Guards', and I think it quite as good.

Fitz made a fine and flattering speech in which he recounted the exploits of my ancestors and observed that 'in all history the pure blood-strain of those who sat upon the Gaddi had been preserved against every tyrannical attempt to impose a foreigner'. Whether or not I deserved the kind words he spoke is not for me to judge, but I set them down for the record: 'To the instincts of a great ruling race you have added the experience of a man of the world, but your long residence in England and your Western training have never diminished your love of your people and I feel that no Jam ever sat to rule this State better equipped for his task than you are . . . ' And so on.

I was moved to answer in terms which I hoped were equal to his. I vowed that I should endeavour to abide loyally by the traditions of my State in its deep unswerving loyalty to the British throne, and that I felt deeply the obligation which rested upon me never to disappoint my friends. It would be vain to predict that my new career would add to my reputation, but I could only promise to endeavour to play the game so as not to lose whatever credit I had gained in another field. And so forth.

There was much applause and a great blast of trumpets. I doubt whether the ragged townsmen had understood a word of what was said, since few of them can have had any English, but they appeared to have enjoyed the show immensely nonetheless. One by one my guests approached the Gaddi to offer their congratulations and tributes, which varied from silk-wrapped gold coins presented by my fellow princes, to simple flowers and lumps of sugar from the common people. I accepted them all with the requisite courtesy, due no less to the common man than to the highest prince, but of all the kind words perhaps the most gratifying to me personally were those spoken by a smart British officer, who stood before the Gaddi, straight as a ramrod, and said with a most appealing twinkle in his eye: 'I salute His Royal Highness, Jam Saheb of Nawanagar and the King of Cricket.' Truly, I felt at that moment that I had the best of all worlds.

But there was not much time to bask in such good cheer, for as soon as the last of my guests had left I was reminded of the immensity of the task ahead: to transform this rotting place into a city of palaces, to make Nawanagar into a state fit for heroes, second to none of the princely states in India, to turn the wretched men and women in my charge into a progressive and vigorous people, fit to take its place alongside the other peoples of our Empire in the march towards a destiny whose greatness would be without parallel in the history of man. We should stand up to be counted and not rest until Nawanagar was among the shiniest jewels in His Majesty's Crown.

It was so hot in Delhi, the night Inder and I returned from a weekend in Rajastan, that one felt one's own weight as a burden. Inder drank glass after glass of barley water. I had beer and we argued about the concept of decadence. We had just spent several days as guests of the Maharaja of Bikampur, known to his Old Etonian friends as 'Biggles', an odd nickname he did not seem to mind. Biggles looked like a prince in a classical miniature painting: several chins; a moustache that curled over his thick red lips, set in a permanent pout, and hooded eyes, which looked nowhere in particular and noticed everything. He had a house in Delhi, but he retained a floor of the palace in Bikampur, which now served as a luxury hotel, attracting largely middle-aged Europeans: the wives in unbecoming Indian get-ups, the husbands in sandals and shorts.

The palace was one of the grander turn-of-the-century follies, part Gothic, part Indo-Saracenic, part neo-classical Victorian, part Venetian – especially Venetian. It seems that Biggles's grandfather had been much taken by the beauty of Venetian palazzos he had seen when he embarked on a grand tour at the time of the Diamond Jubilee. In his effort to re-create the style in the desert of north-western Rajastan, he imported Venetian workmen to lay a floor of marble mosaic in the Durbar hall. The Venetian effect was heightened by a set of Belgian chandeliers, which seemed to cascade from the gold-painted ceiling. On the outside the palace looked more like a Victorian Gothic railway station or a very grand town hall. It had been designed by an engineer called Martin-Jenkins. The stained-glass windows were made in Paris, the neo-classical sculptures in the halls by an Italian artist living in Birmingham and the heavy oak furniture came from a studio in Kent. The Maharaja, like many of his colleagues, had a taste for Hollywood glamour and loved to travel in the United States. It was perhaps to remind him of his American trips that he had a bar installed next to the billiard-room, with signed pictures of Hollywood stars on the wall – Rita Hayworth, Veronica Lake, Marion Davies. The high barstools were covered in leopard skin, the chairs in red leather and the whole thing was illuminated by two lamps made out of elephant feet.

The old Maharaja, Biggles's grandfather that is, had amassed a decent library of leatherbound European classics, but his great pride was a priceless collection of rare insects, neatly preserved and categorised in glass-topped shelves, which a servant would pull out for one's inspection on request. The spiders were especially fine.

The old man clearly had been an avid collector, but some of his pieces were decidedly odd. He had a collection of Delages and Bugattis, now sadly rusting away in the garage, since Biggles had no interest in cars. But fine cars, like precious stones, were acquired by every desert ruler. More unusual was the Maharaja's collection of razor-blades, which he had kept over the years in small bundles tied together with silk cords. Every blade, of the finest English quality, had a little slip of paper attached, on which the Maharaja had noted down, in his spidery hand, dates of use as well as pithy reviews: 'Smooth as silk, 19–10–03' or 'Dashed rough, 3–4–10'.

What, then, is decadence? We, Inder and I, had been through Rome, Ch'ing Dynasty China, Regency England, fin-de-siècle Paris. 'How decadent were the Indian princes?' I asked.

'Well, look, I suppose . . . well, it is of course very complex. If they were decadent, it was because their lives were strangled by the British Raj, under which they were no more than useful and sometimes amusing ornaments. But if you mean to say that the palaces, the Rolls-Royces, all that, if you mean to say that those were signs of decadence, well, I beg to differ . . . '

'How so?'

'Look, vulgarity is not the same as decadence. On the contrary it is a sign of life. It is the British who are really decadent, especially the British out here, in the tropics, sweating in their crumpled suits, drowning in drink, and despising themselves as much as the natives, whom they abuse at every opportunity. No, my dear, there is nothing so seedy as the corrupted European, clinging desperately to the last vestiges of a dead civilisation. I much prefer the Americans . . . '

'Oh?'

'The Americans have freed themselves from the dead hand of good taste. If they have the money and they want something, they will jolly well go and get it. I admire that. Hearst's castle in San Simeon, is that decadent? It is as crass and as vulgar and as expensive as any maharaja's dream palace, but it was his idea of Paradise. To believe that you can actually create your own Garden of Eden may be naïve and in questionable taste, but it is not decadent. Quite the opposite, I'd say. It is the stuff of life.'

Inder rammed his glasses up his nose, snorted heavily and took a long sip of barley water.

'What in your opinion is the highest form of freedom?'

'Well . . . ?'

'Let me tell you – it is the freedom to reinvent yourself, to transform your own identity. Did you know I wrote a thesis at Cambridge about Beau Brummell?'

I did not know, but wasn't surprised. I asked what his thesis had been.

'Simply that dandyism is an art demanding of the highest discipline. You see, dandies are rebels against the conventions of their time, but in order to raise themselves above the mediocrity of conventional society, they must invent their own rules which are far stricter than those they affect to despise. Dandies are creatures of peculiar and arcane habits, which must be strictly adhered to at all times. They are, if you like, an alternative aristocracy when the old one is crumbling. They are, in short, disciplinarians of a kind, with the important difference that they choose their own discipline.'

Listening to Inder's discourse, I thought of a mutual friend in London. He fits Inder's description perfectly. I once spied into his wardrobe, when I stayed at his very untidy flat – unwashed plates in the sink, books and magazines strewn all over the floor, pictures in broken frames. Only his wardrobe showed an almost obsessive neatness. There were rows and rows of identical, beautifully made, double-breasted suits, pistachio-coloured silk for the summer and pearl-grey wool for the winter. With his suits – there must have been at least twenty – he always wore hand-made, buckled shoes, caramel or chestnut-brown, made in Florence, and the same shirts, cream or lavender, from Charvet. His eating habits were as fastidious and invariable as his clothes: he always ate at the same restaurant, if he could help it, where he would sit at the same table and order the same food. He drank nothing but dry white wine (Pouilly Fuissé) and after dinner, without fail, a pear liqueur. As a connoisseur of dandyism once remarked about the typical Regency bucks: 'a creature perfect in externals and careless of anything below the surface, a man dedicated solely to his own perfection through a ritual of taste'. It was as though my friend suffered from a terrible fear of breaking the outward forms that he himself had created, as though only his external discipline created a wholeness which made sense.

Inder stood up from his chair to find a book in the stacks carelessly piled up in all corners of his room. He soon found it and without sitting down opened it and began to read, striking an actorish pose, a bit like Hamlet holding out poor Yorick's skull: 'Thus we find him at the University, and afterwards in his regiment, constantly attentive, master of himself, watching over the least of his gestures, and soon playing his part as the hero of frivolity with incomparable repose of manner. The ideal man of pleasure is an Englishman. This Englishman has laid down for himself a law of life, and will follow his preconceived idea blindly to the end . . . '

I looked at the title: *Beau Brummell and His Times* by Roger Boutet de Monvel. 'But Inder,' I said, 'that is hardly a definition of freedom.'

'No, no, you see, in a way it is. I think it was Wilde who said that most people are other people. Their thoughts are other people's opinions, their life a mimicry, their passions a quotation. Only the dandy, who understands this, has the freedom to choose his own mask.'

Inder seemed more than usually inconsistent. How could he possibly square his theory of dandyism with, say, his advocacy of the caste system? I knew it was futile to point out flaws in his logic, for he would find some way of wriggling free; no contradiction was ever able to trap this mental Houdini. I thought I should give it a try anyway.

'But Inder, how can you possibly square this with your advocacy of the caste system?'

For the first time that evening, Inder flashed a broad smile.

'It is perfectly clear, my dear boy, the dandy's freedom depends on others sticking to the rules, for there can be no rebels without rules to rebel against, no transgressions without taboos. The dandy breaks the rules to show us the limits of our freedom, limits which are entirely necessary, for without them there would be no civilised life. That is precisely why we need the theatre – it is the freedom of the imagination that keeps us rooted in our place.'

Houdini had got away again.

The duty of a ruler, as you have observed yourself, my dear Charlo, is arduous and seldom pleasant. I felt it to be my first task to clean up the town of Jamnagar, an exercise which would, inevitably, result in the destruction of what was known as the old city, a warren of streets, really quite unfit for human habitation. However, since people were living there nonetheless, I had to exercise a certain amount of caution. I was surrounded by men who advised me against changing even the smallest particle of my rotting domain, so I decided that to get anything done at all, I should need to proceed fairly but firmly.

The wretched nautch-girls, employed by the late Jam Saheb, were a case in point. Their mere presence disgusted me and though dancing was their ostensible art, they were a thoroughly degenerate lot, whose antics encouraged dissolution and beastliness of the worst possible kind. They stood, in my opinion, as the prime symbols of India's present state of degradation, sapping men of their will to do good. Clearly, these females had to be done away with, but when I ordered their stipends to be discontinued forthwith, there was an almighty fuss, not least among the gentlemen who enjoyed their services. Thenceforth I decreed that any dancing-girl found within the city walls would be deported, a measure which led to a pretty procession of gaily dressed houris to the opposite bank of the river, whence for several weeks their wretched wailing could be heard for miles around, until I put a stop to that, too, and they slunk off to find employment elsewhere.

Next to go were the pi-dogs. It was these filthy mongrels that caused the diseases which plagued the town. I was informed that more than two hundred people were dying every day, clearly an intolerable situation that had gone on for far too long. It was suggested to me that lack of food was to blame, but I must dispute this, for the Indian gets by on very little, as you know. No, it was the rabid mongrels that were at the root of the problem, hence my intention to exterminate them. This may sound harsh to the English mind, which prides itself on its love of dogs, but in this part of the world we cannot afford to be sentimental. I am very fond of animals, perhaps, if the truth be told, fonder of some of them (such as my dear Popsey) than I am of people. But it would be as difficult for me to summon up any feeling for a filthy stray cur as to love a flea, for, truly, the Indian mongrel bears so little relation to the more noble strains cherished by Englishmen that one hesitates even to compare them. To me they were no more than vermin, for which a quick, firm solution had to be found. Yet here too some caution was in order, for there were Jains amongst my people, whose faith prohibited the killing of any living thing. And so I hit upon what I thought was rather an ingenious solution: the dogs were rounded up at night, and taken to a special camp not too far from the city walls, where they were fed each day, at my express orders, by Jains – rather a good joke, I thought! That, however, was not the end of it, for I made sure the population of the camp was kept well in hand by employing the dogs as bait whenever we had a shikar. The dogs would be tethered to a post and the panthers, attracted by their scent, and further excited by their whimpering, would do the rest, whereupon we shot the panthers. Thus I arrived at a solution that benefited us all – with the exception of course of the verminous beasts themselves.

The demolition of the old city, alas, had to wait a bit longer, but this did not preclude me from planning the future one. I made designs for the broad, tree-lined streets I wanted, and designated the appropriate spot for the cricket ground. Being a mere amateur of architecture, this was by no means an easy task, but I spent hours with the engineer, a splendid young man called Dilks, who grasped exactly what I wanted and informed me how this and that could be brought about. The building styles of course would have to reflect our own traditions. I envisaged something on the scale of Brighton, something fairly simple, which nonetheless would do justice to the aspirations of my people. Jamnagar, as I saw it, should be a city of progress without disregarding our ancient heritage. I should do away with the narrow, winding lanes, whose dark shadows hid all kinds of filth, and plan the city scientifically, indeed with mathematical precision, combining native artistry with a modern sense of rational order and proportion.

Right at the very start of my reign, I began to receive intimations of future trouble. Already at that early stage of planning my city, petty minds started quibbling about costs. My dear Charlo, as though we could haggle like bazaar-wallahs over the pride of a renascent people! As I saw it then – and subsequent events have not proved me wrong – we were confronted with a clear case of noble ideals thwarted by the pettifogging of small men who, at home, would be more suitably employed as clerks. These government officers were encouraged in their mischief by the native politicians, who availed themselves of every opportunity to harm the cause of the Indian states.

You, Charlo, have observed at close quarters how my

169

subjects regard me as their father, and how I endeavour to behave in a manner which does not betray their trust. The relationship between the Indian ruler and his subjects is far removed from the business of politics. Out here, hereditary leadership of the Crown has been handed down to the present times from a hoary past. Rulers devoted to the welfare of their subjects and their country are still held in great reverence and are even worshipped amongst us. For, indeed, according to our ancient texts, the rulers are here as representatives of the gods. The will of the ruler and that of his subjects are one: a decision made, or any task undertaken by me, can only be based on what I judge to be the benefit of my people. Perhaps it is vain, if not indeed plain absurd to expect the petty clerks and politicians to understand our position, since there is no place for ideals in their bookish and commonplace minds.

Is there any other way to explain the hurtful and unseemly complaints aimed at me after the King-Emperor's Durbar ten years ago? I had put a great deal of time and energy into the preparation for what was surely the grandest event in the history of our Empire, as I was adamant to give the best account of myself, not for the furtherance of my personal standing, to which I was quite indifferent, but to express my loyalty to the British Crown and add lustre to the prestige of my State. To the latter I attached enormous importance, particularly at a time when my people were experiencing some considerable distress, caused by a dry spell which had adversely affected the crops. If I could not offer them riches, I could at least provide my subjects with honour and pride. This assuredly would steel their will to see them through hard times. It was for this reason, and this reason only, my dear friend, that I made some considerable effort – alas, to no avail – to increase the requisite number of gun salutes due to my State. I lay stress upon this point, since I so often have been accused of acting out of personal vanity. Of course, nothing could be further from the truth.

Still, even a thirteen-gun-salute prince (more, I might say, than Radhanpur or Wankaner) is perfectly able to put on a good show! It was a grand thing, there at the Delhi Durbar: a whole city of tents, with the banners of all the princes of India fluttering their colourful salute to the King and Queen. I rode in a silver coach, which I had procured from Tattersall's for the occasion. My camp, outlined in oyster shells for which our coast is justly famous, was sufficiently well appointed to offer hospitality to Lord and Lady Londesborough, the Marquis of Bute, Lord Lamington, and the Viceroy, Lord Hardinge, who spoke most movingly about the Mutiny. Although I could offer my guests little in the way of musical entertainment, let alone those dreadful nautch-girls, so beloved by some of my fellow rulers, I am happy to say our oysters were pronounced first rate, and the champagne quite acceptable.

The festive air in the Durbar Camp was disturbed only once, and rather briefly at that, when an elephant belonging to the Maharaja of Rajpipla ran amok, causing a considerable stir, since it trampled the very tent where the Viceroy was about to take his tea. The incident which, I believe, cost the lives of one or two brave fellows sent out to control the rampant beast, was soon forgotten, however, when the King and Queen arrived and took their places on the dais to receive our mujras.

The first to make his presentation was naturally the Nizam of Hyderabad, who gave the King a ruby necklace, in which each stone was as big as a pigeon's egg. Although my gift to the King, a diamond brooch, was rather more modest than the one borne by the Nizam, it sufficiently expressed, I think, my reverence for the monarch. When it was my turn to walk up to the dais, after the Nawab of Junagadh, I thought my heart should burst. It was a moment that gave me more flutters of anxiety than going in to bat against the Australians at Lord's, and I appreciated the presence of dear Colonel Berthon, who succeeded in calming my nerves. As I started on my way to the marble steps, cheers rolled round the arena, and Berthon whispered in my ear that this was a cheer for cricket. So perhaps, dear Charlo, we were more than mere flannelled fools after all!

However, as soon as the festivities were over, and I returned to my palace in Jamnagar, the bickering about expenses started up again. The Government went so far as to suggest that I should, in future, submit reports on my expenditures, surely an infringement of my sovereignty.

My dear Charlo, I am the first to admit that the behaviour of a small number of Indian princes has been less than impeccable and is thus open to criticism, but as for myself, I believe I have always behaved in a manner that was beyond reproach. My dear friend, an injustice is felt as keenly by a prince as by a peasant. At times I seriously wish that I could get out of my State and lead my own life in peace and quiet. However, being an Easterner, I know I must try and submit to fate, until my Western education rebels in me and I lose all patience. I thank Heaven for giving me a cheery disposition, which has enabled me to carry on without for a moment losing my composure. I realised there was only one thing to do: I should take it up with the Viceroy himself, as the representative of the Crown to which I had pledged my loyalty. Surely, he would understand my position.

I would venture to say that part of my problem was a matter of language. When an Englishman hears the word famine, it conjures up the most lurid images of miserable people dying of hunger and thirst. To be sure, I do not pretend that people in India have an easy time of it, but families offer one another the kind of staunch support that is almost unimaginable to the Western mind, which sets so much greater store by individual effort than collective exertions. Out here, in time of want, the prosperous sacrifice for those who are in distress. This is our native version of Fair Play, so to speak.

Our notions of Fair Play are not always the same as those that apply in the Western world, where human affairs are ordered more often according to the dry letter of the law, a concept as yet hardly developed in the Indian mind, even though British administrators have made sterling efforts to introduce it in this country. We must needs proceed with much patience in India, and with due respect for the native traditions. I wager that should the British ever leave this continent, an event which, as you know, I think unlikely and in any event do not desire, the Indian will soon swap his ill-fitting Western garb for a more congenial form of dress. In my opinion, therefore, the ruler must temper the harsh rationality of law with his personal judgement based on wisdom received through the ages.

Entertaining my friends was the one great relief from my uphill task in Jamnagar. Priestly came out to see me the year of the Durbar and declared that he never wished to leave. This was largely due to his passion for our oysters, which he consumed in large quantities at every meal. I pulled his leg one night by inviting him to sit down for supper and serving nothing but bread and water. This, I explained, with my gravest demeanour, was all we were going to have, since we had plain run out of oysters. I had to do my level best to stop myself from laughing when I saw the look of despair on his face, which changed from its normal crimson to a shocked, pale pink. He announced that in that case he would have to take his leave, as a diet of bread and water simply would not do, would not do at all. I clapped for a bearer to draw a curtain, which revealed, to the undisguised delight and astonishment of our friend, a fully laden table with the largest oysters and capital champagne. Priestly laughed so much, I thought he would burst!

Had it not been for these visits from old friends my new life would have afforded me few joys. I missed England terribly: the trout-filled streams, the green lanes, the Sussex Downs, the smell of honeysuckle and English roses, village cricket, Saturday afternoons at Lord's, the shops of Bond Street and St James's, Vesta Tilley at the Palladium, yes, even, I should say, the English weather, so soft and sweet, so unlike the ghastly heat of our summers. For this reason I decided to return to England that year, a journey which was much enlivened by the company of Priestly. However, our trip was not entirely without worry, for only a few months before, the news had reached us about the unfortunate fate of the *Titanic*. The only cheering thing about that dreadful disaster was the exemplary behaviour of the gentlemen on board, who bravely sacrificed their lives for the sake of the women and children, whilst the band played 'Nearer My God to Thee'. It is a sad fact that it often takes a calamity to bring out the true nobility of Man.

'If you ever go to Calcutta, my dear, you must meet Satish Battacharya. You will find him most interesting.' The way Inder said 'interesting' made me wonder a little; he said it with a hint of gleeful expectation, as though I was to be the victim of some prank.

Satish, fortyish, salt-and-pepper beard, elegant in his finely crumpled dhoti, smoking a black Balkan Sobranie ('wouldn't touch anything else'), had inherited a fortune and published rare books on the nineteenth-century Bengal Renaissance. He was fond of making grand statements, which invariably began with the words 'of course'.

'Of course, there are only two great cuisines in the world – the French and the Bengali.'

'Of course, Calcutta is the Paris of Asia.'

'Of course, the three greatest newspapers in the world are *The Times* of London, *Le Monde* and the *Statesman* of Calcutta.'

And so on and so forth.

He leaned back in his brown suede chair, and crossed his legs. The air-conditioner drowned out most of the din outside: the cows, the rumbling Ambassadors, the hawkers and beggars, the film music from the record shops. Suddenly there was a series of loud explosions. Had the revolution, so long awaited with a mixture of dread and glee, finally come?

'No, no,' said Satish, blowing cigarette smoke from the corner of his mouth, 'India won the cricket match against England.'

News of victory must have been communicated instantly to millions of people, through the little transistor radios which men and boys held to their ears as they walked through the pot-holed streets. The ball-by-ball commentary crackling from the radio all day was like a Greek chorus to the match at hand. I was told that in the case of an Indian triumph, some people decorated their radio sets with garlands, like worshippers at a shrine.

'Of course,' said Satish, picking up where he had left off, 'all the good things that happened in this country during the last two hundred years were the result of the British Raj. I agree totally with Nirad Chaudhuri on this. How did he put it: 'All that was good and living within us, was made, shaped, and quickened by British rule . . . '

He smiled at me, his mouth half open, as if waiting to be fed a morsel of contradiction or at least shock. I said that in an odd kind of way Calcutta reminded me of England: the gentility in the midst of decay, the flight into nostalgia, the snobbish aloofness that masked a steady slide into seedy provinciality. What was very un-English was the intensity of Calcutta intellectuals. There was something repulsive and at the same time marvellous about the men in the College Street Coffee House, discussing the influence of Adorno on French New Wave cinema, while people were starving in the streets.

'Of course you know the famous essay by Malcolm Muggeridge, in which he observed that if Bertie Wooster would come to life again, he would be called Dasgupta and live in Calcutta.'

Satish spoke in a high-pitched monotone, which made everything he said sound even more rhetorical. His statements had a well-rehearsed air about them; clearly, I was not the first to hear them.

'Of course, Bengalis are the last true Englishmen.'

Of course, Satish did not really see himself as the last true Englishman, but as the last true Bengali badhralok, the cultivated Calcutta gentleman, who would quote liberally from Milton, Montesquieu and Tagore. The badhraloks, who made their fortunes as middle-men for the East India Company during the eighteenth and nineteenth centuries, collected everything they could from European civilisation. The badhralok gentleman was a walking repository of European literature, music, painting, philosophy, politics, and out of this cultural mosaic, transferred to the intellectual hothouse of Calcutta, he produced the Bengali Renaissance, which flowered briefly in late-

Victorian times and gradually petered out when the Raj shifted its capital from Calcutta to Delhi.

The typical badhralok monument is the Marble Palace, belonging to the Mullick family: a classicist palazzo in North Calcutta filled with nineteenth-century French neo-classical sculptures of Greek deities, busts of Queen Victoria, Napoleon and the Duke of Wellington, a Rubens with cobwebs hanging from its cracked gilt frame, Ming vases, German clocks, prints of the Battle of Waterloo, marble floors, Persian carpets, Florentine fountains, English gardens filled with squawking peacocks, and Victorian paintings of rosy-cheeked English boys playing cricket.

I asked Satish about cricket.

'Cricket', he said, 'was part of the badhralok way of life. My grandfather was a keen cricketer. He played with Saruta Ranjan Roy, the W. G. Grace of Bengal, and with his brother Sharada Ranjan Roy, the translator of Conan Doyle. Cricket, to them, was like playing the violin, an art, a way to cultivate virtuosity. Winning or losing was of course immaterial. What counted was artistry, style, manners. Nirmal Chatterjee, H. Bose, the Ranjan Roys – they regarded cricket as something cerebral, aesthetic. Of course, that approach doesn't square with the professional game today. That's why there are no more top-notch Bengali cricketers – we are poets, not businessmen. Of course, you haven't seen cricket if you haven't been to Eden Gardens, the Lord's of India.'

As a matter of fact I had seen a match at Eden Gardens: 80,000 Bengalis had screamed for blood, as the Indian captain came in to bowl at the captain of Pakistan. Fire-crackers filled the muggy air with little white puffs, like floating bits of cotton-wool. I looked for, but couldn't find, the radio sets festooned with flowers.

'In this part of the world, cricket is like a gladiatorial combat. You must realise that Bengalis love heroes. When you are always ridiculed for not being martial, for not being cut in the heroic mould, you ... well, you go to the Coliseum called Eden Gardens. Cricketers are the Hector, the Ajax, the Achilles of our time ... '

Satish paused for a bit, his epicurean lips savouring the sound

176

of his words. 'Yes, Calcutta is a bit like Rome, or, perhaps, more like Athens . . . Yes, the Athens of Asia.'

Satish lived in a rather grand house not far from the Bengal Cricket Club. It was white, late eighteenth-century classicist – shades of Inigo Jones in the tropics. The house was decorated in perfect taste: an eclectic collection of Bengali paintings and European prints on the walls, some fine French Empire furniture, rare books bound in Morocco, stacked together with a fine eye for balance and sculptural proportion.

I was impressed, which Satish noted with satisfaction. 'Let me tell you something about the history of the place. It was built for a British civil servant, but by the time we bought it, it was dreadfully run-down, so I gave my architect the following instructions. Look, I said, I want the sort of thing an English gentleman arriving in Calcutta in the 1790s would have lived in. Thank God, we still have the craftsmen here to do it. Of course, in London it would be quite out of the question. Have a drink, I'm a malt man myself.'

The other guest was an elderly Anglo-Indian, who owned race horses. His name was Cecil. He was born in Darjeeling and had spent his entire life in Calcutta. He wore an MCC tie. 'Where do you live 't home?' he asked.

'At home?' I said, not immediately grasping his meaning.

'The UK?'

'Oh,' I said, 'well, England is not really my home.'

'An emigrant, are you?'

'No, not really.'

'Well, then, what are you?'

I mumbled something indistinct.

'A bird of passage, what?'

I left it at that. I remarked on his tie and asked whether he was interested in cricket. Oh yes, he said, he used to follow the game a bit. 'Not many of us left out here, you know.'

'Anglo-Indians?'

'I beg your pardon?'

'I'm sorry . . . you mean people who follow cricket?'

'Oh, no, goodness no, MCC members.'

'Of course, he must meet Asoke Sen,' said Satish.
'Frightful idea,' said Cecil.
'Why?' asked Satish.
'A red-hot Commie,' said Cecil.

Asoke Sen lived on Chowringhee Road, just south of Park Street
– 'the Regent Street of Calcutta' as Satish described it. His
apartment block was a crumbling Gothic affair that reminded
me of the cobwebbed frame of the Marble Palace Rubens. On
the broken pavement outside lay a grotesquely deformed man,
jiggling his stunted limbs like a beetle in distress. A few yards
away from him was an emaciated woman of indistinct age,
whose nakedness was barely veiled by the filthy rag which was
all that was left of her sari. She was covered in flies and too weak
to ask for money. She just lay and moaned.

'Yes, yes,' said Asoke, 'one of the last of the grand apartment
buildings.' There were books everywhere, on shelves, on tables,
on the floor. The French windows allowed very little light to
penetrate the large, gloomy rooms. The ceiling fans hardly disturbed the moist, warm air. There was a strong smell of mould.

'Please do sit down,' said Asoke, a portly, dark-skinned man,
dressed in a dhoti. A young servant was despatched to fetch us
tea. 'The Bengali badhralok', he began, 'is both a rebel and a
toady. Indeed, more precisely, I should say, he is a rebel because
he is a toady and his rebellion is always doomed to fail.'

Asoke rarely answered questions directly. Like Satish, he made
statements, interrupted by moments of hesitation, not, one felt, a
sign that he doubted in any way the validity of his ideas, but
more, perhaps, to wonder whether his words had really sunken
in. And just as one would break the silence to ask him a further
question, he would resume his argument, emphasising his main
points with an enigmatic smile, as though enjoying a little private
joke.

'The problem, here in West Bengal, is really this – we have
never had our own Bengali kings, or an aristocracy of warriors,
or great heroes. This is the background of our contradictions. To
be exact, I should say that the Bengali élite has always accommo-

dated outside rulers. As the Americans say, we made deals with them. But we hate ourselves for doing so, and, so, we erupt in rebellions, which, as I said, always fail in the end.

'It is precisely why we fail at cricket, which must be seen in the context of the decline of Bengal . . . '

I waited for more and was about to ask him what he meant.

' . . . You see, you can divide men into two types – those that applaud and those that are applauded. The Bengalis, by and large, belong to the first category. We applaud heroes, without being heroic ourselves. We lack the grit, the killer instinct, the discipline to be applauded – to be precise, the application is missing . . . '

He took a sip of tea, daintily crooking his little finger. I wanted to ask him the same question I asked K. C. Lewis: was there a connection in his mind between cricket and Marxism? I had heard he was an unrepentant Stalinist. I had seen a picture in his study of Lenin. Asoke smiled when he saw me staring at it. 'A Bengali hero,' he said.

Of course, he never directly answered my question, but came close to doing so nonetheless. 'Indian cricket won't get any better, because we lack the will to win. Indians have no team spirit, no sense of unity. Everybody is out for himself, to make a bit of money. You can't ever win that way, can you?'

He smiled. The interview was over. Asoke politely showed me to the door, where I couldn't help noticing a small marble bust of Napoleon peering from his shelf, which he shared with a little bronze effigy of Indra, the many-armed goddess. I said goodbye, went down in the creaky lift and quickly passed the writhing bodies in the street.

It was, as always, with a sense of pleasurable anticipation that I caught my first glimpse of England, even though, as usual, the coast was shrouded in dark, misty clouds, smudging the white cliffs. Still feeling distinctly liverish from the voyage and rather bronchial to boot, I stood on deck, letting the wind blow the cobwebs away and thinking of the joys awaiting me, not the least of which, my dear friend, would be to see you.

1912 was a particularly memorable year for me, as it was the last time I played any serious cricket in England. I had become far too stout to move around as fast as I ought, which made me rather useless in the field, and since I have always attached the utmost importance to fielding, I knew my days as a cricketer were over. You, however, still resembled more than ever a Greek hero straight from the pages of the *Iliad*, and you acquitted yourself splendidly as captain of England against the Australians.

I enjoyed all the pleasures of English life, to be sure, but it was, to tell you the truth, also a very trying time for me. It was one thing, dear Charlo, to be called a prince, but quite another to be a bona fide ruler. It opened new doors to me, certainly, but this entailed certain obligations. For one thing, I had to entertain in a grander manner than I was hitherto able to do either at Cambridge or Brighton. My State is not without riches, and I was happy to share them with my friends and repay my creditors. But for all that I cannot honestly claim that I always enjoyed the company, since one does tend to attract some distinctly odd birds, whose main aim it is to enjoy the fruits of other men's fortunes. But that is by the bye. I decided to acquire the house at Staines from Sir Edward Clarke, K. C., who wasn't odd in the least, but a delightful gentleman in every respect. He had had rather a rough time of it, since he had been counsel to Oscar Wilde, the noted pederast, whom I have had occasion to mention before.

Thorncote, or Jamnagar House, as we called it, had a splendid view of the Thames and we had some good parties there, as you know. It was altogether a rather good season. I recall with particular pleasure the Duchess of Devonshire's fancy dress ball. You recall how stumped I was as to what disguise I should adopt: a European historical figure would hardly do, nor could I go very well as an Indian prince without seeming to turn my own occupation into a music hall turn. I still owe you thanks for your priceless idea to swap identities, so to speak. I much enjoyed going as C. B. Fry, dressed in your

MCC blazer and that extraordinary blond wig, and you made a perfectly convincing Indian prince. Indeed, I didn't mention this to you at the time and I hope you forgive me for sounding maudlin, but I rather wished that by some divine intervention, the disguise could have stuck forever. But that, naturally, would never do.

Unfortunately, the affair of the missing Fabergé eggs put rather a damper on the seasonal joys. I have always had a weakness for these little gewgaws, which I took some trouble to acquire through Cartier. One day, after a quite boisterous weekend party – Jacker was there, as well as Lord George Campbell and General Sir Bindon Blood – it was brought to my attention that several eggs were missing. I should not have minded so much had they not happened to be ones made for Catherine the Great, which were rather dear to me. Naturally, suspicion immediately fell upon my staff, since there was no reason whatsoever to suspect any of the guests, who may have had loafers in their midst, but surely not thieves. The investigation of the servants was a painful affair, since I had brought most of them with me from India, and had never had any cause to doubt their loyalty or indeed, their honesty.

The servants' quarters were turned inside out by police officers. It really was a most unpleasant business, which created much bad blood, since my English servants put the blame on the Indians, who, not wholly without reason, rather resented the accusations. It is true, as you have often observed, that the native Indian occasionally has difficulty grasping the British notion of truth, but my staff were very well trained. The long and the short of it was that the culprit was not found, so, much though it grieved me, I had to sack my butler. He was an Englishman with perfect credentials, but since it was he who was formally responsible for running the house, I had no choice but to let him go. And for the sake of fairness I also sent one of my most trusted Indian servants packing. Even King Solomon was never so sorely tried.

You might imagine, then, my shock when a package was delivered a month after the incident, containing the eggs and a note of apology. It turned out that a gentleman, who will of course remain nameless, had pocketed the jewels and would have kept them, had he not been found out by a mutual friend, who persuaded him to return the treasures to me. It appeared that the gentleman in question had a history of doing this kind of thing, despite being a scion of one of the best families in England. Naturally, I accepted his apology, and invited him to come down for my next party. However, the damage had been done; two honest men had been disgraced, and I had learnt a valuable and melancholy lesson: even men of the highest breeding can not always be trusted to live up to the standards which they publicly espouse.

Increasingly, that summer, I sought to escape from the madding crowd by going fishing. Such quiet moments, enjoyed in the sole company of my dear, faithful Popsey, were a great comfort to me. I am by nature a gregarious creature and require the company of others, yet I try to find refuge from my fellow men in solitary activities. It is truly a strange paradox, which I believe you can understand perfectly well. You are a hero, my friend, and heroes are not like other men, for they are lonely figures who are never alone, like actors on a stage, prevented by the lights from seeing their audience. Forgive me, dear Charlo, for these melancholy meditations. They are the price you must pay for hearing me out.

Before I describe my last cricket match, I cannot resist mentioning my love affair which began that summer; indeed it was more than an affair, for my love was to last forever. The object of my ardent affections was that most excellent of singers, Ella Shields. Whenever I heard she was performing, I made sure to be there, sitting in a box, watching her with the ardour of the young Romeo courting his Juliet – although, naturally, my love was never declared, and certainly not reciprocated. It was known only to myself, and to Popsey, whom I tried to teach the words of Miss Shields' most famous song, wholly without success, I might add. No doubt you know the one I mean:

I'm Bert, Bert, I haven't a shirt,
But my people are well off, you know.
Nearly ev'ry one knows me, from Smith to Lord Rosebery –
I'm Burlington Bertie from Bow.

Apart from the sweetness of her voice, there was a purity about her which made her songs speak to each person in the audience. It was truly as if she were singing just for me. This, I think, is the key to her genius. It is certainly what inspires one's love. Of course, one loves the performer, not the person behind the grease paint, which is why I never wished to meet Miss Shields in person. Quite what constitutes the genius of a born performer, who is at once wholly artificial and absolutely genuine, will, I suspect, always remain a mystery. Why do the simple words of her song, little more, really, than a cheap vaudeville ditty, still reduce me to tears every time I hear them? It is partly, I think, because I can hear Miss Shields' voice singing it, sounding so sweet, so innocent, so pure. And I suppose that these echoes of her voice, more than anything else, remind me of a better, less troubled age, when the world was at peace, when England was still the England that I knew.

I do not wish to sound like a sentimental old fool. Yet that is precisely what I feel like when I think back to my last cricket match of the season, which effectively ended my cricketing career. I chose, for the occasion, not the match at Lord's against the Australians or the Players, nor a match for my beloved County at Brighton or Hove. I wanted nothing so exalted as that. Instead, I decided to take up the invitation to play a charity match in a village near Horsham. The charity was for the old church bell, which was to be restored to its ancient home in the Norman steeple – a worthy cause, if ever there was one, especially for a 'heathen Prince'!

Village cricket – this, I feel, most truly represents the unsullied and noble spirit of our game, which, in more metropolitan venues, had become a highly professional enterprise, to do as much with commerce as with sport. I am not saying this is wrong – though I have my own ideas on the matter. I realise that the world changes. It is inevitable, they say. But that does not mean I have to change with it. For if we all did that, how frightfully dull the world would be.

And so, on a beautiful English summer's day, we motored down to Bucks Barn, where the match was to be played. You could not be of the party, alas, for I seem to recall that duty in the formidable form of Madame beckoned. But I contrived to persuade P. G. H. Fender, H. P. Chaplin, Jacker and W. J. Whitty – over in England with the South Africans – to come down and put on a bit of a show. The countryside was lovely, smelling of freshly cut grass and summer flowers, and I kept the chaps entertained by singing my favourite Ella Shields songs. We were, in short, having a marvellous time.

A most touching thing happened as we approached the village, for word had got around that I was coming, and the road was lined with simple people bidding me their welcome. Even the surrounding hills were filled with locals waving their hats in the air, shouting all the while. I was deeply moved, of course, and when Jacker turned to me and said this showed how the people of this country loved me, I found it quite hard to control my feelings – but control them I did, for what could be worse, my dear Charlo, than a blubbering prince! The village was a vision of Eden, with no ugly buildings to mar its ancient beauty – only trim cottages and well-kept gardens radiant with summer bloom appearing on every side. The cricket ground lay in the shadows of handsome, drooping limes, which rose majestically from the old churchyard adjoining. The gaily striped tents snapped and fluttered in the breeze, as did the flag of my State, proudly displayed on top of the marquee. Never had I felt prouder of the lion in our crest, the sign of our loyalty to the British Crown.

All was bliss and perfection, with Jacker making a few runs and Fender showing some lusty hitting, once carting the ball so far over the tents that it took some considerable time to retrieve it. When it was my turn to bat, the entire crowd rose to salute me on my journey to the crease, expecting, no doubt, to be royally entertained by a glorious, last knock. The sky was cloudless, the freshly-rolled wicket fragrant and flat. The bowler, a lanky, clean-limbed young man, with curly blond hair, was ready to start his run-up, when suddenly I was overcome by a deep weariness. My bat felt heavy and all I really wanted to do at that point was to take a long nap. It put me in a frightful pickle, for I knew the crowd expected a show. I could hear that familiar hush of anticipation around the ground. How could I disappoint them with a show of weakness? To gain some time to pull myself together, I asked the bowler to wait, and looked around as though to check on the field he had set. My eyes wandered from the Downs in the distance, to the tents, the flags, the blur of faces, all watching me in awful anticipation. I stood there, too stupefied to move. At the same time my heart was beating like a drum and I was quite out of breath. To have thrown in the towel, however, would have cast doubt upon my sportsmanship.

How I contrived to carry on I cannot say, for the simple reason that I no longer remember. I made some shots, even hit a few sixers, I am told, but it was as though it was another man batting, or, rather, it was me going through the motions, like a puppet with someone else pulling the strings. I do not know how long I batted, or how I got out (caught at the boundary, I think). I was barely aware of the crowd as I retired to the tent in a trance. Once inside, I must have collapsed, for I did not awake before the end of the match, when Jacker shook me out of my stupor. Oddly, I felt right as rain again, but when I asked him how many runs I had made, he roared with laughter, as if I were trying to pull his leg.

We had a splendid dinner, attended by all the players and their families, who sang most beautifully. Toasts were exchanged and speeches made. Most gratifying of all was Jacker's speech in which he compared the Indian princes with British nobility. He made the most flattering point that you cannot be a Ranjitsinhji unless you have the blood of the lion in your veins, whereas you may join the old nobility of England if you have made a brilliant speculation in rubber, or exploited the gold of Transvaal. This, of course, was a slight exaggeration, though I must admit, with some degree of anguish, the truth of his reflection on the quality of some of the men who have gained prominence in the colonies. How often have I wished that all the leading men in the Empire were cricketers! For if they had undergone the training and the discipline of the game, they would find it easier than they appear to do to think first and last of the team. The princes of India have been very old members of Great Britain's teams; and both on easy and difficult wickets they have tried their best to play with a straight bat for the Empire. I am not at all sure this has been appreciated sufficiently in the places where the most momentous decisions are made. I tried to make this point in my speech, as well as other observations in a lighter vein. To remember the occasion I presented every man with a golden snuffbox, and the ladies with brooches of Burmese rubies. They appeared to appreciate this small gesture, for at the end all stood up and sang 'For He's a Jolly Good Fellow!'

It was, I repeat, a splendid occasion. But had I known what had occurred that very same day at the other end of the world, in my native village of Sarodar, I should not have been able to endure it. For on that same evening, just as I went in to bat in the Bucks Barn village cricket match, my dear Mama had breathed her last. As soon as I heard the news, I knew what had happened to me at the wicket: in a mysterious way the human mind cannot possibly fathom, my dear Mama had sent me a signal of her imminent death. To my eternal shame, I had failed to heed her call.

Without Mama I was but half a man. Even Popsey noticed my despondency, for the dear bird, usually so talkative, didn't issue a single squawk for several days. I do believe that our animal friends are sensitive to human moods, indeed more sensitive than most of our fellow human beings, who think largely of themselves. In Sarodar, that winter, even the crows were quiet.

I shall not speak further of my mother's death, for the memory is too painful to endure. Let us, instead, remember happier days! It is fortunate that, no matter how adverse the circumstances, I remain an optimist in life, fortunate, because the circumstances in my State were very adverse indeed. Despite the fact that I did my level best to improve my people's lot, many still died of ill health and lack of nourishing food. Outbursts of plague, in particular, cut rather a large swath through the population. The Government, most unfairly in my opinion, insisted on blaming me.

You were with me, however, to keep me in good cheer. I have especially fond memories of our long nights together in Gir, silently passing notes to one another whilst waiting for the panther to come for its prey. It was as though our silence bespoke thoughts that went far deeper than mere words could express. This profound bond between us: could one call it love? To be sure, it is not the love that binds husbands and wives, nor is it the love of man for another living creature, such as his horse, his dog, or, indeed, his pet parrot. There is, however, a unique quality about the companionship of men, a quality which I believe transcends the physical feelings such as men might feel for women – which are, after all, of a trifling and passing nature. I love women as mothers and daughters. I have cherished their companionship. Indeed, in these last, trying years, the friendship of Miss Scott, whom you have met out here, has been a great comfort to me. But the idea of physical intimacy would debase the whole affair, reduce something pure and beautiful to mere beastliness. But our friendship, my dear Charlo, based as it is on deep respect and the willingness at all times to sacrifice our own selfish interests, is on a higher plane even than my friendship for Miss Scott; it can be called a form of love; indeed, I would go so far as to say it is a purer love than any other kind.

Nothing brings men together like a good shoot, preferably in the rough. Although I never doubted your credentials as a pukka English gentleman, your behaviour at your first shikar made an enormous impression on me. It must have been a considerable disappointment to you, when, instead of the expected gentleman, a lady panther insisted on appearing in our sights. I offered you the chance to shoot her, and a less noble man than you would have availed himself of the opportunity without a second thought. I know, for I have seen no lesser men than viceroys do just that in their haste to bag a trophy. If truth be told, there was precious little sport in some of these shoots, for it was only common courtesy to make sure that my guests did not return empty-handed. This we could manage, but we could not always be choosy as to the gender of the beast. Not that people gave it any mind, for they were far too pleased with their own prowess. You, however, were different, my dear Charlo; you would never shoot a lady. This I appreciated more than I can say.

Of course, to sit and wait for one's adversary in a kotah was one thing, but shooting a panther walking about in broad daylight was really quite another. It is thus that men's nerves are most sorely tested. I remind you of our rough shoot not only to go down memory lane, though it affords me immense pleasure to do so, but to make a confession – the first of two confessions, in fact, but more about that later.

It began, if you recall, like this: you were yet to shoot your first panther, when I announced to you that you were in luck, as a panther had been spotted by villagers. We set off in the motor car to find it. I brought along my best shikarees, which, as it turned out, was a great blessing, and instructed the village men to drive the beast out of its hiding place. Unfortunately, one of the men wounded the panther by hurling a stone, which meant that we had an enraged and very dangerous animal on our hands. If the fellow you called 'Redbeard' had not thrown himself in the panther's way without a moment's hesitation, we might well have been badly mauled. He sacrificed his life, because I was his bapu. Such is the loyalty of my people. It was a damned shame, for he was one of my pluckiest and ablest shikarees. But you stood your ground and without flinching shot the panther just behind the ears.

It was very soon after that, I think, that you had your religious experience. As a man who prides himself on having a scientific mind, I have, perhaps, never paid sufficient attention

188

to matters of the spirit. Which is not to say that I am lacking in faith, for that would be quite untrue. Indeed, I have always respected our gods, just as others respect theirs. But in most things I tend to favour the reasonable explanation over the more mystical flights of fancy, unlike, I might say, most people of my race, who detect the hidden hand of otherworldly forces in practically everything they see or do.

It was, of course, precisely that aspect of India which caught your imagination. You never stopped talking about the spiritual quality of India and it was plain to see that you were longing for a religious experience, quite as much as for a shot at the panther. Alas, much as I endeavour to accommodate the wishes of my guests, this was one thing I could not provide. However, when I was informed by the High Priest that he had met you at Lord Krishna's pool and blessed you in the usual manner by pressing a flower to your forehead, it seemed an opportunity sent, as it were, by Heaven. I instructed your shikar servant to anoint your forehead with a fresh ticka every morning before you woke. When you came to me later, telling me in a state of high excitement about the Brahmin's blessing and the resulting red mark, I could not bring myself to tell you the truth. I confess it even afforded me some private amusement, and I take this opportunity to beg your pardon for playing my little trick.

But don't be disappointed, my friend, for one cannot say that your religious experience was not perfectly genuine. In fact, it most probably was, for such things take place in the mind alone. I only provided an external mark, no different from an actor's grease paint, which surely detracts not an iota from the spirit of the play. Like absolute beauty, there can be no such thing as absolute truth, for both are matters of perception. It is why the Indian can live happily with ideas which, to the modern mind of the West, would be regarded as quite contradictory. Let me repeat, my dear Charlo, that the truth of your experience cannot possibly have depended on a bit of red pigment.

I can almost hear you say it: 'But Ranji, if your mind is as rational as you say it is, how can you possibly set so much store by the predictions of your Pundit?' And I could only answer that you are perfectly right to point out the paradox. Here, then, is an example of the contradictions that lodge side by side in the Indian mind – and my Western education notwithstanding, I still retain the mind of an Indian, that I cannot deny. Perhaps men such as I are destined to live with a never-ending battle between science and magic, between the rational mind and the mysteries of the spirit. However, it must be said in all fairness that my Pundit has been proved right on so many occasions that it does not take any faith in magic to take seriously anything he says. The problem is that one does not always grasp his meaning. To give you an example: that summer in Bombay, in 1914, he predicted that I should embark upon a long journey, from which I should return in good health but with one of my senses impaired. I must confess I could make head nor tail of it, but the Pundit was not one to furnish explanations.

It was barely a week later, in that sweltering August (how I hated summers in India), that the Great War broke out in Europe. I realised instantly that in this hour of peril, there was but one thing for it: petty differences with the Government had to be put aside and we should all stand up to be counted, for if India had stinted for even one moment, the judgement of history would have gone against us forever. I gave orders that every asset of my State would henceforth be put at the disposal of the Empire. Naturally, I was not unaware of the difficulties then borne by my people, for there had been another year of drought, but I was absolutely confident that where honour was at stake, every man and woman would pull their socks up gladly and give of their best.

As it turned out, my people were unstinting in their generosity. The cowherds from the Barda Hills, where I had enjoyed so much good sport, donated ten thousand pounds worth of clothes, cigarettes, blankets, rugs, sheets, gloves, shoes, and pig-sticking spears. Fourteen thousand pounds went to the Red Cross, seven thousand into buying aero-planes, and ten thousand into ammunition. We contributed tents, motor vehicles, and bullock carts. My entire stock of port was sent to France to be used as alcohol in field hospitals, and my house in Staines was turned into a hospital for officers. And the Nawanagar State Imperial Service Lancers boarded at Bombay to fight shoulder to shoulder with the British Army. This they did proudly, since it afforded every man the oppor-tunity to show that Rajputs still had the old fighting spirit burning within their breast, whether they be clad in the sombre raiments of the West or the luxurious silks of the East.

It was, for us, as for every true-born Englishman, a time to pay the supreme sacrifice in maintaining intact our great Empire and its untarnished name. Naturally I volunteered for the Army myself and was delighted to be accepted as ADC of Field Marshal Sir John French. We were shipped out from Bombay and despite the rather rough seas I can honestly say that for the first time I enjoyed the voyage immensely. I got on like a house on fire with the men of the Inniskilling Dragoon Guards, though some of them lacked manners and finish. Their high spirits and superb morale were an education to me. Despite the seriousness of our purpose, the men never lost their sense of humour. We had some splendid charades. Of course, all the chaps knew who I was and a song was com-posed, entitled 'Ranji Hits the Bloody Huns for Six', sung to the tune of 'John Brown's Body'.

I was so much at home in the Army that I felt at times as though I had missed my true calling. The military life seemed to me like a great brotherhood, a real freemasonry. To share the hardships of a great body of men gave one a unique sense of worth. Of course it was not all a bed of roses, and one had to obey orders instead of giving them. Patience and fortitude are essential in the Army, which is why fishing is so useful, for they are the requisite qualities for baiting an elusive trout no less than for putting up with the vagaries of superior officers.

My career in the Army started off on the wrong foot, however, for I became dreadfully bronchial as soon as we arrived in London. Thank goodness the General was a brick to me and I was soon fighting fit and ready to go to France. However, to my bitter disappointment, I was not sent to the front lines, but ordered to stay back. I failed to see what useful purpose was served by being quartered in a perfectly comfortable French hotel drinking claret with senior officers, whilst there was so much fighting to be done at the front. Truly, I felt as though my presence was treated as rather an encumbrance and that the Army had more use for my cars than for myself. All the while I was itching to join the fray and have a go at the Huns, if only to make very clear that I was not merely a tin soldier, there for a ride, but a useful army officer, able and willing to do my bit.

It seemed only fair that I should at least see how the Indian soldiers were faring, so I was most pleased to be granted permission to visit them at the front. And I must say they acquitted themselves superbly of the great task at hand. Their spirit and pluck earned them the respect of all the British officers. I shall not forget the sight of these men, fighting like heroes, whilst their ranks were depleted daily, through enemy fire as well as sickness and the freezing cold. There was a smell of death in the air, denoting supreme sacrifice for the common good. The sight of these brave men, so cold, so tired, so far from home, doing their manly duty without flinching, was enough to make one weep with pride. I watched as wave after wave rushed over the top, as yet unprotected by helmets, laying down their young lives for the honour of their King-Emperor, their country, and their Empire.

When we were accorded the honour of a royal inspection by the Prince of Wales, I made absolutely sure that every man looked as smart as was possible under the circumstances. On this occasion, a flag and shield were prepared on behalf of the women of England to be presented to the Indian Army in recognition of their services to the Empire. I had the honour of accepting the relics on behalf of the Army. The speeches were fine, though, alas, much remained inaudible, as the German shells made a fearful row.

I could not stay long with the men, for soon I was recalled to the Commander-in-Chief's HQ. Moreover, the bitter cold brought on a bad attack of asthma, even though I felt and looked like a cotton bale with all my warm kit, clothing and overcoats on. Back at HQ I was put to work as the Field Marshal's bridge partner, which, I suppose, was not entirely useless, since the game soothed his sorely tried nerves. Certainly it was an exhausting task, for the C-in-C was a very keen player, which meant that I had to be on standby day and night, ready to be summoned whenever he wanted another rubber. Because the C-in-C would be in a frightful temper when he lost and his skill did not necessarily match his keenness, it was my task to boost his morale by letting him win without giving the impression of doing so. The C-in-C's morale was of course of the greatest importance, but it was not what I had come to France for, and it rendered quite meaningless the flattering references to myself in the British papers: 'What would Ranji like to do with the Germans? He would like to drive them to the boundary.' I would indeed have liked to do just that, had I been offered half a chance.

That first year of war was the occasion of another great sorrow, the death of Field Marshal Earl Roberts, Commander-in-Chief of the Indian forces. He was loved by all Indians, since he had grown up in our country and knew the native customs intimately. Hence, when his mortal remains were being taken to the seashore for embarkation to England, it was thought appropriate for an Indian to sit in the motor-lorry with his corpse. Several of us volunteered for the task, which eventually fell to Sir Pratap Singh, who squeezed in proudly between the driver and the late Field Marshal, sitting straight up, still dressed in full uniform, to all the world as though he were still alive. The great soldier was saluted by his loyal troops as they saw him pass by for the last time, and Sir Pratap smartly acknowledged the salutes, though many of the men might well have wondered who the devil he was.

Not long after, I found myself back in England, too, nursing chilblains and asthma. How I wish I could have been in

France. What a useless passenger I felt myself to be, the eternal twelfth man, sitting out the great match in the dubious comfort of the pavilion. To say that Sir Pratap, kept equally idle, and I were chomping at our bits would be putting it mildly. You at least had your hands full with the training of boys and could pride yourself and Madame on turning out fighting men by the hundreds. It must have been a source of great pride to you both to see the fruits of your labour show the world what they were made of.

As for myself, my friend, what was I but a mere ornament, a pretty thing whose only role was to provide entertainment for heroes fighting the greatest war in the history of Man. Still, such was my destiny, my bad luck if you like, and there was precious little I could do about matters preordained by fate.

My friend Subhas had an interesting theory about Victorian cricket. 'Cricket', he said on several occasions, 'is an Indian game accidentally discovered by the English.' Whenever he said this, he would give me his sly, sidelong glance, waiting for me to ask him what he meant. (This was our little ritual.) I asked him what he meant. Whereupon he frowned, crossed his hands on his stomach and explained:

'Because, my friend, Indians believe in fate. In no game are the fortunes of the players so much subject to fate as in cricket. Of course, of course . . . skill is a factor. One can't deny that.' He frowned, as though challenging me to deny it. 'But so is the weather, the state of the wicket, the sheer bad luck of the one unplayable ball, which seals the batsman's fate. The batsman only has one life but, as the philosopher Ramchandra Gandhi put it, he has the possibility of a reincarnation in the second innings.' This *trouvaille* clearly pleased him, for his frown turned into a radiant smile.

But wasn't that true of many games, I asked. What about baseball?

'No, no, absolutely not. Baseball is quite different.'

Why was that?

'Look here, much less is left to fate in baseball. I should repeat fate is the first signifier of cricket. The cricketer must learn how to deal with fate, to cajole it, to appease it, even to yield to it. You see, for one thing, in baseball, as in most games, there is always a result. In cricket, one team can be much stronger than the other and play much better and yet fail to win. The most exciting games often end in a draw, frequently for reasons beyond human control, fate, in short. Now, if success, in Weberian terms, is not necessarily a matter of winning the game, then what is it?'

Well, what?

'It is a matter of character, a matter of how the actors play their roles, how they cope with fate. To be a good loser is very much part of the game. It shows character, a stoic acceptance of fate. It shows, as an eminent scholar once said in another context, the nobility of failure. That, my friend, is why cricket is an Indian game – it is, if you permit the pretension, the Bhagavad Gita performed in the guise of a Victorian English morality play. A far cry, wouldn't you agree, from C. L. R. James's belief that a fine batsman is, as he put it, a "genus Britannicus". No, my friend, he is a "genus Indicum", for we have retained what the modern Britishers, with their professionalism and materialism, have lost – an appreciation of the game's classical purity. We, you must understand, are the last amateurs.'

Speaking of bad luck, let me fill you in on my own mishap, about which legends abound and few people know the truth.

What actually happened was this: I decided to visit the Vicar of Gillingham, who had been my tutor at Cambridge. He was a rather keen shot and since I was feeling liverish myself, I rented a shoot and invited a group of local sportsmen to join. The weather was cold and damp, and the terrain so muddy that we had to get the beaters to lay down wooden planks, lest we slip off our butts. I shared mine with the Vicar's daughter, a most charming young lady called Clara. Now, I had noticed the first time the birds were sent over that our neighbour was a somewhat erratic shot with an excitable temperament. He kept shouting, as though the birds were his mortal foes, and in his excitement he forgot to stop shooting, even as his gun was pointing almost straight down the line. I was worried that Clara might get hurt and made sure the second time round that I stood between her and our keen friend, and a good thing I did, too, for this time the birds flew over like bullets and the air exploded in gunshots. My neighbour shouted something about killing the bastards and ended up pointing his gun at me. I tried as best I could to protect my face with my arm, but with my usual luck, one pellet must have found a gap and hit my right eye. There was a bit of blood; however, since I had no intention of disrupting the shoot by making a fuss, I kept going until the end. It may interest you to know that in spite of feeling faint I continued shooting from the left shoulder and bagged ten birds out of twelve shots.

I believe I behaved in a manner you would have expected from a friend of yours, and in which my dear Mama would have wished me to act in like circumstances. It was with deep gratitude and some considerable pride that I received a most gracious letter from His Majesty the King's representative. I hope you will forgive my immodesty in quoting from it, but it is not often, you must admit, that I blow my own trumpet: His Majesty, it said, sent his congratulations 'on the remarkable success which attended your efforts in shooting from the left shoulder, after having received a serious wound to the right eye. It was indeed courageous of you to continue shooting and then to walk three miles home.' I lost my eye, of course, but my only regret is that I didn't lose it, or any other part of my body, in France.

As to the fellow who shot me, I never disclosed his name and made sure he was invited to my next shoot. I can tell you now, though, that I slipped the shooting volume of the 'Fur and Feather' series into his room, with several passages marked in red ink. I am told he took this with good grace, and placed it on his drawing-room table – though I am not sure he ever bothered to open it!

Meanwhile the great battles were being fought in Europe

and the Indian chiefs were still not allowed any part of it. Bikaner was so sick of the whole thing that he returned to India and, with great reluctance, I soon followed. The reason was that my sister was getting married to the Maharaja of Jodhpur, a most fortuitous match to be sure, and the Government insisted that I preside over the ceremony personally. I can only surmise that my presence in England was regarded as a nuisance, for there could have been no other reason for removing me from the battlefields of Europe, where the future of our civilisation was being defended against the forces of barbarism. I am pleased to say, however, that family honour was redeemed magnificently by my nephew Dajiraj, who fell in France, after having greatly distinguished himself at Ypres. Poor Dajiraj! His loss was very acute. But he has left an imperishable name and memory and made us feel so proud of him, of our line, our house, and race. He lived and died a true Rajput – I can honestly say I envied him.

I heard Inder speak about death only once. Not that he was too young to think of his own mortality, for people of any age can be prone to morbid obsessions. But Inder was not morbidly obsessed. I heard him speak of death late one night in Delhi, after we had dined with an old Englishman of letters called Rigby. He was an acquaintance of Inder's, an elderly homosexual who had roamed the earth restlessly for most of his life in quest of Arcadia, which is to say, boys, boys and more boys; particularly native boys, eager to please a rich white master in exchange for some crumbs off his admittedly sumptuous plate. An amusing old buffer to us, to them he represented immeasurable wealth, adventure, the wide open world. It was a fair exchange of dreams: one Arcadia of innocence and native beauty and guiltless sex, for another one made of streets paved with gold. It is hard to say which was more elusive.

Anyway, Rigby told us he was finally returning to England. After years of living in Borneo, Baghdad, Cyprus and Bangkok, among other places, he was retiring to a pleasant cottage in the West Country. There, he thought, he would find happiness at last, pruning roses and entertaining the vicar for tea. It sounded like the mythical England that used to haunt colonials in the lonely outposts of Empire: the little patch of England, which always beckoned and always disappointed. I was reminded of my grandparents' house in Berkshire, near the village where Tom Brown was born. I remember life there as an endless round of village fêtes held on my grandparents' lawn, drinks on New Year's Eve, cricket matches, afternoon walks in muddy fields, the tinkle of tea cups in the drawing-room, the neighing of horses trotting down the road, the smell of mackintoshes in the soft rain, and my grandfather dressed in his white tropical suit, declaring the curry the best since India, acting out his Englishness with a gentle irony.

But Rigby seemed too sophisticated for the mawkish dreams of colonial outposts, so I asked him why he was going back. He looked at me askance with a watery twinkle in his grey eyes and said he wished to die in England and expected this to happen rather soon. We laughed uneasily and nothing more was said about the subject. Rigby repaired to his hotel and Inder and I had a nightcap.

Suddenly, quite out of the blue, Inder remarked: 'Of course he's quite right.'

Who was right, about what? I asked. It was as though Inder hadn't heard me.

'I shall die in Punjab,' he said, staring past me at his wall.

But, Inder, I said, you weren't even born there. Again he paid no attention, but rambled on as if in a trance: 'I realised it when I was in Lahore. It was as though I saw for the first time the landscape of my own mind. I had seen it before in my dreams, and it was exactly as I had imagined it – the ochre-coloured streets, the red stone of the old city, the gardens that smelled of roses. My mother never forgot the city of her childhood and passed it on to me. She implanted the images in my dreams. She will never be able to return, but I shall die there, I know I shall.'

I said no more. But when I enquired after Rigby, about six months later, I was told he was in Manila. He didn't last more than one summer in the West Country, hating every minute he was there.

It was with a much troubled mind, my dear Charlo, that I returned to my palace in Jamnagar and nothing I saw there helped dispel my sense of gloom. That year's drought had caused enormous distress and my people were going hungry. Nonetheless, there was no question of slacking in our efforts to help the war effort, at some considerable cost. Our State was second to none in the number of young men that had laid down their lives in His Majesty's services. It seemed, therefore, eminently reasonable to ask for a loan from the Government to see to it that my sister's wedding could be held in the appropriate manner. This was indeed granted after the usual procrastination, but had I known what trouble lay in store for me because of it, I surely should not have bothered.

The affair had been too extravagant, I was told, as though the wedding between two major Rajput houses can be arranged in a miserly fashion. But then how could these men possibly understand such considerations – most of them are hardly even gentlemen. A gentleman is not so much the product of his birth as of his breeding. His credentials are his manners. It is that quality that is so sorely lacking in the cads sent out to administer our Empire.

The drought was of course terribly bad luck, but then I was always unlucky. More and more I feel destined to struggle. I was as distressed as the next man to hear about hundreds of people dying every day and horrified at the thought of their corpses lying out in the open to be devoured by vultures and beasts. (In fact I issued orders to clean the streets before dawn.) But to have made me responsible for the famine was too absurd for words. The Government of India was taking unfair advantage of a famine year to impose conditions on me which were frankly dishonourable. One such was that I should have thrust upon me a Britisher as a permanent financial administrator. The letter informing me of this measure was marked confidential, but everyone in the State knew it. I was deeply hurt and decided that if I had to have loans on these conditions, I frankly didn't want them, for I should rather pinch ourselves than borrow more from this Government.

To take my mind off mundane affairs, I decided to start the rebuilding of my city in earnest. I was fortunate to enlist the help of Sir Edwin Lutyens, who came down for a look when my new palace was halfway to being completed. He was a most delightful man, with a great sense of humour. But his manners could be distinctly rum. He was met at the station with the usual pomp, but instead of standing still when the State anthem was struck up, Lutyens waved his topi and sang along with the band. He then loudly declaimed 'Topi or not topi, that is the question!' donned his hat and marched to the waiting motor like a tin soldier, saluting every person in sight. I roared with laughter when I heard about it, but my people, unused to such puckish behaviour, didn't know what to make of our distinguished guest.

Naturally, I was interested to know what he thought of my new palace, and when he advised me to pull it down and start anew, I thought this was another of his jokes and laughed heartily. Alas, he was absolutely in earnest – at least I hope he was, you never knew with Lutyens – for if he was not, it would have been one of the most expensive jokes in history! I ordered the palace to be pulled down the very next day.

He rather liked the old palace, however. I couldn't think why, for I hardly visited the place. The late Jam Saheb's bedroom, which was left exactly as it was when he died, as is our custom in these parts, seemed to amuse him. 'Don't change a thing,' he said as he brushed the cobwebs from his face.

He then turned his attention to the city itself, assuring me that he could dig something out of his bag of tricks. It didn't take him more than a day or two to come up with a most impressive plan. One of his fancies was a Chinese tea garden in the midst of what he called a Wrenaissance square. He was mightily tickled and said there was nothing like a bit of tradition. Naturally, I agreed, since I regard myself as a traditionalist, too, but I was interested to know how he thought the spirit of the past could be translated most authentically into the forms of the present.

'Your Highness,' he said, 'what is authentic?' I must confess he had rather stumped me there. He lit his cheroot and chuckled to himself. 'With respect,' he said, 'all tradition is forgery of one kind or another. We all make of the past what we want, and that is as it should be. Byzantine, Corinthian, Tuscan, Ionic, Gothic, Palladian – Your Highness, it is all ours, ripe for the plucking, like peaches that never spoil. Were the great columns of Sir Christopher Wren any less authentic than those built by the Romans or the Greeks? Of course not. I repeat, what is authentic? Are the noble minarets of the Jami mosque in Delhi less authentic than their models in Medina or Baghdad? Surely not. Is this authentic?' He held out his cigar for my inspection. I replied that it seemed authentic enough, but no sooner had I said it than the damned thing exploded with a bang, whereupon the great architect laughed so much he got hiccups.

I clapped for some more tea and buns, which he consumed in great quantities. After his laughter had subsided, he lit another cheroot, a real one this time, and resumed talking: 'The spirit of the past, you say. I know not what that is. So let's not be too solemn about history and keep our sense of humour, for history is the most wonderful bag of jokes available to man. It is priceless, Your Highness, and bottomless, absolutely bottomless.' He stopped talking and dug into the warm buns, scooping a generous chunk of butter from the dish. 'Butter late than never, Your Highness,' he said and both of us laughed and laughed.

Lutyens' advice was, I dare say, sound, even though we were not able to incorporate all his ideas in the final scheme. The Chinese tea garden, alas, was not to be. He did, however, drive a rather hard bargain, which once again got me into trouble with the wretched pen-pushers and agitators. But I shan't bother you with any more of that. The important thing is that the task was completed; I had built my city just the way I wanted, and though I say it myself, it was a most handsome place, in no way inferior, indeed in many ways superior, to any city in the princely states. A crescent was named after Lord Willingdon, the Governor of Bombay, and the finest square, the *pièce de résistance* of our town, so to speak, following the Wrenaissance model of Lutyens, was named after the Viceroy, Lord Chelmsford. I can recall with great pride how hard my people worked to complete construction in time for the Viceroy's visit.

Lord Chelmsford is, as you know, a most honourable man. We always got on since I first knew him as Freddy Thesiger, when he was captain of cricket up at Oxford. On India we saw very much eye to eye. It was he who told me of his great regret that Indian political leaders had not been to Eton. So, naturally, he could not fail to see the injustices done to me by his subordinates. It was not, however, my own honour that concerned me so much at this point as the honour of my people, who had sacrificed so much and so willingly for the sake of our Empire, and it seemed to me churlish in the extreme that proper recognition should be denied them. It is my strong conviction that the British Empire should treat all its subjects alike. Indians, after all, are as worthy of being first-class members of the Imperial family as South Africans, Canadians or Australians. The Viceroy, as I expected, absolutely agreed and promised to confer the appropriate decorations on those who were worthy of them.

Finishing the preparations in time for his visit was no easy task. The new palace was made spick and span and the camp near Sarodar, where I had planned some shooting, was turned into a veritable town, complete with electric lighting and green lawns to remind the Viceroy of home. We would have a comfortable lodge with fireplaces to keep us warm at night, marquees for the guests to dine, bathrooms, kitchens and ice-rooms to keep the food from spoiling. To transport the guests, as well as the French wines which didn't stand at all well the rough and tumble of Indian roads, a brand new road was built from Jamnagar. The builders worked day and night to complete the job, a test they passed with flying colours and, considering their fatigue and the amount of dynamiting, a minimum of injuries. They were of course rewarded with extra pay and a splendid party with more food and drink than they had ever seen. An excellent time was had by all, although, unfortunately, some of the chaps fell victim to their own greed, for a few succumbed to overeating – a rather sad end to a most sterling effort.

It was, all in all, a splendid show. Indeed, it would have been perfect had it not been for a most embarrassing hitch. I wished to show the Viceroy and his party our modern port at Rozi, to which end I borrowed Patiala's yacht, *The Star of India*. We set off early to enjoy a hearty breakfast on board whilst viewing the new harbour, and just as we were about to tuck into our scrambled eggs and oysters, the bad luck that I had come to expect caught up with me once again: with a ghastly sound of splintering wood, the yacht hit a sandbank and we were absolutely stuck in the middle of the harbour, water gushing in. There was no recourse but to shunt everyone ashore in rowing boats, an operation which took considerable time and caused a great deal of discomfort. I suppose that now I look back upon the sorry affair, it had its comical side, but I assure you it was no laughing matter then and the Viceroy was furious at missing his breakfast.

Thank God we managed to lay on a shoot within twenty-four hours, during which I contrived to have the Viceroy kill a leopard, which did much to brighten his mood. And Lady Chelmsford, riding in a Japanese chair, was much amused by the equestrian skills of my ADC, who contrived to, as he put it, 'make his horse dance'. Over and over Her Excellency would ask him to dance, and this he did, and she laughed merrily in her chair the while. This was followed by a superb display of fireworks. The racket was indescribable and went on most of the night, somewhat reminiscent of the attack on Neuve Chapelle which I was privileged to have witnessed at very close quarters the year before.

The Viceroy, despite the misadventure at Rozi, declared the visit a great success and graciously invested me with the KCSI, with which I was much pleased, although my number of gun salutes remained the same – still two less than the Nawab of Tonk, despite the fact that his was the smaller state, or Kishengarh, which was smaller yet. I was, however, more than delighted when the Viceroy took up my suggestion and honoured several Indians who had contributed to the war effort. I had personally designed the medals, adorned with fine emeralds. That this very same Viceroy would not long after fail to stand his ground against political agitators caused me considerable grief, but perhaps one should blame Montagu and his wretched reforms for that – a most charming and able man, no doubt, but a Jew who in my opinion lacked the requisite backbone for holding the fort against the dark forces bent on attacking it. But more about this anon.

That I should be attacked for extravagance after the Viceroy's visit was only to be expected. I can only say that once again the petty clerks had failed to understand the Indian mind – so unlike the Viceroy, who showed himself to be entirely in sympathy with it. For it might be mentioned in my defence that not even the most humble resident of an Indian bazaar would consider that a viceroy had been properly honoured unless a small fortune had blazed into the sky in the form of rockets and elaborate set-pieces. Here, my dear Charlo, is a gesture particularly Indian – to rejoice in the spectacle of the next month's revenue being expended in a series of brilliant explosions. Revenue, by the way, which could be recouped easily by the sale of a few bonbonnières.

But, as I said, this carping about money I had come to accept as my destiny and moreover it is our belief that to be punished in this life means less grief in the hereafter. An infinitely more hurtful blow was struck by those who accused me of chicanery in obtaining honours for my men. I do not wish to rehearse the malicious gossip levelled at me. Suffice it to say that Indian agitators used the occasion to blacken my name and thus attack the very foundation of my State. I was accused, quite absurdly, of having secured the honours by flattering and bribing the Viceroy. My dear Charlo, think about it, if you will: the very idea that the chief representative of the British Crown should hold out his hand for baksheesh in the manner of some lowly bazaar urchin! It was too ridiculous for words, but of course mud sticks, as you know. Truly, if I had not felt so strongly my responsibility towards my people, I should have been more than happy to renounce my claim to the Gaddi and spend the rest of my life fishing trout. I suffered fearfully from asthma in that awful climate – even my dear Popsey stopped her usual cheerful chatter and her feathers drooped like a fur coat in the rain. Thank God for the small diversions that kept me in sound mind. Whenever I felt weary I would have my musicians play my favourite Vesta Tilley tunes, of which, after much practice, they gave a slightly rum but perfectly proficient rendering. Ah, my dear friend, whenever I feel low, I remember those cheering words:

> The Army is Today's All Right!
> Who said the Army wasn't strong,
> Kitchener proved them wrong,
> On the day he came along.
> So let the band play and shout 'Hooray'
> I'll show the Germans how to fight . . .

Ah, marvellous! Still, my dear Charlo, even the memory of Misses Tilley and Shields could not entirely dispel my sense of impending doom, as I endeavoured to persuade my fellow princes to stop their eternal bickering and stand in the breach for our interests. I was much worried (correctly, as it turned out) that the so-called Chelmsford-Montagu Reforms posed a severe threat to us, since they opened wide the doors of government to all kinds of native riff-raff. It pains me to say this, for I regard myself as a patriot. I was brought up among the English and have a great affection for them, as you know, but I am still an Indian at heart, and would not hesitate to advocate the withdrawal of the English from India if I thought it wise. I did – and do – not think so, however, and I had hopes that the firm partnership between the King-Emperor and the princes would continue indefinitely. However, when I realised what was in store for us after the War and calculated the consequences of the reforms, I was, I must confess, not at all reassured.

Indeed, it would have been no more than just if our influence in India had been increased, considering the staunch loyalty of the princes to England in her hour of need. Instead I saw a steady erosion of our traditional powers and privileges even in our own domains. More and more often I heard of fellow princes being replaced without ceremony by common politicians with no understanding whatsoever of the traditional loyalties which have worked perfectly well here for thousands of years. And mark my words, dear friend, when these loyalties disappear the very fabric of our country will be torn asunder.

Sad though it is to say, these considerations cast a shadow upon my rejoicing at the defeat of the Empire's foes. Gandhi, whom I had never regarded as anything but a common troublemaker, not only was quite prepared to incite violence amongst the Indian masses, whose political sophistication was at the level of infants, but he had managed to bamboozle a considerable number of otherwise sensible Englishmen into thinking that India was ready for self-rule. Not only did I foresee incalculable harm being done to those very masses whose interests Gandhi claimed to have at heart, but the word of Great Britain, which was pledged to the princes, was in danger of being broken. All I asked for was that just as we have played the game and will continue to play the game by Great Britain, with unswerving loyalty and attachment to the Crown, so Britain should play the game by us in the spirit of true sportsmanship.

Tell me, my dear friend, if this is too bold a request? To be accused by the clerks and clubmen of profligacy, even to have them impose a British adviser on me, humiliating though it is, I can just about take in my stride – for what choice do I have?

But to be let down by the representatives of the Crown itself surely would be too much to bear. For, just as the reign of the British King-Emperor is ordained by God, so do we, the Indian princes, represent our gods on earth. To tamper with that, my friend, is to tamper with the life-blood of our civilisation.

I still refuse to believe that this will happen. I trust the word of an English gentleman too much, for if one cannot trust even that, my dear Charlo, what will be left in this sad world of ours but unholy barbarism?

To struggle against barbarism on the battlefield is a necessary evil; how much better would it be if we could thrash out our differences on more civilised grounds. It was therefore with considerable enthusiasm that I took up the offer to represent India at the League of Nations, for not only did this allow me to work towards a lasting peace for mankind, but it afforded an excellent opportunity to impress upon some of the most influential figures in the world the special problems of India. It had always been a source of regret to me that so few people had any more than a superficial understanding of India, her people and her hereditary rulers. Here, at last, was a chance to rectify some of the false impressions bred from ignorance.

The invitation came when I was in Staines. This was, as you will recall, the summer of 1920. I had left India feeling very jumpy and tired out, so I decided to have a rest. It was not much of a rest, of course, what with all the entertaining, although I did get in some fishing. I also visited the Academy, where I acquired some superb paintings by Tuko, who is, it seems to my untutored eye, at the height of his artistic powers. The picture of the young boys bathing – the one now hanging in my bedroom in Jamnagar – is too beautiful for words; what splendid specimens of young manhood! And how well he expresses their clean joy in being alive and young. I must say it makes me feel old and jaded. I suppose that is why we have art, so that its beauty can revive for us, even fleetingly, the memories of our youth.

Not the least of my pleasures at Geneva was having you

there as my companion. I chose you, my dear friend, because you spoke French and you were the kind of English gentleman who would not be afraid to try, however high the obstacles put in your way. What is more, I knew I could trust you to put your case, as well as promote harmony and peace, with the maximum effect and the minimum of fuss. If I have learnt anything from my public life it is the utmost importance of propaganda. Reality, it appears to me, is influenced to a great extent by the way people perceive it. If we can shape these popular perceptions in a way conducive to harmony, order and peace, that, surely, would be half the battle. War and peace are after all entirely dependent on the human will. If we wish to live in peace we must stick to the rules. This is no different from a game of cricket or tennis: the players cannot be forced to abide by the laws through force of arms; they have to do so of their own volition, for otherwise there is no game. Which is why I thought the attitude of the French delegates to be so wrong: there is no point in having an international army, for if the individual nations cannot agree willingly to play by the same rules, they will certainly refuse to fight in one army. Far better, I thought, to convince the national leaders to behave according to an agreed code of conduct. And with sufficient propaganda, their respective peoples surely will fall into line.

So far as I am concerned, and this is where your assistance was an invaluable asset, the keynote of the League was rubbing together with strangers over the port. You think at first that some of the others are savages, and then you find out they are gentlemen. Of course I never had any doubts about such excellent personages as Wellington Koo from Shanghai, and his charming wife, or H. E. Monsieur Paderewski, but even the Japs, despite the fact that they had snuffled our suites at the hotel, turned out to be quite civilised. Baron Hayashi's knowledge of horses was most impressive, I thought. However, among the individual personalities of Geneva, the English delegates always seemed to me to stand out in a class by themselves for force of character and power of presentation. But I should also say that the one man who impressed me most was Monsieur Paderewski, the great pianist and statesman.

We hit it off immediately, for we had much in common, despite our vastly different backgrounds. I have especially fond memories of playing billiards with H. E., at which he was a past master. He played his game casually, but brilliantly, a cigar in his mouth, his hair flying in all directions like a huge white bird's nest, and his sensitive hands gesticulating as he made his points; for he loved to talk, even as he dispatched the balls on the table with consummate ease. He made the game look easy, which is the true mark of genius. After one especially memorable soirée at his villa on the lake we fell into a long talk about the nature of genius. This was after the other guests had left and Madame Paderewski had retired for the night. You, I believe, had gone off carousing with that Egyptian prince you were so fond of. At any rate, Paderewski and I were left alone, drinking brandy in his library, which smelled pleasantly of polished leather and charcoal. The fire lent a warm, orange glow to his animated features. Paderewski was exercised by the question of whether genius is there at birth, or whether it is acquired through circumstances and application.

I shall repeat his argument as best I can: 'Of course,' he said, 'it must be both, for a native gift has to be polished in order for it to blossom and shine. But where in the balance lies the heaviest weight: the gift, or the acquired skill? If it is the former, what then does this gift consist of? What *is* genius? Is it simply physical, in my case, good hearing and skilful hands, in yours, quick reflexes and good eyes? Or is there something more to it? After all, Your Highness, good ears, even superbly good ears do not explain a Mozart, although they might explain a Liszt. You know Liszt's three requisites for a great pianist?'

I confessed I did not.

'Technique, technique, technique. But that cannot be all there is to it. It showed Liszt's limitations. Biology and practice determine talent, perhaps, but not genius. There is unquestionably a spiritual dimension, and when the spirit matches the flesh, and given the right circumstances, genius can flourish. Now the question is whether the fusion between body and mind can be cultivated, as one cultivates the perfect flower. In other words, can one breed a race of geniuses? It is my opinion that one cannot, for genius is unique, while superior training breeds uniformity, skilled uniformity perhaps, but uniformity, and uniformity is always mediocre.'

Monsieur Paderewski spoke with his eyes closed, in deep concentration, a bit like my Pundit, but with the difference that whereas the Pundit spoke as though his words came straight from the depth of his soul, Paderewski's seemed to emanate from his formidable brain. I couldn't keep my eyes off the huge dome that was his forehead and I imagined his brain ticking away like a Swiss clock, and his great mane of hair sprouting like so many great thoughts. It was no easy task keeping up with him, and I do hope I have done justice to his brilliant talk and recorded his words accurately – after all, my memory is not infallible.

He was interested to know what I, as an Indian, thought of his ideas. This I found a difficult question to answer, for, as I have told you before, I am Indian at heart, but my mind is English educated. That is to say, I believe instinctively in the power of fate and what we call karma, or reincarnation. And this, I suppose, would explain the superiority of certain men, even certain races over others. It is, as they say, but the luck of the draw. But then the English part of my mind tells me that achievement, and indeed all forms of progress, are the result of will, science and application. This, however, got me no closer to answering Monsieur Paderewski's question. I cannot deny that once I had a gift for batsmanship – now, alas, long gone – but was this a matter of training, or was there indeed, as some English writers liked to think, an element of magic involved, perhaps handed down to me from a previous incarnation? Or was it in my blood, or perhaps inhaled with the air of India, so rich with magic?

'Magic!' said Monsieur Paderewski. 'That's it, genius is magic! A trick of fate, God's little joke on mankind.'

He thought this highly amusing and couldn't stop giggling. Although I pride myself on my sense of humour, for once I could not share in the laughter. Indeed, the idea that I should be the butt of some cosmic joke rather chilled me, for it entirely cancelled out my own free will. Now you might say that my belief in fate has the same effect, but there is a difference, for fate is impartial and affects everyone, much like the weather, whereas genius, if indeed there is such a thing, which I am still inclined to doubt, would single out a chosen few, who might not at all welcome the heavenly gift. Indeed, I have felt at times that to have received one special gift is to be cursed, for without it one is lost but while it lasts one is but a slave to it. Is it not far better to be one's own puppeteer, however modest the role, than the choicest puppet, playing the king in the hands of an unknown master?

'Well,' said Monsieur Paderewski, as he slapped his knees with both hands, 'let us put our theories to a little test. Genius, after all is said and done, is the power of invention. Why don't you give me a tune and I shall turn it into something else. I shall transform it, render it mine, unique, never heard before. In short, Your Highness, let us have magic!'

I thought it a splendid idea and racked my brains for an appropriate tune. Anything would do, said Paderewski, but I could not think of one. I am, I must admit, not well versed in the classics and rendering a tune was quite beyond my powers. After a prolonged silence, the great musician asked me what my favourite music was and I could only reply that my knowledge did not stretch much further than the music hall. He asked me for an example and suddenly – how strange are the workings of the human mind – an old tune sprang to mind, one I hadn't heard sung for many years: George Leybourne's 'Champagne Charley'. And so I sang it for Monsieur Paderewski, who had sat down at the piano, listening with his eyes closed, tapping the rhythm with his long, pointed fingers.

Then he began to play, picking up the tune with ease, and as

I sang the words the most extraordinary thing happened: for whilst not changing the rhythm for one instant, the tune began to change, subtly at first, until it had become a different one altogether. I was absolutely enchanted by this demonstration, for he had indeed transformed the tune, but the remarkable thing was that something of the original music was still discernible. I cannot express quite what it was, but it was there, almost but not quite beyond recognition, behind the disguises contrived by the composer. Truly, I felt in the presence of genius.

'Magic?' shouted Paderewski, after he had brought his improvisation to a stop. He laughed like a man possessed. 'No, Your Highness, it is but a cheap music hall trick.' I felt a little let down, I must confess, a little deceived, but the great Pole had such charm that I forgave him. He smiled, took my arm, and suggested a game of billiards, which, with his customary nonchalance, he contrived to win with ease.

And this, my dear Charlo, is where we get to my second confession. I was reminded of it by the memory of Monsieur Paderewski's musical disguises. I refer to the famous Albanian episode, which is, I am sure, still quite fresh in your memory. You will recall how it was mooted in the corridors of the Hôtel de la Paix that Albania was in need of a monarch to replace the unfortunate Prince Wilhelm of Wied, who had vacated the throne during the Great War. You will also remember that the Albanians were especially keen to fill the post with an English country gentleman who could pay ten thousand pounds a year. Well, that much of the tale was absolutely true. What followed, however, belonged more to the world of Gilbert and Sullivan than the great affairs of state.

When I asked you casually whether you would like to be King, I meant it in jest, but you expressed such enthusiasm for the idea that I could not resist carrying the joke a little further. It was indeed not so far-fetched a notion, since you fitted the bill quite admirably – though I'm not sure you had any idea where the ten thousand were going to come from; I rather

suspect you had hopes of assistance from the coffers of Jamnagar . . .

Your ensuing interview with the Bishop of Albania, who
bore such an uncanny resemblance to W. G. Grace, was, if I
may say so myself, staged with some finesse. My footmen
looked absolutely splendid in their gold-braided Nawanagar
uniforms and the Bishop, with a taste for malt whisky, acquitted himself of his task wonderfully well, as did you, my dear
friend, as the aspiring monarch. Indeed, you might well have
become a great king, had it not been for one small detail: the
Bishop, far from being an Albanian man of the cloth, was in
fact my jeweller in Geneva, whose knowledge of emeralds and
diamonds rather surpassed his acquaintance with Albanian
affairs!

I hope you can forgive me for my little jest which I can see
now was perhaps carried a bit far. But had I known how keen
you would be on the prospect of ruling a minor Balkan state, I
should not have indulged in the charade. In fact, I felt rather
sorry for you, which is why I decided to keep the secret to
myself, fobbing you off with vague excuses all the while. I dare
say, however, that you are better off as you are, my friend,
firmly rooted in English soil, than you would have been as a
tinpot monarch of a tinpot nation. But all that is now by the
bye.

I cannot hide my disappointment at the lack of progress
achieved as yet at the League, despite the great exertions of
many worthy men. Propaganda remains the essential thing
and it is a matter of regret that the Press continues to be
cynical. I would make an appeal to the Press to use its gigantic
power worthily. The Old World crucified Christ. Will the
New World crucify the spirit of Christ? His was the spirit of
all great teachers, that, already, dwells latent but potent in the
League. The League is still far from full power. What is
needed is more propaganda and a self-sacrificing spirit among
delegates. The temptation to compromise must be resisted. It
is not true statesmanship to compromise merely to gain time,

for soon there will be nothing left to defend. If this was my message in Geneva, exactly the same applies to my fellow princes in India. To be overwhelmed by the pressure of noisy agitators and compromise on fundamental principles is the height of foolishness.

Time and again I told the British administrators in India that although the country may seem to be in heavy waters, the unpropitious elements now visible are but the froth and foam which ever appear on the surface when progress rides the waves. But one might as well be talking to a brick wall, my dear Charlo, for they will not listen. Instead they cower under the ludicrous intimidation from the likes of Mr Gandhi. Now, more than ever, the hand of princely rule ought to be firmly on the tiller. From slackness of discipline and the divisiveness of politics only chaos will ensue.

Gandhi talks about helping the unfortunate Untouchables, but all he thinks of is how to exploit these simple people for his own political ends. You should have seen the tears when I appeared at the feast of the Untouchables during my anniversary as Jam Saheb. I rode to the palace in a silver coach, dressed as a Kshatriya king. I fed 80,000 poor people at my own expense. I had myself weighed in the full armour of the founder of Nawanagar against ingots of gold, which I gave to the poor. I visited the feast of the Untouchables and allowed them to touch me and they cried with gratitude. How can it ever be said that we are no longer loved by our people? My dear Charlo, we princes are loved by our people, nay, more than that, we are worshipped, we are gods!

It is perhaps too much to expect that the mediocre clubmen now sent out to rule our Empire should understand the deep human bonds forged over thousands of years of civilisation, but I felt confident that a direct appeal to the British Crown would not fall upon deaf ears. Of course I knew perfectly well that others would conspire to stifle such an appeal. It was of the utmost importance therefore that HRH Edward, Prince of Wales, should be royally entertained in my State on the occasion of his visit to India. Despite our rather precarious finances, I could count on my people to tighten their belts and do their very best for me. If only I could speak to the Prince, privately, man to man, preferably during a good shikar, which affords the best possible opportunity to get to know one another, I knew I could get him on our side. He is a sensible young man with sound political instincts, who would never do anything to jeopardise the ancient exercise of kingship.

It was a perfect time to realise the plans that I had made for a larger palace which could serve, not as my own quarters, since my personal needs were modest, but to house distinguished guests in the comfort to which they were accustomed. Lutyens' designs would finally find their natural home in the Lal Palace, which was catholic to a degree in its conception: ancient Rajput craftsmanship added a local flavour to a thoroughly modern building, whose Indian provenance was further enhanced by the Mogul-style domes, which blended beautifully with the classical columns and the Italianate loggias. In regard of HRH's known fondness for billiards, the billiard-room would be second to none in India. And since I knew that HRH had a weakness for German music, I had my musicians trained to play the prelude to Wagner's *Lohengrin*. Our food would be provided by the best Indian and French chefs, who would be on hand day and night. I also saw to it that plenty of game was about in the area and the tanks were replenished with fish. Since it would be the first time our State was to be honoured with a royal visit, my Lancers were put through special drills and I personally designed brand-new uniforms, based, you might be interested to know, on the dress of the Albanian Royal Guards. HRH would arrive from Rajkot by special train and I had arranged for a cow to be freshly milked without noise during a halt in the early hours so that HRH might enjoy his morning tea.

I mention all this, not to boast of my hospitality, but as proof that we were absolutely prepared for the royal visit and that all rumours to the contrary were utterly absurd. I also have it on the highest authority that HRH was looking forward enormously to visiting my State, which can only mean that the decision to change the royal itinerary at the last minute was made by his subordinates on the basis of slander spread by local agitators. The idea abroad that there should be a malaria epidemic here is of course absolutely baseless. I was yet again accused of profligacy, but be honest with me, Charlo, if I was not to be trusted with money, why was I nominated in Geneva to the Finance Committee? I cannot believe this was done in jest. And as to that slanderous suggestion that I engaged in gem smuggling, all I can say is that I am appalled by such vicious rumour-mongering. It is a direct attack on my authority. Worse even than that, my friend, it is a deliberate attempt to blacken my name in the face of my own people, to crush their love for me, as base an act as separating a father from his children!

What have I done to deserve this, Charlo? Why has fate dealt me such a fearful hand – me, who have done so much and sacrificed so willingly for the sake of the glorious Empire? Why did I have to be insulted so, nay, more than insulted, kicked in the teeth by the country I loved so well? Perhaps I could issue an appeal to the English people, perhaps I could try my hand at cricket once again. But, no, even I, having been an eternal optimist, realise that this is fanciful. I can no longer feel much hope for the future. On the contrary, I am fearful that things might get still worse, which is why I have stopped consulting my trusted Pundit – I admit it, it is sheer funk, but I can no longer face the prospect of further misfortunes. I should rather not know about it. Hence, when I received a telegram from the Pundit only the other day I put it away, unopened, for fear that it might contain a portent of doom. I turned for solace to my dear Popsey, as is my wont, but she, poor, sweet, innocent thing, has gone quite deaf and hardly utters a word these days.

You are my last friend in this world. In your company I could still put on a brave face and a good show. How I wish you could be here, at my side for ever. I'm sure I could find a spot for you as my personal secretary. We should both be so happy. Together we could stand in the breach of a civilised world which is rapidly going under. My friend, I do feel that a pall is descending on all that we have treasured. The way things are going, the Great War was but a prelude to a far darker spectacle, which, when the forces of barbarism are finally let loose, will engulf the entire world. To have let down the princes of India may seem a trifling thing, but it is no less than a betrayal of all that civilised men have always lived and died for. We have carried the torch of tradition for thousands of years, and now the flame is guttering. I need you by my side, my friend, now more than ever, and I shall guard this account of mine until I can hand it to you personally.

But I realise this is too much to ask. After all, you have other obligations, not least towards your Madame. I quite see that I shall have to face death alone. It is curtains for the old flannelled fool. So farewell, my dear friend. Here is where I'll sign off. I have nothing more to say, except that I am so very, very disappointed. God bless you.

Your affectionate friend,
Ranji

I tied up the papers in their Cambridge-blue ribbon and wondered about the contents of the unopened telegram. I knew it still existed, for I remembered seeing it in Ranji's room.

The palace was of course the same as when I had last been there, but it was almost as if the place, so like a neglected tomb before, had been infused with a spirit of life. The Landseers, the Tukes, the glass domes with the stuffed birds inside, the old brown cricket bats, the hunting trophies, Napoleon's copy of Tacitus, somehow all this seemed to belong less to a museum than to a man I knew; it was his collection, his life. I thought it would be a kind of sacrilege to disturb it further.

'He was a fine gentleman, a very fine gentleman,' the old retainer said, after having appeared quite suddenly, silent as a ghost. His voice broke the spell and I became the researcher once more. 'About this telegram,' I said, 'do you think we could open it?' The retainer did not answer my question, but said: 'Come, I shall be showing you his music. The Jam Saheb was always playing it in the night-time, many, many times, always the same music. He was sitting alone, wearing his dark glasses. Kumar, he would be saying, kindly put on the record again. And I would be doing so and he would be listening and coughing and talking to his parrot.'

He stopped at a low cupboard made of teakwood, which contained an old phonograph and a small pile of records. Kumar lifted one of them from the pile and put it on the turntable, which he cranked up with the easy motions that showed a lot of practice. Then he gingerly placed the old needle on the record. It was Ella Shields singing 'Burlington Bertie'.

We listened in silence to the scratchy voice and when it was over, he asked whether I wished to hear it again. I looked out of the window at the sun-baked ground that had once been a green lawn and had long ago turned into khaki-coloured dust. A white cow was poking around, looking for something to eat. I said that once was enough.

'Now about that telegram . . . ' The retainer hissed nervously and asked whether I had the Raja's permission. I said I would take full responsibility. He led me through a long hall and told me to wait in a lugubrious room with a large billiard-table, covered in moth-eaten green baize. I waited for what seemed like ages, looking into the staring glass eyes of the stuffed tigers protruding from the wall. I was about to give up and look for Kumar when I noticed a small side-table. On it was a faded copy of a book entitled *Courts and Camps in India*. And next to it, as though by sheer chance, lay the telegram with a silver paper-knife on top. I opened it.

It had been sent from Bombay by Pundit Ram Krishna. It read: 'One year after the celebration of your Jubilee as Jam Saheb, Markesh will come.'

As I read this cryptic sentence, I became aware of Kumar, who had entered the room once more. I asked him who or what Markesh was, but he stiffened and mumbled that the Jam Saheb had been a very fine gentleman. I had the impression he wanted me to leave as quickly as possible, since my presence was an embarrassment, as though I should disturb slumbering spirits. I complied and did not see the inside of Ranji's palace again.

I went to say goodbye to kindly old Mr Patel and his rock and roll family, and asked him about Markesh. 'Markesh?' he said. 'Ah yes, Markesh.' He flicked his wrist dismissively. 'It is just one of our symbols of death. Why do you ask?'

I told him about Pundit Ram Krishna's telegram. 'Oh, my goodness,' said Mr Patel, 'that dreadful man. He was a complete charlatan who pretended to be able to read horoscopes. He was always after Ranji's money. Unfortunately Ranji was rather credulous so far as these matters were concerned. Or it may be that he paid these fellows out of the goodness of his heart, for he was awfully generous, you know.'

I pointed out that the prediction had turned out to be true. Mr Patel was not impressed. 'I'm afraid that must be a matter of pure coincidence.'

It was time to leave Jamnagar and I decided to take the train to Bombay, where Inder had promised to introduce me to some friends. We passed through the same landscape Ranji had seen on his way to England when the weather became too hot. Little can have changed: the same arid plain, dotted with houses of mud, the same parched river beds with vultures and kites flying circles in the toffee-coloured sky. The same smell of spices and excrement and sand.

To pass the time I read about Ranji's funeral. A long procession of mourners dressed in white had walked barefoot from the palace to the burning ghat. People had ransacked their houses, chopping up furniture and ornaments to supply sandalwood for the funeral pyre, whose sweet smell could be detected from miles away. Ranji's eldest nephew, Raj Kumar Pratabsinhji, collected the ashes, after being bathed and shaved by priests. Five months later, on a date determined by the joshis, he travelled for a thousand miles to walk into the Ganges with the urn in his arms, until the river swilled over his head, and the ashes floated off into the sacred waters.

There had been, it seemed, some unpleasantness about the circumstances of Ranji's death. A report appeared in a British newspaper saying that Ranji had actually committed suicide. In 1933, the year of his death, Ranji was Chancellor of the Chamber of Princes. He was deeply worried that a scheme for a Federated India would further erode the princely powers. When he expressed this fear in Delhi to Lord Willingdon, who presided over the Chamber, he was publicly rebuked. This, the article implied, snapped his spirits so fatally that he bade farewell to all his friends, went once more round all his favourite places, and took his chosen successor, Digvijaysinhji, for a tour of the State capital.

'Let us go through our Jamnagar for the last time,' he said, and smiled when his nephew asked what he could possibly mean by that. He instructed the younger man to build a bank here, a market there, six new roads in yet another place. And when he was satisfied that he had said enough, he retired to the palace to die, alone with the deaf and bald Popsey.

Absolute nonsense, wrote Ranji's official biographer, Roland Wild, in a letter to *The Times*, Ranji and Lord Willingdon had been great friends. There was no question of a death wish. Those who said there was, were political saboteurs. Ranji had simply died of asthma.

I put the book aside and looked out of the train window. Dusk was turning the sky saffron, giving the landscape and my fellow passengers a jaundiced air. Sand and dust filtered the light that slanted into our carriage. Rajput women in bright red and yellow saris were digging up roads in the distance. The old woman sitting opposite stared at me silently, munching a betelnut, crimson juice dribbling like blood from the corners of her mouth.

I listened to Mozart's Requiem on my Walkman, which had the odd effect of heightening the melodrama of my surroundings by providing a kind of soundtrack to the imagery. The rather agreeable sense of unreality dredged up sentimental thoughts; of home, childhood, lost loves, church bells ringing on frosty Sunday mornings, death.

Home, I knew all too well, was but a dream. Yet I wondered what I was doing there, in the desert, the land of the dead. I felt a sudden need to hear a familiar voice, something to retrieve my bearings, a confirmation that I was alive and not alone. So I called Inder in Bombay and found nobody home. He might be in Goa, said a friend of his. He has gone up to Delhi, thought another. At this time of year he is usually in Mussoorie, I was told by yet somebody else. No one expressed the least surprise that he had ignored our arrangement to meet. That was just like Inder, always off somewhere, usually on a whim. One had to be lucky to catch him.

It didn't seem terribly important at the time, for I knew I would have the chance to see Inder again on my next trip to India. I still had a standing invitation to spend time with him in Mussoorie, where we would write our respective books and discuss the world in the evenings.

But it was important for I was never to see my friend again. After returning to London I did not think of Inder for some months. Then, one afternoon, I ran into a mutual friend in Charing Cross Road. I asked her whether she had heard from Inder recently. She opened her eyes wide and went pale. 'Didn't you know?'

'Know what?'

'He was killed, in Jaipur, during a riot . . . '

It had been a nasty business. Members of a fanatical Hindu group, whose professed goal was to create a purely Hindu India, had set upon a leader of the Muslim community, who, with equal zeal, struggled to protect what he called the Muslim identity. The attack caused an uproar amongst the believers and what followed was the usual sort of thing: Muslims smashed a Hindu shop, Hindu thugs went on the rampage against the Muslims, and the army was left to pick up the mutilated corpses. Inder, decent, gentlemanly Inder, had apparently tried to protect a terrified Muslim jeweller from the mob and got so badly beaten that he died in a clinic after lying for hours in a pool of his own blood, surrounded by a crowd too blinded by rage to do anything to save him.

Inder's mother was shattered at first, but when the shock passed, she quickly recovered her usual equanimity. She was convinced, so she told everyone, that her son would come back to her, just as his so-called cousin had suddenly appeared from nowhere. Inder, she said, would live again. Like her son, she believed in miracles.

I thought of the last time I had seen Inder, in Delhi. He wished to show me the site of King George's Great Durbar in 1911. We drove there in an old Ambassador, past the Maidens Hotel, the university, the centre of Old Delhi, and through the outer suburbs of bungalows and shanties, until there was nothing but bush and sand. 'Let me show you,' cried Inder. He tugged at my sleeve and ran to a large marble platform, which looked like an ancient site of ritual sacrifice, something the Incas might have built. Here the monarchs and viceroys had held court to the Indian princes. Here the theatre of Empire had found its grandest expression. It was a windy day, and the sand was getting up our nostrils.

'Absurd,' muttered Inder, gazing at the platform, at the broken Greek columns, at the desert where once the princes pitched their tents, 'totally absurd.'

'Yes,' I replied, 'but without all this you wouldn't be who you are. You wouldn't have sat on your mother's lap at the age of three, listening to her reading Shakespeare. You wouldn't have written English poetry. You wouldn't have your sense of irony.'

He stared at me with a look of irritation and bewilderment. 'Absurd,' he repeated, 'and irrelevant. Come along, I'll show you something else.' Again he tugged at my sleeve and we headed for what seemed like scrubland. There was a rusty iron gate, behind which stood some stunted trees and bushes. Rolls of tumbleweed clung to our ankles like tenacious little dogs. 'Look!' said Inder.

I looked and at first I saw nothing, but then I could just make out, sunk into the sand between the trees, a number of large grey statues of men in Roman togas. They stood about like flashers in a park, with weeds growing out of their feet; some were without hands, or noses; all were covered in layers of hard sand. I read the inscriptions on the classicist plinths: Lord Curzon, Lord Linlithgow, Lord Willingdon, Lord Chelmsford . . . They looked sad and lost, like ghosts who, having wandered into the wrong place, were condemned to stay there for ever.

Inder explained that these statues came from the former state capitals of British India. They had been removed after Independence, and put to rest in this desolate spot, once meant to be a park. 'You see,' said Inder, who had recovered his sardonic good humour, 'it was all irrelevant, a blip in the timeless universe, a ripple in the ocean, a mere interlude in an endless play. The Raj wasn't just absurd, it was meaningless, it had left nothing behind.'

I said nothing, awed by the ghostly spectacle of these petrified great men, stranded in the desert.

'Go home,' said Inder. 'You can only find meaning to your life when you go home to the place whose history you share, and whose language is in your soul. Only there will you find poetry, and sense. All the rest is skimming the surface. Go home.'

'But, Inder, you know I have no home. And neither do you. We are on the road for ever and to assume otherwise is to chase illusions.'

'No,' shouted Inder, 'no, no, no. India is my nation, my home, the home of my ancestors . . . '

'Which ancestors? The Muslims from the north, the Aryans, the Dravidians, the tribes in the northwest? Be honest, Inder, India always was a hodgepodge, its history a free-for-all. And so, for that matter, was Europe. Home is where we choose to make it, where we have our friends, and our books. Home is in our minds. All tribes are now lost. The ancestors are long dead . . . '

'But,' said Inder, almost howling with rage, 'but you cannot be a complete cosmopolitan. That's like saying you're nothing, a man without a past, without identity. To deny your identity is simply arrogance. It's as bad as the Empire builders, who thought the whole world belonged to them . . . '

'They built their Empire precisely because they believed in their race, their ancestors, their home, even though few of them really wanted to live there. Anyway, Inder, why can't you forget your identity, or mine, for a moment, so we can just be friends.'

Inder's anger had passed like a short burst of tropical rain, and he spoke softly now, as though more in sorrow than in anger: 'That will be impossible, as long as you persist in attacking me for who I think I am. Look, maybe they are illusions, but they are my illusions, so you must respect them. As long as you can't do that, we cannot be friends.'

I nodded, but said nothing. I looked again at the chipped images of the old viceroys, and at the great marble platform in the middle of the old Durbar ground, and thought of the illusions of Empire and how they were still with us. Silently, sadly, we walked back to the Ambassador, feeling the sand harden in our noses.

Epilogue

'Did he really happen? Or was he perhaps a dream, all
dreamed on some midsummer's night long ago.'

Neville Cardus on Ranjitsinhji

LEAFING THROUGH DOZENS of photographs of Ranji, in
England and India, it struck me as odd that certain people kept
appearing whom he never mentioned in his letter to Fry. There
was, for example, a young European woman, often seen sitting
next to Ranji and stroking a cat. I saw her in pictures taken in
Jamnagar in the Twenties, at banquets or shikars, as well as in
photos of scenes at Ranji's Irish castle in Ballynahinch. She was a
handsome woman of a certain age, with dark hair and a thin,
slightly curved nose.

I came across her identity quite by accident one day when I
visited an old Irishman who had been Ranji's bridge partner. He
had gone out to India to seek adventure and found himself in
Ranji's employment, ostensibly as an engineer, but in fact as a
full time bridge player. His only other duty had been to rinse
Ranji's eye socket in the evening when the physician was away. I
should have realised when I heard his name, but the penny failed
to drop.

Mr Scott was a spry eighty-five-year-old when I saw him at his
house in Hove, which he shared with his much younger wife, a
mannish woman dressed in tweeds. He was wearing a dapper
cream-coloured suit.

I asked him how he first got to know Ranji. His eyes blinked a
little mischievously behind his tortoise-shell glasses: 'I never
knew the Jam Saheb. Nobody really knew him. I certainly didn't,
even though I lived with him day and night, for many years.'

Well, then, I asked, how did he first meet him? 'Ah, you see,
the Jam Saheb was in love with my sister. Nobody knows about
this . . . In fact, I do believe you're the first person I've told.' He
chuckled softly to himself. 'Oh, this is taking me back a long

way. What memories! Oh, I'll have some nightmares tonight, to be sure.'

I was surprised to hear about this love affair, which seemed, to put it mildly, a little out of character. I decided to broach the subject delicately: Had Ranji thought of marrying Mr Scott's sister?

'Oh yes, I do believe he did. Yes, very much so. Indeed, he was about to abdicate from the Gaddi, but then, of course, he sadly passed away. It was a most beautiful funeral, you know. The people in white, the chanting, the flowers, and the shrouded corpse bathed in the water of the holy Ganges . . . '

I asked Mr Scott whether he had any pictures of his sister. Indeed he had, but looking at them was sure to provoke a nightmare. Still, it wasn't every day that he had visitors asking him about the Jam Saheb, so he would show me his albums. Together, knee to knee, we went through a leather-bound scrapbook of old menus, dance cards and photographs. There were photographs of Ranji in a tweed hacking jacket standing behind a mountain of dead game, his head turned sideways to conceal his false eye, of Ranji at a formal dinner, Ranji in Durbar dress, Ranji in a train, Ranji on a steamship. In every picture he showed only his profile, while the people surrounding him stared at the camera. And there she was, the dark-haired woman, Mr Scott's sister. And Mr Scott himself, of course, a wiry young man, smiling in the background.

'Now, don't get me wrong,' he said when I asked him for more details about his sister's relationship with Ranji, 'there was a romance, undoubtedly, but entirely Platonic. I am sure that's all it was. Nothing physical. You know, I don't believe Ranji had a sex-life. He never talked about it, never a word about sex.'

What did he talk about?

'Oh, nothing much, really. Yes, superficial things.'

Superficial things?

'Yes. You know, he smoked a tremendous amount, always Turkish cigarettes. And if you asked him a difficult question, he would blow smoke-rings and watch the smoke rising, saying nothing, just smiling and watching the smoke go up and up.'

Mr Scott held out his pipe, his watery eyes looking up, as though in a trance. The grey smoke spiralled towards the yellow-stained ceiling.

We turned our attention back to the scrapbook. I was interested in a picture taken somewhere in Europe, on the terrace of what looked like a grand hotel. Ranji, dressed in a dark suit, looked straight at the camera, unusual for the time but then he was wearing sunglasses. Behind him were three Indian servants and a smiling Mr Scott and next to Ranji sat a distinguished-looking gentleman in a white suit, leaning on a cane.

'Aix-les-Bains. The Aga Khan. I suppose the Jam Saheb was there to borrow money or something of that sort. Don't know whether he ever got it. Probably did. You know, he could be a little unscrupulous, smuggling pearls and diamonds, that sort of thing. Of course, the princes were exempt from custom duties in those days. He was terribly extravagant, but also very generous. There's many a time I saw him take out jewels and those Easter egg things from his pockets and simply give them away to his guests, smiling, always smiling. Ah, he was a real gent was the Jam Saheb . . . '

To spare Mr Scott the effort of getting up, I took the album and put it on the table. 'Ooh, not there,' he said, almost panic-stricken, 'that will never do. My wife, you see, is very particular, very particular indeed. Won't have any books lying around on the table. Must put it back where it came from.' The wife, much to my relief, was out shopping.

Mr Scott sat back in his chair and stared into space. 'No,' he said softly, 'nobody really knew the Jam Saheb.' And then, with a jolt, as if awakening from a trance: 'Of course, he was a great joker, always full of jokes.'

Did he ever get angry?

'Angry? No, not really, well, once in a while, at bridge. He could be terribly abusive to his ADCs when they played bridge with him. Called them stupid idiots, and so forth. And then there was the time . . . '

He fell silent. I urged him to go on. And he quickly said: 'Well, you see, he was a very proud man, a very proud man indeed. We were on our way back from India and took the Blue Train from Marseilles. And the Jam Saheb was informed that Charlie Chaplin was on the same train. He loved Chaplin flicks and sent down his card with an invitation to come up and see us. After a short while a message came back from Chaplin saying that he would be delighted to meet Prince Ranjitsinhji, but only in Chaplin's carriage. The Jam Saheb said nothing but I could see that he was furious, for he went pale and seemed breathless, as though he was having one of his asthma attacks. He often had those, you know. Of course, he absolutely refused. Terrible shame, really. What a missed opportunity to meet a great man . . . '

Yes, indeed, I thought.

' . . . How could he have turned down an invitation from a great prince.' Mr Scott shook his head in disbelief. 'What a great, great pity . . . '

Absolutely, I thought.

The old man shrugged his shoulders and sighed: 'But of course Charlie Chaplin was just a pleb.'

Ballynahinch in the rain must be as bleak as Tierra del Fuego: a stony, desolate, grey landscape, where only the mustard plant grows in profusion round the rocky pools. It is a wild landscape, uncultivated, primeval, seemingly untouched by human hands. Ranji by all accounts found a kind of happiness there in the last years of his life.

I was driving through the Irish countryside in my Japanese car, listening to the radio. Housewives spoke about family funerals and priests defended murders committed in the name of patriotism. There was also an almost obsessive concern among the radio announcers and their listeners with identity – the identity of a small nation existing always in the shadow of a larger one. Resident foreigners were trotted out to say how much they loved Ireland. There was a special quality to Irish life, they said, unique and wonderful. It reminded me of similar sentiments expressed in Holland: the insistence on being different, special – physical smallness turned into a special virtue, provinciality as a kind of cult. I found it both touching and depressing.

I pulled up at a pub for lunch. It was dark inside. A plump young woman with grey streaks in her carrot-coloured hair was reading a paper behind the bar. At the table next to mine sat a middle-aged man in a cable-knit jumper and a slightly younger woman, presumably his wife. They spoke softly, but I could tell at once that he was British. Since we were the only customers, we struck up a conversation.

'Travelling through, are you?' he asked.

Yes, I said.

'Your first time in this country?'

Yes, it is.

'Ours too,' he said. Then, with an air of discovery: 'Awfully nice people.'

Yes, I said, they are.

'Don't seem to mind us at all, really, do they?'

Us? I thought . . . us?

'No, they don't, do they?' I said.

'One hears that they dislike us, but I haven't noticed it, have you?'

Not in the least, I said, still thinking of 'us'. I liked the feeling of us, of being included without thought. It felt cosy. Perhaps that's what it's like, to be home. But I knew the feeling would pass. Home, us, isn't that what one tries to get away from? Do you have a choice in the matter? Like Lot's wife, there is no looking back once you've hit the road. Memories are what you are now, your own private collection, the accumulated riches, kitsch and junk that make up your identity. There were times, during my pursuit of Ranji's enigma, that I felt he had become a part of me, as though some of his riches, kitsch and junk had, if only in the imagination, become mine. The fluttering silk shirt, the glass eye, the green parrot, they are in my collection now.

Ranji's castle in Ballynahinch, which is really a large, grey, gabled house on a river filled with salmon and trout, is now a hotel owned by Americans. In the distance loom the blue-grey cones of the Connemara Hills, and in between there is nothing but peatbogs and loughs.

The castle was built as an inn, but renovated in 1813 and turned into a grand house by Richard Martin, also known as 'Hair-trigger Dick' or 'Humanity Martin', the former because of his fondness for duelling, the latter for his kindness to animals. Humanity Martin was a Regency dandy and spent his fortune on grand parties. He was often in debt and process-servers were beaten or drenched in bog-water. He loved animals, though, and imprisoned anybody suspected of mistreating them. He almost killed a man called 'Fighting Fitzgerald' for being unkind to a wolfhound. Humanity Martin died penniless in Bologna, where he had gone to escape from his creditors.

I was the only guest without fishing tackle. The others were mostly hearty Americans and their wives. I had heard that there was one local man still alive who had known Ranji. I asked the young woman at the reception desk and she knew all about him: 'Oh, yes, he can tell you a lot of stories about the old Maharaja. He was his ghillie, you know. He's a very old man now, but still quite hale.' A meeting could be arranged that very afternoon.

At five o'clock Martin O'Halloran shuffled into the saloon bar, supported by a steel walker. He had a cheerful drinker's face: crimson nose, red cheeks, watery blue eyes and tufts of white hair protruding from his ears.

'A drink?' I asked.

'Oh, Christ, yes, and then another, and another.' Martin's drink was brandy.

When had he first met Ranji?

'The first time, let me think now. It was on my first day of work, planting potatoes. His Highness – we always called him His Highness – was sitting at his favourite spot on the river, fishing. Oh, for hours he sat there, quite still, waiting for the fish to bite.'

Was he alone?

'Alone? Christ, no, he would have a grand English lady with him, a handsome lady she was, with dark hair. And then there was an Indian we called the Major. He was here all the time, never said a word, not a word.'

I asked Martin whether Ranji had been well liked by the local people.

'Oh, Christ, yes. Oh, Christ Almighty, yes, he was a fine man, a fine English gentleman. But simple, you know, quite simple.'

What did he mean by simple?

'Very polite to the working man. He never ignored us like some people do. Always had a kind word. And a great sense of humour. Oh, Christ, what a sense of humour . . . '

Martin ordered another brandy which he gulped down. He looked round the bar, greeting the regulars. We were approached by a thin Indian lady in a sari, who asked if she could join us, since she could not help overhearing our conversation. Who, she asked, was this maharaja? 'Oh, he was a fine gentleman . . . ' started Martin. I wished she would go away.

'India has such a great culture,' said the lady. 'Have you ever heard our music?' I told her that I had. Martin stared blankly into his glass. 'And our miniature paintings, have you had the opportunity to see those?' Yes, I said, I had. 'We may be a very poor country,' she bubbled on, 'but we are rich in spirit.' Her husband, an amiable American in a pair of tartan trousers, arrived to take her into dinner. 'Well, I'll leave you two to it, then,' she said, as Martin politely touched the peak of his tweed cap.

'Yes, a fine gentleman, and that's God's truth,' Martin resumed.

He used to give parties here, didn't he?

'That he did, that he did. Oh, Christ, yes. Every year, September – His Highness's birthday. The billiard-room was cleared out and forty-five tables laid. At eleven o'clock we would all come in and leave at about four, and His Highness would give us all a tip, one by one, according to our rank. Oh, Christ, they were good parties. We sang Irish songs and the young men danced and the whiskey flowed and His Highness would be there watching and laughing, enjoying every minute. After lunch he would propose a toast. Now, he knew perfectly well that a toast to the King did not go down well in our parts, so he stood up and toasted the Emperor of India, and that's God's truth.

'Yes, they were good times all right. I remember it as though it were yesterday. When it was time for His Highness to leave – he had a special carriage all the way to Dublin, you know – we would see him off at the station and many of us cried, for he was a fine, fine gentleman. The last time we saw him off was in September 1932, and that's God's truth . . . '

Martin took out a red handkerchief and wiped his eyes. He emptied his glass of brandy.

'April first, 1933, is when we got word here that His Highness had died. Now, His Highness had a grand sense of humour and April first is an important day in Ireland, so we thought it was a joke. Oh, Christ Almighty, we thought it was a joke and we laughed and we laughed and we laughed.'